# Daring to Love You

Sharon C. Cooper

Amaris Publishing LLC

DARING TO LOVE YOU
By
Sharon C. Cooper

ISBN: 978-1-946172-61-7
Paperback

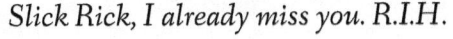

*Slick Rick, I already miss you. R.I.H.*

# From Author

# Blurb

***She agreed to fake date her brother's best friend, but is being with him supposed to feel so real?***

Lynix Mathews knows Dorian Priestly is the woman for him, but she won't give him a chance to prove it. His man whore reputation doesn't help. Even his millionaire father is demanding he settle down—by pushing Lynix toward an arranged marriage. But that can never happen. Not when Lynix's heart only beats for Dorian. He'll have her or no one.

Dorian hasn't had the best of luck with men, and her mother's matchmaking schemes make everything worse. The only thing left to do? Fake a relationship with Lynix—her brother's best friend. It's a win-win for both of them until she falls in love with him.

Lynix is a known player, and Dorian is stressed with indecision. Should she break things off with the man who's captured her heart? Or will choosing what she wants—him—leave her shattered in a thousand pieces?

# Chapter One

"When are you going to stop running from me?" Lynix asked, his voice a deep rumble, causing goosebumps to skitter over Dorian's skin.

Chest heaving with her nerves on edge from literally running from him, all she could do was stare at him. He had kissed her near the private lake that was on his parents' property, and Dorian had run to the pool house with him hot on her heels.

She wasn't sure what made her run, but...

No, that wasn't true. She knew exactly why she had taken off. It had everything to do with her experiencing the most electrifying, soul-stirring, make-you-want-to-drop-your-panties kiss of her life. He did that. He made her feel things she had never felt, and she wasn't sure what to do with the sensations still thrumming through her body.

Dorian might've wanted a repeat of that lip-lock, but she wasn't sure what to do with these needy, lust-filled feelings swirling inside of her. All she could think of was that Lynix

1

"frickin" Mathews, Mr. Playboy himself, had kissed her senseless.

The most gorgeous, sexiest, and infuriating man she knew. A guy who was so far out of her league that this moment, this incredibly arousing, scary moment, didn't seem real. More than any of that, though, Lynix was her brother's best friend. Meaning, he should be off-limits for that alone. Yet, her body craved him in a way she had never craved another man.

There was so much wrong with this situation that Dorian wasn't sure where to start dissecting it to make it make sense. Lynix currently had her backed against the door with his arms on either side of her, blocking her in, making her escape impossible. But if she was honest with herself, she didn't want to escape. Nor did she want to keep pushing him away.

Except she had to. She had to keep her guard up when it came to Lynix. He was the epitome of a bad-boy, and no way was she letting him near her heart. She'd done that with her ex, and she still had the mental and emotional scars to prove that getting involved with a player was a bad idea. A really, really bad idea.

At over six feet tall and built like a linebacker, Lynix towered over her, his presence confident and domineering. As a Chicago police officer, he probably intimidated the hell out of perps. Yet, he didn't scare her. The only reason she was nervous was because of the way he made her feel. Out of control. Needy. And she wanted more than just to kiss him again.

She was also nervous because it was only a matter of time when someone in her family wondered where she'd gone. They were on the Mathews's family estate. Her brother and his new wife had gotten married on the property, and the reception was currently going on. Dorian had slipped away to get some air and had ended up at the man-made lake that was quite a ways from the main house. That's where Lynix had found her. One thing had led to another, and before she'd known what was going on, he'd kissed her.

Now here they were, a heavy silence filling the space in the small foyer.

Dorian's hands moved of their own accord and settled on Lynix's hard chest, then moved to his thick biceps. He had shed his tuxedo jacket and bowtie, leaving him in a white tuxedo shirt and pants. The man was hella fine, and from what she could tell, he had a powerful body that felt as if it had been carved from stone.

Between the way he was staring down at her with those smoky brown eyes and the intoxicating scent of his cologne, all she wanted to do was kiss him again. Which again would be a bad idea.

His left eyebrow quirked, as if he could read her mind. "What? Nothing to say?"

Dorian swallowed hard as her breathing slowly went back to normal. "What was the question again?" she asked, trying to buy a little time.

He chuckled. The deep, rich sound was as potent as his scent and settled around her like a cozy blanket. "I'm sure you remember the question, but just in case, I asked, when are you going to stop running from me? I know you feel what I feel whenever we're within a couple of feet of each other. Why keep fighting the inevitable?"

Dorian narrowed her eyes at him. "And what exactly is the inevitable?"

"That you'll one day be mine."

After a slight hesitation, a slow smile kicked up the right corner of Dorian's mouth, and she started to let it make a full appearance. However, he wasn't smiling. "Wait. You're serious? You honestly think I'll one day be yours?"

"There's no doubt in my mind. You and I are meant to be together, and I'm prepared to do whatever it takes to prove that to you," he said in all seriousness, as if he were an attorney putting the final touches on his closing argument.

Dorian had known Lynix for years, and she could admit to enjoying their playful banter and lighthearted arguments. But he was arrogant, too fine for his own good, and more than that, he was a babe magnet. Whenever he stepped into a room, it was as if he had a silent beacon that lured women to him. She'd seen it with her own eyes, which had a lot to do with why she'd been able to resist him. She didn't need another player in her life.

Nope, she wasn't going down that road again. When it came to Lynix, she planned to continue to resist the temptation. Sure, her body might lust after him, but her brain was protecting her heart. That's why she only dated nice, safe guys. Not sexy, wealthy bad boys who were used to women falling at their feet.

Of course he made her want to walk on the wild side, but doing so was outside of her comfort zone. Yet, their attraction for each other was getting harder to resist.

"Lynix, I like you, but you already know you and I aren't a good fit. I'm nothing like the women you usually date. I'm looking for forever... and you're not."

She lowered her gaze. She had just turned thirty-three, and she was ready to find her special someone and have a family. Though he and Zion were best friends, Lynix was older than her and her brother. At thirty-five, from what she knew of his dating life, it didn't seem like he had any intentions of settling down with one woman. Let alone her.

Lynix gently cupped her chin within his large, calloused hand, forcing her to meet his gaze. He studied her for the longest, and then his expression softened. He really was a handsome man with intense eyes and skin the color of cinnamon. She had never dated anyone with facial hair, but the well-groomed scruff along his jawline made her want to rub her hands over it to see what it felt like.

*Stop. I have to stop this.* She couldn't keep looking at him like he was a treat she wanted to devour. No, she had to stay strong and hold on to her resolve.

He released her chin and went back to caging her in. "Dorian, sweetheart, no matter what you're telling yourself, you and I are perfect for each other. You just have to give me... give us a chance to find out."

She folded her arms over her chest, and his eyes followed the move. His gaze lingered on the swell of her breasts in the low-cut, gray dress she wore, and she rolled her eyes. He didn't meet her gaze again until she dropped her arms to her side.

"You have too many women," she blurted.

He snorted and shook his head. "There are no women in my life. Granted, yes, I'll admit to being seen with women, but there's nothing serious between us. Besides, I haven't been out with anyone in over a month because I'm saving myself for you."

She stared at him for a moment, then burst out laughing. "Yeah, right. I just witnessed one of the catering staff flirting with you."

He shrugged. "So. If you saw that, you also saw me walk away without a backward glance."

True, but still. She couldn't imagine him giving up anyone for her.

"For the record, if you've seen me with anyone in the past, that's exactly what it is, in the past. I've never been emotionally available to anyone I've gone out with, and they've known that going in."

"And what? That would be different with me? Am I

supposed to believe I'm somehow special, somehow different from all the others who came before me?"

His expression turned even more serious than it had been a moment ago. "Yes," he said simply.

Dorian shook her head and pushed against his chest to move him away, but it was like pushing against a brick wall. He was immovable and didn't budge.

"Give me a chance to prove to you that I've changed, that I want you in my life as more than just my best friend's sister. And as more than just my verbal sparring partner. You're the one I want to be with, Dorian. *Only you.*"

She shook her head. "I can't," she said weakly, despite meaning it. This time when she tried pushing him away, he moved easily. She skirted past him, putting a little space between them. "I don't want to get hurt again, and you, Lynix Mathews, have the ability to crush me."

"I would *never* hurt you," he insisted.

"Maybe not intentionally, but I'm not willing to take the risk. Now, I need to go and rejoin the wedding reception. I'm sure someone in my family is wondering where I'm at."

He huffed out a loud breath. "Fine. Then I'll just have to show you that I'm serious about you and me. I'm going to prove to you that you're the only woman for me." He opened the door and stood back, and as Dorian hurried out of the pool house, she heard him say, "I don't mind working for what I want."

Dorian tucked his words into the back of her mind as she headed to the main house. She had to be strong when it came to Lynix, but she wasn't sure how much longer she could resist him. He made her body hum with need whenever she was around him, and she wanted him. She wanted him in every way a woman wanted a man, but...

*Nope. Not going to happen. Stay strong, girl.*

# Chapter Two

T wo *months later...*

Dorian was starting to hate anything involving weddings, engagement parties, and happy couples.

Bitter? Maybe.

Jealous? Definitely.

*No. Wait.* That's not right.

She sighed at the route her thoughts had taken and shook off the sudden bout of negativity. She wasn't bitter or jealous. As a matter of fact, she loved love and respected anyone who could keep the excitement growing in their relationship. Yet, there were moments like this evening, being surrounded by loving couples, that reminded her of the sad state of her love life. It was pitiful at best, and finding her soulmate was like looking for a goldfish in the Atlantic Ocean.

Why did it seem impossible to find a wonderful man, fall

madly and passionately in love, and then live happily ever after?

She strolled into the kitchen of Moody Days, her sister Nyla's jazz club, where several people bustled around washing dishes, plating up food, and taking care of a host of other things. She grabbed a batch of lemon pepper wings and mini quiches and headed back out to the huge room full of guests who were dancing, talking, and laughing. Basically, having a good time.

Once she set the items on the table, Dorian stood back to see if she could take any empty dishes away. When she had agreed to assist with Nyla and her fiancé's engagement party, she hadn't expected to have to help cook and serve so much food. She also hadn't expected there to be so many people. Then again, what started as an engagement party had turned into a wedding reception as of five days ago. Her sister and now husband, Harrison, had returned from vacationing in Jamaica as a married couple.

Needless to say, Dorian's mom had been livid to find out they had eloped. Especially when she'd dreamed of giving her girls, four of them, a fairytale wedding. Virginia Priestly was used to getting what she wanted, but now that her daughters and only son were grown, they were taking some of her power away.

*If only I could be more like Nyla.*

Instead, Dorian was the one who never stepped out of line. From a young age, she had always followed the rules and was the only one of her siblings who had never given their parents trouble.

The problem was she was tired of being the "good girl"—not that she wanted to be a rebel like Nyla and their sister Cree. No, she was just ready to live a little and stop being so socially awkward and predictable.

"Okay, it's time to stop hiding out back here," Raven, Dorian's sister-in-law, said after sidling up to her. She had to talk loudly to be heard over the music, but not too loud for the people on the other side of the buffet table to hear.

Raven was another one who'd been recruited to help with cooking along with Dorian's oldest sister, Essence, and their mother, Virginia. Raven had also taken on hosting duties. She was a virtual assistant by trade, but she really could've been a party planner considering all the great ideas she'd come up with for this event.

Raven bumped Dorian's shoulder with hers. "There are a few single guys here from Harrison's tech company. You should be out there mingling and getting to know some of them."

Dorian had spotted a few people who seemed to be there solo, but no one really snagged her attention. Nope. She seemed to only zone in on the numerous couples who were hugged up with their spouses or dates. It was getting tough to watch others who had clearly found the love of their lives. Especially Nyla and Harrison, who were in the middle of the dance floor staring lovingly into each other's eyes as they rocked to "If I Ain't Got You" by Alicia Keys.

Dorian's heart softened as she continued watching them. It was clear Nyla and Harrison were crazy in love and having a good time. She wanted that for them. Wanted them to have a happy and prosperous life together. They deserved it, especially Harrison. His life had literally been a living hell, and she was glad he'd found Nyla and their family.

Still gazing out at the dance floor, Dorian's hand flew to her chest. "Raven, look," she said and nodded to where Harrison had moved across the room and guided his mother onto the dance floor.

"*Aww*," Raven said, and they both watched as he danced with the woman who he'd been estranged from for years.

Harrison and his mother were working on rebuilding their

relationship. Her brother-in-law's efforts were commendable because, the way his mother had betrayed him and left him to rot, Dorian wasn't sure she could've ever forgiven her.

Yet, she loved how Harrison was making the effort. It said a lot about his character as a man and a human being. Despite being a bit envious of his and Nyla's relationship, she was overjoyed her sister had found a good guy.

"Yes! He made it," Raven said excitedly.

"Who made—" Dorian started to say but stopped when she spotted the *he* Raven was referring to. Her heartbeat immediately went into a tailspin, and her breathing increased.

*Lynix "Frickin" Mathews.*

"Who invited him?" Dorian murmured, not meaning to pose the question out loud and with such distaste in her mouth.

Yet, that was the effect Lynix had on her. He was so... so beautiful and a major pain in the butt with his arrogant, God's gift to women persona. That attitude had seemed to multiply over the last couple of months, ever since their conversation during Zion and Raven's wedding reception.

Granted, Lynix was all that and then some, but the fact that he knew he was *hot* got on her nerves. Some of the crap he spewed made her want to punch him. Playfully, of course, because she didn't want to break her hand on his rock-hard muscles. Then other times, she wanted to leap into his arms, kiss him hard, and claim him as hers.

*Too bad I'm not brave enough to do either.*

He had told her he wasn't giving up on them being together. He was just waiting for her to catch up with what he already knew—that they were made for each other.

It was just more of the cocky crap he kept whispering in her ear every chance he got, which had been often lately. With them being the godparents of her niece and nephew, Zion and

Raven's twins, they'd been forced to see each other more than Dorian preferred.

But right now, despite trying to look away, she couldn't help but check him out. As usual, the tall, gorgeous man was hard to miss and practically sucked all the air out of the room with his imposing presence.

Why'd she have to be attracted to him? *Why?* She hated noticing the way his black Polo shirt hugged his muscular upper body, especially his impressive biceps. Or the way his long, thick legs looked in his black dress pants.

*Just stop looking.*

"I invited him," Raven said, snapping Dorian out of her thoughts. Her sister-in-law looked pleased with herself as she grinned. "He was over at the house yesterday hanging out with the babies, and I suggested he stop by the party. He was so gracious in letting us use his family's house for our wedding and reception. The least I could do was invite him to a family gathering since he's like family. Wait. I'd think you'd be happy to see him."

Dorian frowned at the woman who had not only become her sister but had quickly become one of her best friends. "Why would you think that? I can't stand him."

Raven narrowed her eyes and planted her hands on her hips, giving Dorian a *yeah right* look.

"I can't believe you can say that with a straight face. Why are you lying? More importantly, why are you lying to yourself? I've seen you two together, and you guys are always stealing glances at each other."

Dorian didn't respond because she found herself looking at Lynix more often than she preferred. How could she not? The man was too good-looking to be ignored, and the way he made her body stir, even without touching her, was starting to be a problem. He was always a perfect gentleman, but she didn't miss the way his potent gaze always took her in.

"And clearly, you have forgotten how I saw you and Lynix sneaking around on his family's property during my wedding reception," Raven added.

Heat spread to Raven's cheeks as the memory slammed into her like a ninety-miles-per-hour baseball pitch. Yeah, she remembered that night at the lake well. It was one of the few times that she and Lynix hadn't argued, bantered, or got on each other's nerves. He told her a little about the property, which his wealthy family owned, and how he used to hang out at that lake a lot as a kid. He'd claimed the stars seemed a little brighter in that particular spot at night, and after witnessing it, Dorian had to agree.

But then he kissed her.

The kiss had been long, passionate, and there were times, even months later, she could almost feel his mouth on hers. It was hands down the best kiss she had ever experienced, but Dorian knew his type. Heck, she had even dated a man who reminded her of Lynix in some ways. Confident. Determined. And a player. Her ex had been her coworker, which should've been one of many warnings to stay clear of him.

She hadn't. Instead, she had learned the hard way that she should have never dated someone she worked with. Besides, she wasn't cut out to date the proverbial bad-boy, though that was who she was often attracted to. Now, she only went out with guys who were nice, understated, and treated her like she was special. It didn't matter if some of them had been boring, as long as she felt emotionally and physically safe with them.

Dorian took a few steps back, blending into the shadows as if Lynix was looking for her or something.

"Don't even try it," Raven said, grabbing hold of Dorian's

wrist and pulling her forward. "At some point, you're going to have to go after what you want."

"Raven," Dorian started to protest, but Raven lifted her hand and shook her head.

"Whatever you're about to say, don't bother. You might have your brother fooled with your disinterested behavior when Lynix is around, but I know better. Why don't you go over and say hi?"

Dorian shook her head. "Why? The man is a chick magnet. I'll give it ten minutes before a woman is draped all over him."

No sooner were the words out of her mouth, a model-like woman with perfect hair, a slamming body, and a toothpaste-white smile approached him at the bar.

"I rest my case. Besides, I'm not interested in talking to him. We'd probably just argue anyway."

Again, Raven was shaking her head. "Nah, something has changed between you two. I noticed it last week when you were at our place visiting the babies, and he showed up. Even if you claim not to be interested, he is."

Dorian snuck another peek in the man's direction, and her heart sank when the woman moved closer to whisper in his ear. Lynix laughed at whatever she said, and Dorian tried not to let it bother her. He wasn't hers, and she didn't want him anyway. Who cared who he talked to? Not her.

Unable to help herself, she continued watching him and the mystery woman. They talked for a few minutes longer before he shook his head and resumed drinking his beer.

"See, he was just being nice. He's not interested in..." Raven started but stopped when another woman approached him. This time, it appeared he knew her because he flashed her his spectacular smile, stood, and then hugged her before reclaiming his seat.

"Some things just never change," Dorian said and started to move away from Raven, but her sister-in-law stopped her.

"Okay, the woman's gone. Now you can go over there, say hi, and thank him for coming to the celebration. Knowing him, I'm sure he'll take the conversation from there."

"I don't want to talk to him." At least that's what Dorian told herself.

Part of her didn't, but her traitorous body wanted to be near him, and it pissed her off. He was no good for her. Yet, she loved the attention he always gave her.

As if sensing her watching him, Lynix turned slightly, and their gazes locked... and held. The seriousness of his expression and the intensity in his dark eyes drew her in, and it was as if everyone in the room had vanished and left them there alone.

Seconds ticked by before she quickly diverted her gaze.

What was happening to her? She'd been doing so well, but her resolve to stay clear of him was weakening.

"Come on, Dorian. Go," Raven said. "Oops, too late. He's coming over here," Raven said excitedly. "And on that note, I think Zion's looking for me. Bye, and don't feel you have to stick around if you get a better offer."

Raven started to move away, but Dorian grabbed her hand. "Don't leave me," she whisper-shouted, and Raven laughed as she sauntered away.

"Hey, beautiful," Lynix said, and Dorian shivered at the sound of his deep, husky voice. "Come outside with me. I have something to show you."

Dorian narrowed her eyes at him. "The last time you said something similar, I ended up having to run through your parents' backyard to keep from being seen by others."

Lynix grinned, then cracked up. Okay, maybe their encounter during her brother's wedding reception hadn't gone quite like that, but still, the man was a danger to her psyche.

"All right, this is a little different, but you have to admit, the kiss we shared that night was epic."

Yes, it had been, and if she were honest with herself, Dorian wanted a repeat. Then again, that would be too dangerous. Normally, she could stand firm on decisions she made, but Lynix was too irresistible for her not to be on guard.

No, she had to be strong. She'd go with him because she was curious, but there'd be no kissing.

"Let's go," she said, sounding more confident than she felt. "And don't even think about trying any funny stuff. No more stealing kisses."

He laughed again, then slid a hand around her waist and leaned in close, his intoxicating scent making her weak in the knees.

"I make no promises, sweetheart. Especially now that I know how good you taste."

# Chapter Three

"Lynix, don't make me regret going outside with you," Dorian said, and with those parting words, she headed toward the nearest exit.

He stood back for a second with a smile on his face as he watched her sashay away from him. If he wasn't mistaken, he was sure she was adding a little extra swing to her hips, and he was here for it.

Damn, she was *fine*.

Lynix followed a few steps behind her, weaving around people who were huddled together talking and laughing. He was trying not to stare at Dorian's ass, but it was impossible not to. He'd always thought her a cutie-pie, but this evening she was giving off Nubian queen vibes. The incredibly sexy, strapless black dress that stopped just above her knees hugged her curvy, petite body. Add that to the strappy black sandals highlighting her shapely legs, and he was about ready to bow down to her. Or better yet, carry her out of there and straight to his condo.

As they slowly moved across the room, he continued

checking her out. She often wore her hair in long, individual braids, which he liked, but they always made her look ten years younger. However, seeing her with her thick hair, straightened and hanging loose around her shoulders, had him itching to run his fingers through the long tresses.

He couldn't. He had to tread lightly with her.

Dorian was still skittish around him, and he understood some of the reasons why. She'd been hurt in the past by some asshole and had erected an invisible wall to protect herself. Which was making it hard for him to slide past her defenses. Another reason why she was keeping her distance was because she thought he was a lady's man. She wasn't wrong. He used to be. He unapologetically loved women. They were beautiful creatures, and there'd been a time when he welcomed their company.

But something had been missing in his life. He was tired of the chase and tired of the game of dating. Actually, he couldn't even call what he'd been doing dating. He'd just been out here floundering until one day he saw Dorian. Like really saw her. He'd always tease Zion about hooking up with his sister, Dorian, but a few months ago, the teasing didn't feel right. Lynix started to realize he really did want her, and the more he spent time with her, the more he wanted to.

They still bantered, and she still acted like she couldn't stand him, but he felt... No, he knew something had shifted between him and Dorian. Now all he wanted was her.

Lynix caught up with her. "This way," he said, nodding toward the back hallway.

He almost reached for her hand but stopped himself, not wanting to attract too much attention from the party guests. Instead, he placed his hand at the small of her back and guided her to the hallway that led to the backdoor.

Touching her anywhere always sent a jolt of electricity

shooting through his body, and now was no exception. His hand rested just above her butt, and it was taking every bit of control he had not to let it slide lower.

Hell, he was surprised she had agreed to follow him outside, and he was even more shocked that she didn't swat his hand away.

This was a good sign.

The only reason he had even taken Raven up on the invite was with hopes of spending a little time with Dorian. But the way she'd been staring at him while he was sitting at the bar, he figured the best thing to do was get her outside. She didn't like crowds, which was probably why she'd been hovering near the buffet table. Knowing her, she was looking for any excuse to do anything *but* mingle with other guests.

Now that he'd talked her into going with him, he hoped no one stopped them. It was time he upped the pressure in getting her to give him a chance. He just wanted to spend uninterrupted time with her alone. Without one of her family members showing up, especially her brother.

He'd eventually have a talk with Zion about his intentions with Dorian, but not today. Today his focus was to make sure Dorian knew he wasn't going anywhere. He wanted her in his life as more than a friend, and he'd wait patiently for her to come around to his way of thinking.

No matter how she tried to deny it, their attraction was undeniable. For years, he'd always thought her a sweetheart and adorable inside and out, but it was only recently he'd been ready to pursue her. He loved the way he felt when they were together. She was easy to be with and one of the kindest people he'd ever met.

At thirty-five, he was finally ready to settle down with one woman—Dorian—but he'd known he had to come correct. He had to be ready to make a serious commitment. Otherwise, she'd never take him seriously. Which was why he'd started making changes in his personal life. He hadn't been on a date in months, trying to prove to himself that he could be a one-woman man. He was ready because the only woman he thought about these days was Dorian, and no other woman would do.

She reached for the doorknob, but he stepped forward.

"Let me get that," he said, and a second later, they were outside.

It was almost the end of June, and the seventy-degree temperature was perfect. The sun was almost setting, and a gentle breeze brushed across his skin.

Dorian glanced around. Behind the building was a big, green dumpster several feet away from the door, as well as a couple of parking spaces. When she returned her attention back to him, her perfectly arched eyebrows were bunched together as she narrowed her eyes.

She planted her hands on her narrow hips. "Okay, so what was so important that you had to show me?"

He nodded his head to the right, where he'd created his own parking spot. He moved past her old jeep, and on the other side of it was his car. He stood next to the driver's side door with his hand on the roof of the vehicle.

"I heard you've been having car trouble. I wanted to give you something a little more dependable to drive."

Dorian's gaze bounced from him to the car and then back at him. Her facial expression went from confused to shock, and then it transformed into something he couldn't quite identify.

Damn, she was cute.

"You can't be serious."

"I'm dead serious," he said as he opened the door to the 2023 BMW 8 Series 840i. Her brother had mentioned her having car trouble over the last few weeks, and Lynix thought about this car that he rarely drove. He had even considered selling it, but now he was glad he hadn't.

"I don't know how much a car like this costs, but I do know I can't afford it," Dorian said as she walked the length of the vehicle, inspecting it as if she was on a car lot and knew what she was looking at.

"I wouldn't charge you for it."

She stopped and looked at him with wide eyes. "Sooo, what? You're just going to let me have it?" Her tone was incredulous, sounding as if that was the most ridiculous idea in the world.

"Yes." He shrugged. "I have three vehicles, and I really only drive my truck."

It wasn't like he couldn't afford to give her the car. He'd barely touched the trust fund his maternal grandfather had left him for when Lynix turned twenty-five. During the last ten years, since being able to access it, the fund was just sitting there earning interest. The only thing he'd purchased was a luxury condo that overlooked Lake Michigan. As well as investing in a couple of small businesses. Yes, he could afford to let her have the car. Or hell, even buy her one of her choosing.

"Lynix, this is extremely generous, but it's too much. I can't take your car," she said, backing away and shaking her head. "But if you're willing, I might want to borrow it on occasion for when I have a date."

Lynix stiffened, and an involuntary growl rumbled inside his chest as he watched her, trying to determine if she was serious. Her expression never changed, and he was in her face in a heartbeat.

He backed her against her jeep and gently gripped her chin in his hand, lifting it until their eyes met. "If you think for one minute I'm going to let you drive some other brother around in that car, you clearly don't know me at all."

His voice had gone deep as he tried to control the sudden jealousy rearing its wicked head. Now that was an emotion he'd never experienced. Leave it to her to bring it out of him. He didn't care if it was irrational considering they weren't a couple, but the thought of her dating anyone but him had him ready to spit bullets.

"Besides," he continued when she didn't respond, only studying him, "any man who asks you to drive on your dates doesn't deserve to be with your fine ass. You deserve to be catered to, worshipped even, and *I'm* the man who can do that."

Lynix's eyes zoned in on her tempting lips that hung open slightly at his words, and before he could stop himself, he covered her mouth with his.

Dorian froze, but as he moved his mouth over hers, she relaxed and kissed him back. Her hands slid up the front of his body until she wrapped her arms around his neck. That was all the encouragement he needed to deepen their connection. He cradled the back of her head in his hand, and his other hand circled her waist, holding her close.

Having her softness pressed flush against his body made his dick stir with need. No doubt she felt the effect she had on him, but she didn't pull away. Instead, she moaned into his mouth, her arms holding him tightly.

Lynix hadn't planned to kiss her. He'd only planned to spend some time in her presence, talk with her about the car, and then leave. He'd been trying not to come on too strong, trying not to scare her away, but instead of chipping away at the wall she'd built around her heart, his control was crumbling.

She felt too perfect against him and tasted like wine and strawberries as he devoured her mouth. He hated to admit he'd kissed plenty of women—something he wasn't proud of. Yet, he could honestly say none of those experiences matched what he and Dorian shared. And all they were doing was kissing. However, he felt the sensuous caress of her lips to the soles of his feet, and if he never kissed another woman, it would be all right. If he hadn't known it before, this moment would've sealed it for him. Dorian would one day be his.

A door slammed, and Dorian leaped away from him as if someone had burned her. Lynix growled under his breath and ran his hand over his mouth as his gaze shifted to the person who dared interrupt them.

*Shit.* Of all the people to come outside, why'd it have to be Cree, one of Dorian's older sisters. The woman, an entertainment attorney, was fine as hell, looking like she should be gracing the cover of Vogue magazine with the way she was wearing the slinky red dress. But when he looked into her eyes, she reminded him how she had the ability to put fear into the most hardened criminal with just a look. Yeah, she was that scary.

Cree looked from him to Dorian and then back at him before narrowing her eyes.

"I guess I don't have to ask what's going on out here," she said, her husky voice deceptively calm, while her gaze was hard enough to chop him into pieces. Then she turned her attention to Dorian and so did he.

Lynix couldn't stop himself from smirking when he looked at his sweet Dorian. She might've been a sweetheart, but he sensed there was a bit of a hellcat inside of her, considering the way she was glowering at Cree.

But of course, there was. She came from a family of strong, outspoken women. There was no way some of their strength and boldness hadn't rubbed off on her. Why would he think otherwise?

*Because she's so damn sweet,* that little voice in the back of his mind said.

"I know why I'm out here," Dorian snapped angrily, her arms folded across her chest. "But why are you? Are you following me?"

Seconds ticked by before a slow smile spread across Cree's lips, and she pointed at Dorian. "Don't get snippy with me, young lady," she said, humor in her tone, something Lynix had never heard from her before. "I came looking for you because they're getting ready to toast the happy couple, and I didn't think you'd want to miss that." She turned and glared at Lynix. "Then again, I could be wrong. Maybe you'd prefer to have Lynix's slick talking tongue down your throat instead."

"That's none of your business," Dorian said, her words not as confident as they'd been moments ago. "So you can leave."

Cree waved her hand dismissively. "Fine, I'll go, but Lynix, I don't care if you are some rich, entitled prince. Hurt my little sister, and I will destroy your ass."

*Prince?* She'd known him for years and knew he wasn't some damn prince.

"And after I destroy you financially, then I'll cut off your balls and feed them to a junkyard dog. Think about that the next time you kiss my sister at a family event."

"Seriously, Cree?" he said, struggling not to laugh at her dramatics.

Without responding, she turned on her red, sky-high heels and went back inside as if she hadn't just threatened to castrate him.

Lynix looked at Dorian. "Should I be afraid?" he asked jokingly, trying to lighten the mood, and Dorian didn't disappoint when she burst out laughing.

She laughed for a solid minute before saying, "Umm, *yeah*. You should be *very* afraid. You know she don't play."

Smiling, Lynix nodded and pulled her back into his arms.

He kissed her sweet lips and then asked, "Will you have dinner with me next weekend?"

Dorian sighed and placed her hands on his chest, oblivious of the effect her fiery touch had on him. Her hands were like a hot poker against his skin, but he loved when she touched him.

"Lynix, I—"

"Don't say no," he said quietly and brushed the back of his fingers down her soft cheek. "Even if you're not ready to date me exclusively, tell me you'll have dinner with me in the *very* near future."

"Okay, I won't say no. I'll say... maybe."

She smiled at him, and it was like watching the sun burst through clouds on a rainy day. He wanted to see that smile every day of his life, and all he had to do was figure out how to make that happen. How to get her to let down her guard with him.

He gave her another quick peck on the lips. "I'll take that. Just know I'm not giving up. I'll be asking again soon."

She nodded, still smiling as she walked backwards toward the door. "Take care, Lynix, and thanks for the offer regarding the car." Were the last words she spoke before disappearing inside the building.

Lynix rubbed his hand over his short beard as he stood there a moment longer. He needed a plan. It was time to show her what she was missing by not giving him a chance.

Feeling encouraged, he walked to the driver's side of his car and climbed in. He'd think of something. He always did.

# Chapter Four

Lynix smiled to himself as he drove north along Sheridan Road toward his parents' estate. The picturesque views of Lake Michigan, just before nightfall, was a beautiful sight and matched his mood. He always felt lighter after spending time with Dorian, whether alone or when they hung out with their five-month-old godchildren.

It had been an honor when Zion asked him months ago to be his twins' godfather. Of course Lynix accepted. He loved kids, and those two were perfect little humans. He loved spending time with them and watching how they were growing and developing so fast.

Then there was the fact that Dorian was their godmother, which gave him more opportunities to see her. That was probably why Lynix's feelings for her were growing more intense so quickly. He got to see the real her when she was with the babies and not being overshadowed by her large family. Or running around taking care of things for her parents' bed and breakfast where she worked.

Yeah, running into her today, with her looking absolutely gorgeous, and getting to spend a couple of minutes one-on-one with her, had been a treat. But he wanted more of her and more of her time.

Another glance at the lake gave him an idea. An early morning date with Dorian to see the sun rise over Lake Michigan would be perfect. Especially if they were on the roof top of his condo eating a light breakfast and drinking coffee. She would love that.

Lynix had planned his share of dinner, theater, and even weekend getaway dates. Yet, he had never looked forward to being with a woman the way he looked forward to being with Dorian.

*Soon.* He'd get his chance soon, but for right now, he needed to get mentally prepared to spend the evening with his parents. Specifically, his father.

His parents spent the winters in Palm Beach and had arrived in Chicago last night with intentions of staying in town a few months. Hearing from his mother this morning, asking him to come for a late dinner tonight, hadn't been a surprise. Whenever she was in town, she insisted on seeing her boys, and she'd see him more often if it weren't for his dad. Too bad they didn't get along.

His mother, however, was his heart. There was nothing he wouldn't do for her, even agree to spend a couple of hours with his father. Just thinking about the man had Lynix gripping the steering wheel tighter. It was because of his dad, Weston Mathews III, that Lynix had joined the police force. Mainly to piss him off.

Lynix grinned at the memory of the day he'd told the old man he wouldn't be going into the family business. Instead, he was joining Chicago PD. Talk about a legendary argument. His pops had been livid. It was right after he'd graduated from college. Instead of sticking to the plan that his pops had laid out for him, Lynix rebelled.

The old man had wanted all four of his sons to oversee the numerous businesses he had started or taken over. Businesses that he had built over the years and turned into a multimillion-dollar family empire. Everything from hotels to manufacturing companies, they had their hands in a lot and were very successful.

As the youngest, Lynix was the only one of his brothers who hadn't fallen in line with their father's plans, which also included him getting an MBA. Not just a bachelor's degree in business. That had been one of many plans of his father's Lynix had squashed, which was a big reason their relationship had been on shaky ground for much of his adult life.

As he neared his parents' neighborhood, he turned the volume up on the radio. He bobbed his head and tapped his fingers on the steering wheel as Usher's "Good Good" flowed through the car speakers. Normally, he'd blast some rap music, the raunchier the better, to help get him into a certain frame of mind to deal with his father. Not today, though. Today he was in too good of a mood for even his father to get on his nerves.

Lynix pulled up to the gated entrance of his parents' home and punched in the code. When the tall iron gates slid open, he drove along the tree-lined driveway until he reached the six-thousand square foot home. Parking behind his oldest brother's Range Rover, he realized another one of his brothers had arrived. There was only one car in the long, circular drive that he didn't recognize.

Lynix had barely made it to the door before it swung open, and his mother stood smiling in the doorway. Normally, the housekeeper would be the one opening the door. So this was a surprise.

"You made it," she said, smiling and opening her arms to him.

"Hey, Mom. You look as amazing as usual." He wrapped her in a bear hug and soaked up her scent, as well as her gentle spirit. His father might be an asshole, but what his pops lacked in common decency, his mother made up for with her sweet and calming presence.

"Thank you, honey. I'm glad you're here," she said, ushering him into the house and closing the door behind him.

Standing in the foyer that had a twenty-foot ceiling, marbled floors, as well as an elegant double staircase, Lynix's senses were bombarded by several things at once. The smell of curry and ginger, as well as a host of other spices, had his mouth watering. Apparently, his parents' live-in cook had made the trip. Smooth jazz—John Coltrane's "A Love Supreme"—played through the home's sound system, and the other thing that snagged his attention was the strange vibe he was getting from his mother.

Nervousness.

Anyone who knew Bridget Mathews knew she didn't get nervous. She owned whatever space she was in and wore her confidence, as well as her regalness, like a badge of honor. So the unusual emotion he was picking up from her was different. She had her cell phone in hand and was quickly typing out a message as he studied her.

She was always well put together, and tonight was no different. Her salt and pepper hair was pulled up on top of her head in an intricate twist with long strands framing her face. At seventy-years old, her face was free of wrinkles and that was without any cosmetic surgery. He couldn't help thinking of her whenever he heard the phrase, *black don't crack.*

His mom favored African attire, and she looked regal in the

multicolor halter maxi dress. The bold colors accentuated her beautiful sepia skin tone and gave her a youthful appearance.

As if feeling him staring at her, she finally lifted her head, then shoved the cell phone into a hidden pocket in her dress. "Sorry," she said and patted her hair which looked perfect.

Moving closer, Lynix whispered, "What's going on? Are you okay?" he asked, his protective instincts going on high alert. He didn't think she'd just be standing there if she was in danger, but...

That's when he heard laughter coming from the living room to his right and about twenty-five feet from the entrance. The way the room was positioned, he couldn't see into it, but he could definitely hear several voices. He had temporarily forgotten about the additional vehicle he'd seen outside.

His mother gently grasped his arm and guided him to the huge dining room that was on the opposite side of the house from the living room and steps away from the kitchen.

"So you don't feel ambushed when you walk into the living room, I wanted to give you a heads-up," she said in a low voice, and Lynix went still.

"Who's here?" He folded his arms across his chest wondering what was going on. Whoever it was must've been someone he didn't like. Otherwise, his mother wouldn't have pulled him off to the side. This explained why she'd met him at the door.

"Your brothers are in there, but your dad also invited Karsten and Marisela."

Lynix dropped his arms to his side as anger crawled through him. His first thought was to get the hell out of there. He didn't need any drama tonight, and he sure as hell didn't want to see Marisela. Or her father, Karsten Baldwin, for that matter.

Yeah, he needed to leave. However, seeing the pleading

look in his mother's eyes kept him in place. He also didn't want to make a scene because there was no doubt in his mind the Baldwins knew he'd be there tonight.

"I had no idea your dad invited them until ten minutes before they showed up. I would've called you, but I didn't want you to turn around and go home. I wanted to see my baby," she said, cupping his cheek, and Lynix leaned into her touch and released a long sigh.

He tried tamping down the fury swirling inside of him. Yeah, had he known who'd be there for dinner, returning home was exactly what he would've done.

"I'm sorry, honey. I know how you feel about them, but I'm hoping we can have a lovely dinner. I haven't seen you boys in months, not since my birthday in March, and I wanted all of us to catch up. I guess I should've told your father my intentions. Then maybe he wouldn't have invited anyone over tonight. With that said, hopefully everyone can leave the past in the past."

"Seriously?" he ground out. His anger now mixed with frustration. "You honestly think Pops and Mr. Baldwin won't bring up the past?"

Before she could answer, Lynix heard footsteps heading in their direction, and he braced himself, thinking it was his father. But when he turned, he was glad to see it was his oldest brother Weston IV, who they called Wes.

"What's up, bro?" his brother said and switched the drink he was holding to his other hand before giving Lynix some dap. Then he pulled him in, and they bumped shoulders in lieu of a man hug.

"Hey, man." Some of Lynix's frustration subsided, but he was still tempted to make a break for it. At least a couple of his brothers were there. "Sorry about not calling you back this morning. I had to work, and then I just got busy. You said something about needing to talk about the hotels."

The family owned numerous hotels around the country and had recently taken over ownership of one near downtown Chicago.

"Okay, I'm going to let you boys talk business but for only ten minutes," their mother whispered, looking between the two of them before settling her gaze on Lynix. "I'm sorry about tonight, honey, but I expect you to be on your best behavior."

"Mom..."

She squeezed his hand. "If for nothing else, do it for me. You have every right not to want to spend time with the Baldwin family, but I want you to stay. I promise to keep your father in line," she said before kissing his cheek and walking away.

His mother was probably the only one who could control Weston Mathews III. She was the one person his father adored, and though his dad was a hard-ass, he always showed his wife the utmost respect. It was everyone else he didn't give a damn about.

Then again, he'd held his father-in-law, Lynix's grandfather, in high regard until he passed away almost twenty years ago. Lynix's mother's side of the family came from old money, and his dad was always trying to prove himself worthy. As a young man, he had big dreams and barely enough money to pay for rent. Let alone his college education.

After hearing about his plans to take over a manufacturing company, Lynix's grandfather had invested in his father's very first business. According to the stories heard throughout Lynix's childhood, his Pops had worked his ass off to be a success, mainly so he could pay his father-in-law back within a year. He'd done that, and had since become a self-made multimillionaire, but not without a lot of sacrifice. Which was probably why he was such a jerk.

"Come on. I have ten minutes to tell you why I called this morning," Wes said, snagging Lynix out of his thoughts. "Want a drink?"

"Definitely. The stronger the better."

They went to the family room at the back of the house that used to be their game room when growing up. Their mother had converted it shortly after he moved out, and it looked like a totally different, more sophisticated space.

Lynix headed straight to the small bar. He needed a little calming elixir to help him get through the night. But nothing too strong to where he risked embarrassing himself or his family.

He grabbed a tumbler and a bottle of cognac. Once he poured his drink, he took a healthy swallow.

"I take it you didn't know the Baldwins would be here," Wes said.

"Of course not. I wouldn't have come if I did. I know that whole crazy situation is in the past, but I wouldn't put it past Pops to start some mess tonight."

"I wish I could disagree, but he is who he is."

"True, but anyway, what did you want to talk to me about?" Lynix knew if they didn't show up in the living room in ten minutes, their mother would come find them. She might be sweet, but when she told you to do something, she expected it to be done.

"How attached are you to Chicago PD?"

Lynix lifted an eyebrow, wondering where this was going. "I wouldn't necessarily say I'm attached, but I like my job well enough."

He could honestly say every day was different, and there was never a dull moment. Still, there were days when he thought about doing something different with his life. Especially since he'd been thinking about a future with Dorian.

"I want you to come work with me," his brother said and sipped his drink.

Wes mostly oversaw the companies that fell under the family's hospitality ventures, including restaurants they owned around the country.

"Before I hire another executive, I figured I'd see if you'd be willing to come on board. You can finally use that business degree of yours, and before you ask, I promise to keep dad away. To be honest, he hasn't been micromanaging as much as he used to. He calls himself semiretired, but Thane and Omari say otherwise," he said of their brothers.

Thane was the Operations Manager of their father's very first business, a manufacturing company that had recently gone international. While Omari was the Operations Manager of their tech company. Wes oversaw the hospitality leg of the family's holdings, but he also owned a few businesses of his own. Lynix honestly didn't know how he did it all.

"I find that hard to believe," Lynix said as he gently swirled the liquid in his glass while thinking about his brother's offer.

"Believe it. We had a big blowup last year, and I told him either he backed off or find a new CEO. He conceded, and I haven't had any trouble... Well, I haven't had many issues where he's concerned."

Lynix nodded. That was good to know. Surprising, but good, nonetheless.

"And I'm prepared to triple whatever you make with the city," Wes added, looking pleased with himself.

"You know I'm not motivated by money. I have enough to live comfortably for the rest of my life." Especially if he was careful with his investments. "It would be cool and a nice change of pace to work with you and in the family business.

However, I'm going to have to wait for an official offer before I say yes. Can't have you saying one thing with the intention of going back on your word," he joked, knowing Wes was one of the most honorable men he knew.

His brother chuckled. "I'll get on that. In the meantime, I have some pressing issues that need to be handled. Things you can probably do while still with Chicago PD."

"Yeah, just let me know what you need." He finished off his drink and set the empty glass on a table, knowing the housekeeper would take care of it. "But if I do decide to leave the force, I'd want to give a few weeks' notice."

They continued talking as they left the room, and as they strolled down the hallway, the door to one of the guests' bathrooms opened.

They slowed, and the first thing Lynix saw was a black, high-heeled sandal attached to a dark, shapely leg. When the woman's full body appeared in the hallway and they locked eyes, Lynix's heart slammed against his chest.

Marisela—his ex-fiancée.

# Chapter Five

"**H**ello, Lynix. It's good to see you."

"Too bad I can't say the same," he ground out, clenching and unclenching his fists at his side.

Ignoring the way her dark eyes gave him the once over, Lynix moved around the woman and headed to the main foyer. He feared that, if he opened his mouth to say more, he'd say something extremely disrespectful because that's how much he hated her.

So instead of risking making a scene, he was leaving. Seeing her again brought back a host of memories he didn't want to relive. Memories that had messed with his head years ago and were currently pissing him the hell off. He thought he had moved on. Forgive and forget, but...

"I see you still haven't forgiven me," Marisela said as if reading his mind.

Lynix stopped at the end of the hallway and slowly turned to her. She was still standing just outside the bathroom door, but now she was leaning with a shoulder propped against the wall and her legs crossed at the ankle. She looked as if she didn't have a care in the world.

"I think this is my cue to get lost. Holler if you need rescuing," his brother said with humor in his tone.

If only Wes knew what happened in college with Marisela, he wouldn't leave him alone with her. Nor would there be humor in his tone. Only two people, besides Marisela, knew about the worst night of his life during his freshmen year of college. That was his brother Omari and Lynix's college roommate, Jake.

Omari was the closest in age to Lynix. They shared a bedroom growing up, and he was one of Lynix's best friends. His brother had come through for him big-time that night, and they hadn't spoken of the situation since.

That had been fifteen years ago, and Lynix had no intentions of ever discussing that night again. It had been the scariest and most humiliating day of his life.

He stiffened when he realized Marisela was walking toward him, but she stopped suddenly. He wasn't sure what she saw on his face, but whatever it was had her rooted in place. Good. He didn't want her nowhere near him.

"Lynix, what happened back then was a long time ago," she said quietly as she started walking toward him again. "I don't know how many times I have to apologize, but I really am sorry about all that went down. What do I have to do to get you to move past my horrible mistake? We were stupid freshmen in college. I'm sure there were things you did back then that you aren't proud of."

*Not back then,* Lynix thought. Thanks to her, he had changed schools, anything to put some distance between them. Then he spent the rest of his college life keeping his head down and doing everything he could to get through the next three years.

As for his early adult life? Yeah, there were things he wished he could take back. Namely his hoeing ways. He loved women and they loved him, and these days, that wasn't something he was proud of. But he had changed. Changed for the better so he could win the heart of the most incredible woman he knew—Dorian.

"Well, you can keep pushing me away, but now that we're adults and have moved on from that night, I want you back."

Heart pounding loud enough to wake up the dead, Lynix looked at her as if she had lost her damn mind. He moved closer so he wouldn't have to raise his voice, and he didn't want anyone else to hear what he was about to say.

"Let me make this clear once and for all," he said, hearing the lethalness in his own voice. "I don't know what type of game you're playing, but I don't want you. You are the lowest form of human life, and as far as I'm concerned, you can go straight to hell where you belong."

She held his gaze and lifted her chin in defiance. In that superior way she used to do, as if she was beyond reproach. "Baby, I know you don't mean that." Her voice was low and sultry as if she truly wasn't getting what he was saying.

"Oh, I sure as hell do mean it, and if you don't believe me, fuck around and find out what happens." Rage clawed through his body, and he was struggling to keep it in check because this woman had a way of stirring the beast within him like no other.

He shortened the distance between them. Close enough to get a whiff of her floral scent, and it almost made him gag, but he needed to make sure she understood him. Standing several inches taller than her, even in her high heels, he used his size to intimidate her and leaned in.

"We share a secret, and if you want to keep it that way, I suggest you stay as far away from me as possible. I heard about your new fashion line, and I'm sure you wouldn't want your potential investors or buyers to find out what type of person you really are. I guarantee if they knew what I knew, you wouldn't be able to sell shit."

Concern flashed in her eyes, but it was gone as fast as it appeared as they stood staring at each other, but then that spark of mischief had returned to her dark gaze.

"Oh, Lynix. I guess that means you really haven't forgiven me yet." She ran the back of her bejeweled fingers over his chest, and his body jerked as if burned, and he grabbed hold of her wrist in the process.

"No, that means if you *ever* come near me or touch me again, you're going to wish you were dead."

Approaching footsteps sounded in his ear, and he released her, then cursed under his breath. He might've missed his opportunity to flee the house without an audience.

"Oh good. I see you two kids have kissed and made up," Mr. Baldwin said.

The smiling multimillionaire was a big guy with a receding hairline, light-brown eyes, and a broad nose that took up the majority of his face. He had raised Marisela after his wife died from a rare disease when their daughter was only four. Lynix couldn't even imagine how hard that had to be, especially after losing his wife. It all probably played a major role into why Marisela was a spoiled brat who had mean-girl tendencies. Still, the older man adored his daughter.

And right now, the huge grin on the guy's face was grating on Lynix's nerves.

"We haven't kissed and made up yet, but I was suggesting to Lynix that we should do just that," Marisela said sweetly, and Lynix gritted his teeth so tightly it made his jaw ache.

Yeah, she was up to something, and for all he knew, her father was in on it. So Lynix needed to shut whatever this was down immediately.

"That's *never* going to happen for so many reasons, but it mainly won't happen because I'm involved with someone." The words flew from his mouth before he could think them through, but most of them were true.

He turned away from Marisela and strolled past Mr. Baldwin with every intention of walking out the front door without looking back. But before he could reach it, his mother and father stepped into the foyer.

"Well, if it isn't the prodigal son," his father, Weston Mathews III, said.

He and Lynix had similar builds with his dad being an inch or two taller with salt and pepper hair neatly cut and a full, perfectly trimmed beard covering his face. Dressed in a black shirt and pants with a lightweight tweed jacket, he looked more relaxed than Lynix had ever seen him. Maybe it was true. Maybe he really was trying to retire.

"I'm glad you're here, Son," his dad continued, surprising Lynix by referring to him as *Son.* Usually his father preferred terms like, *idiot, pain in the ass, bane of my existence,* when it came to Lynix. "Did Karsten tell you that he and I want to talk to you and Marisela after dinner?" he asked of Mr. Baldwin.

"*Weston,*" Lynix's mom said in a warning tone. "Not tonight. We're going to have a nice meal together, and there will be no talk about business... or marriages."

Lynix's hackles went up. So he was right, Marisela and her father were up to something, but he wasn't about to stick around and find out what that something was.

"Sorry, Mom. I can't stay," Lynix said, and he didn't miss the disappointment in her eyes.

His father threw up his hands and scowled. "There he goes running like the punk ass he is," he said, disgust dripping from his words.

And that was the father Lynix remembered. From what he

could tell, the only thing that had changed was his style of dress. Other than that, he was still the self-serving, controlling, bastard he'd always been.

"I raised you to be a strong, respectable man," his father continued. "Yet, you continue to embarrass me and disappoint your mother. We have guests here, and Marisela came to see you. You're not going anywhere."

Lynix snorted, then started laughing. He couldn't help it. The old man actually thought he could tell him what to do, and he'd listen. Those days were long gone, and it was time he reminded him. But not wanting to embarrass or disappoint his mother any more than his leaving would do, Lynix didn't speak the words that were dangling on the edge of his tongue.

No, he'd save them for his father's ears only. Because whatever he and Mr. Baldwin were up to, Lynix was sure he'd hear about it sooner or later. When that happened, he'd be ready to shoot it down without remorse.

He approached his mother who was moving toward him. Reaching for her hand, he squeezed it and kissed her cheek. "I'm sorry, Mom. I can't stay."

She released a long breath and nodded. "I know, and I'll walk you out."

Lynix knew his brothers probably heard everything from wherever they were, and he'd talk to them later. Once he and his mother were outside, she pulled the door closed behind her.

"I'm sorry, honey. I'll be having a long talk with your father. I don't know what he and Karsten have planned, but I'll make sure they keep you out of it."

She might try, but knowing his father, he'd still find a way to rope Lynix into something. He would try it more with his brothers if he could get away with it. He definitely couldn't insist on them being a part of some stupid marriage scheme since Wes was married, Thane was engaged, and Omari had a longtime girlfriend. That only left Lynix.

Instead of telling his mother that she probably couldn't stop whatever his father had in motion, he said, "Thanks, Mom, and sorry I can't stay."

"It's okay, but did I hear you say you were dating someone?"

*Dammit.* She wasn't supposed to hear that. Hell, he wasn't sure why he'd said it in the first place. Yet here he was now, having to explain himself. He could lie, but his conscience wouldn't let him. Instead, he gave her a half-truth that he hoped to be true sometime in the very near future.

"Yes, I'm seeing someone, but we're taking it slow."

The smile on his mother's face could've lit up Times Square during a blackout. She never tried to push him and his brothers into relationships, nor did she demand they give her grandchildren, but he knew that's what she wanted.

"That's wonderful. I hope you're planning to bring her to the fundraiser gala next month. Or better yet, you can bring her by here so I can meet her," she said, and he didn't miss the hopefulness in her voice.

Instead of saying yes or no, he kissed her on her cheek and said, "We'll see."

Now all he had to do was get Dorian to come around to his way of thinking.

# Chapter Six

**D**orian pulled the chicken parmesan from the oven and sat the pan on the counter. Her job at her parents' bed and breakfast was to cook the meals, as well as prepare desserts and snacks for the guests. Tonight, along with the entree, she had made pasta, baked homemade bread, and made a large Caesar salad to go with the meal.

She opened the door of the second oven and peeked at the apple pies baking. A few more minutes and everything should be done.

Years ago, after her parents opened the B&B, Dorian never imagined she'd one day work alongside them. However, over a year ago, despite plans of one day becoming an executive at the company, she had walked away from her marketing job. She hadn't wanted to leave, but the drama she'd been caught up in while there forced her hand. It turned out that leaving and joining her parents at their quaint B&B had been the best decision she could've made.

She had always enjoyed cooking and baking, so working there was a good fit. Her parents had once feared none of their children would want to keep the B&B going after they retired, but Dorian was looking forward to overseeing the business someday.

"Baby, you should go ahead and get changed so you don't be late for your date," Virginia Priestly said as she strolled into the kitchen carrying several rolls of paper towel and a large pack of napkins.

She stored them in the pantry. When she came back out, she was putting on a red apron over her colorful sundress. Though her mother was in her sixties, her flawless dark skin, stylish updo, and welcoming smile made her look years younger. Her vibrant personality also helped with that and made her perfect for hosting guests at the B&B.

"I can finish up dinner, and Gwendolyn Renee will take care of cleanup this evening," she said of Dorian's aunt who also helped out at the B&B.

"I appreciate that." Dorian removed her apron. Then she grabbed her duffel bag from a cubby in the back of the pantry which held her change of clothes. "The dinner is done, but the pies need a few more minutes. I set the timer, and they should be ready to take out in ten minutes. Oh, and there's a bowl of fruit in the refrigerator to set out tonight, as well as pastries." She pointed to the counter on the other side of the baker's rack.

The B&B was full to capacity, which wasn't unusual for the summertime, and she tried to make sure there was always extra food and snacks available for the guests.

"Got it," her mother said and smiled as she approached with her arms outstretched.

The woman was a hugger, and normally Dorian craved her hugs, but she knew what this was about. Her mother was in the *let-me-get-all-up-in-your-business* mode. She felt she was entitled since she was the one who introduced her to her date, Glen.

Her mother was still on her matchmaking kick, and Dorian was a little sick of it. It wouldn't be so bad if she wasn't just focused on her, instead of Dorian's two older sisters, Cree and Essence. But nope, she was the one getting all the attention, and telling her mother to back off was akin to telling her to try harder. Virginia felt it her duty to find the perfect man for her baby girl.

Her words. Not Dorian's.

Her mother hugged her tightly before releasing her and stepping back. "I'm so excited you and Glen are going out again. This is a good sign. It means you two must be getting serious."

"Mom, don't get ahead of yourself. Glen is nice and all, but we're just friends. Right now, I'm keeping my options open and not limiting my dating life to one man."

Her mother waved her off. "Oh hogwash. Glen is perfect for you. Nice-looking, great job, well-mannered, and he always smells so good when he delivers our packages here."

He worked full time for a shipping, receiving, and delivery company, and the B&B was a part of his route.

"Besides, I asked him all the important questions months ago," her mom said as if it was perfectly normal for a mother to vet her daughter's dates in advance. "Never been married. No kids. Owns his home, and he adores his parents. I can totally envision the two of you having a long life together. All I ask is that you don't elope. Don't be selfish like your sister, Nyla. I want to be a part of your big day. I even want to help plan your wedding, and your dad and I will pay for it when you're ready."

Dorian rolled her eyes, knowing she should run from the room right now before her mother continued.

A loud sigh came from the entrance into the kitchen and Dorian perked up when her aunt, Gwendolyn Renee, who she called Aunt GiGi, strolled in. "Ginny, leave the girl alone," she said. "She's thirty-three years old. She doesn't need you butting into her love life. That's probably why Nyla and Harrison eloped. They didn't want to put up with you and your helicopter parenting and know-it-all self."

"Oh hush," Dorian's mother said, smiling and not looking deterred in the least, but she did stop with the wedding talk.

"Thanks, Aunt GiGi," Dorian whispered as she hugged her fashionista auntie whose makeup was done to perfection, including the red lipstick she favored.

Dressed in tight blue jeans and a light strapless blouse, she looked as stylish as usual. She was a retired educator. Now she helped out wherever needed at the B&B, and she always looked amazing. She had once told Dorian that it was more important to be ready for an opportunity to meet a man than to have a man show up and you look a hot mess.

"I appreciate you sticking up for me, but you won't have to after tonight. I've already made a mental note to myself to never let my dates pick me up from here."

She had mainly done it these last few times because she hadn't been ready for Glen to know where she lived. He was nice enough, but she didn't feel a spark when they were together. It was safe to say he might stay in the friend zone.

Dorian left her mother and aunt in the kitchen, then headed to the bathroom at the back of the huge home. After leaving their corporate jobs, her parents had remodeled the Chicago Greystone, maintaining its Italian architectural charm. The ornate, old world style building, with its historic and modern amenities, had been featured in several magazines over the years.

The home was stunning inside and out with dark woods and grandeur artwork and furnishings. It had seven huge bedroom suites, a large eat-in kitchen—which happened to be Dorian's dream kitchen, a dining room, living room, and a library. What made it even more perfect was the two-bedroom, two-bathroom innkeeper's cottage directly behind the main building where her parents stayed.

Dorian entered the bathroom and wasted no time in getting changed into a deep pink, cold-shoulder blouse and black skintight jeans that molded over her hips and butt. She paired the outfit with black wedge heel sandals and silver jewelry. Once she finished getting dressed, she freshened up her makeup. Going for understated but alluring, she added eyeshadow, black eyeliner, and mascara, and in the end, it did what she set out to do.

Now all she had to do was get through the evening without thinking about a certain someone else. The someone who made her tingle inside and who kissed like he created the activity.

*Lynix.* No matter how she tried, thoughts of him kept creeping in and whenever that happened, memories of their kisses dominated her mind. The man definitely knew how to turn her on with his lips and tongue.

*I wonder what else he can do with his mouth.*

The wayward thought came with an erotic visual that slammed into Dorian like a powerful wave, and she gripped the edge of the vanity as her body trembled. It was as if she could actually feel Lynix's warm mouth on her, sucking and teasing her nipples into tight buds before peppering kisses down the center of her body. Once he reached the apex between her thighs, his tongue began its exploration, doing wicked things to...

*Gawd!* She slammed her eyes closed and breathed in and out a few times. What the heck was wrong with her? She didn't normally have sexual fantasies, but they'd been coming more often, usually while she was asleep.

All of this was a first. She never imagined herself with a man the way she'd been imagining herself with Lynix. She had no right fantasizing about how he could please her in places she had no intention of ever letting him near.

Nope. She wasn't going there, and neither was he. It was time to stop torturing herself with these thoughts. No sense in thinking about being intimate with the man unless it was going to actually happen, and it wasn't. *Ever.*

She just had to forget about him.

They hadn't spoken in a couple of weeks. The last time had been a week after Nyla's wedding reception. He had called and asked Dorian out to dinner, but she'd already had plans—a date —and turned him down. He didn't seem too disappointed and told her that he wasn't giving up, but she hadn't heard from him this week. Which was probably for the best.

All she had to do was remember why it wasn't a good idea to hook up with Lynix. He might be sexy, funny, and easy on the eyes, but he was also a player. Granted, he insisted he had changed, but she didn't believe him. Besides, dating her brother's best friend was taboo. Or at least that's what she'd heard.

But man, her mind kept circling back to Lynix's delicious kisses. As well as the way her body sparked to life whenever he hugged or touched her. Dorian hoped going out with other men would distract her from her sensuous thoughts of Lynix. Clearly, that wasn't working, but hopefully it would eventually.

Unfortunately, that last thought made her think of Keenan, a blind date she'd had a few days ago. He was the cousin of a former client, who insisted they were perfect for each other. Wrong!

Keenan, an investment manager, was a nice-looking guy and a great dresser. Yet, he'd been unbelievably boring. He had taken her to a high-end restaurant, and the food had been amazing. Yet, the conversation had been stilted, and she found herself counting down the minutes until the date was over.

No more blind dates, and she also planned to put an end to

her mother's matchmaking. The latter wasn't going to be as easy, but Dorian had to do something. Her mother was clearly getting obsessed, and it didn't help that she rarely took no for an answer.

*Well, she's going to have to start getting used to me saying "no" because I'm not letting her fix me up with anyone else. I can find my own dates.*

The alarm on Dorian's phone chimed, informing her that Glen would be there in fifteen minutes. She grabbed her stuff, and checked to make sure she had everything, then left the bathroom.

Voices and laughter from somewhere in the house sounded. Hopefully, it was her mother talking to guests. That way Dorian could sneak out the front door without running into her —but no such luck. When she rounded the corner, her mother was standing behind the registration desk working on the computer. As if sensing her, she glanced over her shoulder.

"You look wonderful, baby. Do you know where Glen's taking you tonight?"

"I do," Dorian said. She pulled her small purse from the duffel bag, then shoved the large bag into the cabinet under the desk. "But I'm not telling you. Can't have you showing up on my date."

"I wouldn't do that," she insisted, and Dorian just looked at her. "Seriously, I wouldn't."

So far, she hadn't done it to her or any of Dorian's siblings, but she wouldn't put it past the woman.

"I'm going to wait outside," Dorian said, and her mother grabbed her elbow, stopping her.

"That's not what I taught you," she said with authority. "You wait until the young man comes to the door and gets you."

"Normally, I would, but knowing you, you'll intercept him and ask him more questions that aren't any of your business."

"If it involves you, it's my business."

"Mom, I know it's hard to believe sometimes, but I'm a grown woman. You have to stop this. Otherwise, you won't know who I'm dating until after I'm engaged. Is that what you want?"

"No."

"Then please stop with all the matchmaking and inserting yourself into my love life."

"I'll try, but sweetie, I can't help it. I want the best for you and yes, maybe I get carried away, but you're my baby."

Dorian huffed out a breath. "Why do I even bother?" she mumbled just as she heard the front door open and caught sight of Glen. "Bye, Mom." Dorian rushed away before her mother could say another word. Glen looked at her in surprise when she grabbed his hand and pulled him back out the door.

Yes, it might've been rude not to let Glen at least say hi to her mother, but it was for his own good.

"Umm, is everything all right?" he asked, confusion in his expression.

"Everything is fine."

Like her, he was dressed casually. He had smooth fair skin, deep brown eyes, and his best feature was his friendly smile. He didn't have movie-star good looks, but with his buzz cut fade, clean-shaven face, and a tall, runner's build, he would definitely catch the eye of other women.

"Sorry, I'm a couple of minutes late," he said as he placed his hand at the small of her back and guided her to his Toyota Supra. "Traffic was a little heavy."

"No problem. You were actually right on time. Let the fun begin."

# Chapter Seven

D orian watched as the eight ball slid into the left corner pocket, and Glen did a fist pump in the air before grinning at her.

She had learned a lot about him tonight. One: he was an only child used to getting anything he wanted—according to him. Two: He was looking forward to being invited to her house so she could cook for him. Because her mother suggested it, saying *"Dorian is the best cook in the country. Get her to cook for you."* And three: Glen was competitive and an awful winner.

"I've beat you four games, babe. Maybe we should stop now before I embarrass you too much," he said with a laugh. Then he reached for her cue stick and hung hers and his back in the rack against the wall.

"I'm not embarrassed at all. I told you when we started I didn't play often. You beat a rookie. Must make you feel real good."

She grabbed her purse from under the table and strolled to where he stood. Between the music, the talking and bursts of laughter from other patrons, it was hard to hear in the small building.

"I asked you to give me some pointers, but you acted like if you did, I might turn around and beat you."

He moved closer, looking at her with a frown. "I didn't think that at all. There's no way you would've beat me, and I did give you pointers."

He had, reluctantly, as if her asking was a bother. He'd suggested she hold the stick differently, and there were a few times when he'd explained how to hit a particular shot. All that was during the first game, and it helped. But when she started making more shots by herself, he stopped helping.

Dorian just chalked it up to him wanting to focus on his own game. Shooting pool with him was supposed to be fun, but he had turned it into a competition. Which was fine, but it did take some of the fun out of the evening.

Earlier, they'd gone to an Italian restaurant and dinner had been delicious and conversation flowed easily between them. Which was when she learned more about his mother and father who had him late in life. He also talked about how much he loved his job, and it was refreshing to hear someone speak highly of their place of employment.

Everything was going great until Glen brought up her mother and told her about a conversation the two of them had. According to him, Virginia said she was determined to find Dorian a husband. Claimed she had vetted a few men already, but Glen was perfect for her baby girl. That had been only part of the conversation. By the time he was done telling her all that her mother had shared, Dorian was ready to strangle the woman who had birthed her.

Talk about embarrassing. She wasn't sure if everything Glen said was true, but enough of it sounded like Virginia that Dorian believed him. She was more determined than ever to keep her mother out of her love life. Assuming she ever talked to her again.

Unfortunately for Glen, this only added to the short list of reasons why Dorian wouldn't be going out with him again. He was too friendly with her mom, and it would be weird dating him knowing they talked about her.

If that weren't enough of a reason to make this the last date, her decision had been solidified once they arrived at the pool hall. It was as if Glen had turned into a different person.

Dorian wasn't sure if he had been showboating for someone in particular or just being a jerk while they played. The way he loudly celebrated himself after each shot he made had been a bit over the top.

Then, whenever *she* missed a shot, he made a big show of it by saying stuff like, "*Aww, babe, you'll get it next time.*" Or "*Not bad for a beginner.*" And there was the time he wrapped her in a hug, kissed the side of her forehead, and told her, "*With more practice, you might get as good as me someday.*"

"Dorian, are you listening to me?" He touched her arm, and her gaze snapped to his.

"Oh, sorry." She leaned a hip against the pool table. "What did you say?"

"I did try helping you with a few shots during our first game. But you got all weird when I put my hands on you or my arms around you."

"Oh, you mean when you were trying to grind against my ass," she said through gritted teeth, trying to keep her cool. "Because I don't see how that was supposed to help me."

Glen shrugged. "What can I say? You have a nice ass." He cracked a smile and nudged her playfully. "But seriously, I'm sorry if I made you uncomfortable. I like you, and I like being with you. Since we were on a date, I figured I'd try to get a little more up close and personal."

Yeah, she knew what he meant. They were on their third date, and if she'd been into him like that, a touch, a hug, and even some kissing would've been accepted. Except she wasn't feeling him like that. She was okay with a little touch here and there, but not when he invaded her personal space the way he had.

"Also, I know I've been an ass since we got here. I can get a little competitive when it comes to pool or any sport for that matter. I'm sorry if I embarrassed you. How about we get out of here and go next door for some ice cream?"

Dorian nodded. Maybe she was making a big deal over nothing. It's not like they were destined to be together. After tonight, she might never see him again, except when he dropped off packages at the B&B. And even then, there was a slim chance because he usually delivered to their location in the middle of the day when she wasn't there. So, she might as well try to enjoy the rest of the evening.

An hour later, after some of the best ice cream she'd ever had, they were heading back to the B&B. It was almost eleven o'clock, and Dorian couldn't wait to climb into bed. It had been a long, exhausting day, and now she wished she'd had Glen pick her up from home. Then she could get to bed quicker. Instead, she had to go back to the B&B to pick up her truck.

Rap music boomed through the speakers of the small sports car, and Dorian tried to recall who the artist was. She liked music as well as the next person, but the rapper's words were so mumbled, she couldn't understand a word he was saying, but at least the song had a nice beat.

As Glen bobbed his head to the music, he maneuvered his car in and out of the busy traffic as if he was part of Formula 1, racing along the Circuit de Monaco through the streets of Monte Carlo. Dorian appreciated him being a skilled driver, but he was driving too fast for her comfort.

While heading to the restaurant earlier, she had asked him to slow down, and he had. But she shouldn't have to ask him every time he got behind the wheel of the car. Yes, he'd driven faster than needed during their other two dates, but tonight was worse.

Dorian gripped the door handle with one hand and the center console with the other. Not only was she holding on for dear life, but she was pressing her feet to the floor as if she was able to control the brake and gas petals.

She took the liberty of turning the volume on the radio down before saying, "Glen, please slow down. You're making me nervous the way you're driving fast and weaving in and out of traffic."

"Relax, baby. Loosen up, I got you," he said, his speed remaining the same.

At least he wasn't cutting off other drivers anymore, but she was still holding her breath while he flew down the highway. Maybe he was right. Maybe she should just relax. At the rate he was going, he'd have her back at the B&B in fifteen minutes versus the twenty-five minutes it would normally take.

Glen slammed on the brakes, and Dorian screamed and braced her hand on the dashboard when it looked like he wouldn't be able to stop in time. He jerked the steering wheel to the right, barely missing the car in front of them, and jumped into another lane. He slowed down some, but he was still going above the speed limit.

Glen chuckled. "Whew, that was close. See, I told you. I got you."

Anger clawed through Dorian as she gritted her teeth and her chest heaved. Part of her wanted to tell him to just pull over, and she'd find her own way home. The other part of her didn't want to call a family member or a car service to pick her up. If she just hung on a little while longer, she'd be back at the

B&B and away from this jerk. That's assuming he didn't kill her first.

"These people can't drive worth a shit," he mumbled, still zooming through traffic.

As he talked about inexperienced slow drivers, she stared out the passenger window. It was self-absorbed buttheads like him who made her want to stop dating. Instead of a man, maybe she'd just get a dog or a cat to keep her company. Being in a relationship might be overrated, and if she was honest, she was getting tired of the dating scene. Asking men numerous questions while trying to get to know them was getting tiring. Maybe she'd just take a break and regroup.

She startled when Glen touched her thigh, and she pulled away.

"Are you okay?" he asked.

"What do you think? I asked you to slow down, yet you're going even faster than before. It's too much traffic out here for you to be driving like a maniac. You keep this up, you're going to get us killed!"

He laughed as if she told a joke. "Dramatic much? I'm just keeping up with traffic."

Dorian had the sudden urge to slap him, and she wasn't even a violent person. Yes, some other drivers were driving more than the speed limit, but Glen was passing them up. Besides, he was driving more reckless than anyone.

No sooner than she thought that, Glen cut off another driver and was met with the blaring of horns. All he did was chuckle as if this situation was funny.

"Don't worry, I'm going to get you home safely," he said, splitting his attention between her and the road. "Speaking of home, when are you going to invite me to your place?"

She looked at him as if he'd lost his mind. "Never," she said, then thought maybe she shouldn't have said that until he dropped her off. They were still at least ten or fifteen minutes from her parents' place.

"Oh, so it's like that. I've taken you out three times, and you can't even cook dinner for me or invite me over? These dates weren't cheap."

"I appreciate you taking me out, but you've just ruined a fairly decent evening. So no, I won't be inviting you to my house or anywhere else. I'm not hanging out with someone who doesn't care that his reckless driving scares me. As for the cost of the date..."

She opened her small purse and pulled out all the cash she had on her. Which probably only amounted to fifty dollars, but it was better than nothing.

"This should cover my portion." She stuffed the money into the cup holder, then folded her arms, and stared out the side window.

Glen huffed out a breath. "I shouldn't have said anything about the cost of our dates. I wanted to take you out. You don't have to pay for..."

A booming siren wailed behind them, and they both jumped. Dorian jerked her head and glanced over her shoulder. That's when she saw the police car right on their bumper and the blinding flashing red and blue lights.

"*Aww*, hell!" Glen pounded on the steering wheel, cursing up a storm.

After some maneuvering across several lanes, Glen eventually pulled onto the side of the highway. He made quick work of grabbing the car's registration from the glove compartment and pulled out his driver's license.

He glared at Dorian. "If I hadn't been arguing with you, he wouldn't have gotten the jump on me!" he growled.

"If you weren't driving like a lunatic, you wouldn't have gotten pulled over in the first place. I hope your ass gets a big fat ticket that you can't afford. Better yet, maybe they'll arrest you for reckless driving!" she snapped, then slammed the back of her head against the headrest.

No more dating. No more spending her precious time with an idiot.

Frustrated with herself and the situation, she closed her eyes and inhaled deeply, then released the breath slowly. This wasn't her. She didn't wish bad things on anyone, and she sure as heck didn't say crap like that to people. But Glen deserved her anger and more.

When Dorian heard the electric window slide down, she glanced at the driver's side just as the police officer approached the door.

"License and registration," the cop said as he leaned down slightly and looked into the car.

Dorian groaned. Of all the people to pull them over, it had to be Lynix?

*Seriously?*

# Chapter Eight

Lynix wasn't sure how long he stared at Dorian, but someone could've knocked him over with a feather. His gaze did a slow sweep over her face and down her body, and she was as pretty as usual. Except the extra makeup and the low cut of her blouse led him to believe she was on a date. *A damn date.*

He tried not to let the fact that he'd asked her out more than once taint his opinion of her decision-making skills. Yet, she'd chosen to go out with this, this... idiot who came close a couple of times of ramming into other drivers.

That bothered Lynix even more now that he saw Dorian was a passenger in the vehicle.

He glanced around the interior of the compact sports car, not seeing anything that raised any red flags before his attention went back to Dorian. Her eyes were watery, and he didn't miss the way she wrung her hands in her lap. Nervous. Anxious. Part of him wanted to ask if she was okay, but then she nibbled on her lower lip and glanced away.

*Okay, then.*

He'd start with doing his job, and then he'd figure out what to do about her. Accepting the documents from the guy, Lynix skimmed over both. He had already checked, and the car registration was good, and the driver didn't have any outstanding warrants or tickets. He did, however, have a driver's license which had expired a week ago, and there were a few ways Lynix could handle this. It all depended on how Glen Smith answered his questions.

"Where are you two coming from in such a hurry? Do you realize you were going 105 in a 65 mile-per-hour zone?"

"I'm sorry, Officer. I was keeping up with traffic and didn't realize I was going that fast."

Dorian mumbled something that Lynix didn't catch, but whatever she'd said had Glen glaring at her. Interesting. Definitely trouble in paradise.

"Where are you two coming from?" Lynix asked again, though he didn't have a professional reason for asking. Right now, his questioning was more about seeing how this guy responded.

After a slight hesitation and looking as if he was getting ready to mouth off at Lynix, Glen said, "We're on a date, and I was taking her home before you stopped us."

"A date, huh? Well, I'd think you'd want to take better care of your *date* than to be driving recklessly the way you were. Speeding, weaving in and out of traffic, improper lane changes, following too closely, failing to use turn signals, and cutting other drivers off seems a little risky when trying to get your *date* home safely. And if all that wasn't enough, you're driving with an expired driver's license."

"Dude, I'm not trying to hear a lecture. Can't you just give me a ticket so we can leave?"

It was taking all Lynix's self-control not to snatch this bastard out of the car and throw him into oncoming traffic. He couldn't do that, but it would serve the asshole right for driving erratically. Maybe if he saw what could happen to someone who got hit by a car or in an accident, he'd take his driving more seriously.

Lynix's body camera was on, so he wanted to be careful not to do or say anything that could bite him in the ass. However, he had decided to give his three-week notice at the end of his shift. So he wasn't too concerned with being reprimanded at this point.

Without another word, he took his time writing out the citation. With the offenses listed, the fees were going to eat up a huge chunk of the man's cash, but that was better than the alternative. He could arrest the guy and let him spend hours in county lockup until someone bailed him out. Yeah, he should really do that, but instead, he was going to warn him with a ticket, then give him a second chance to get his shit together.

The main reason Lynix didn't want to haul the guy away was because of Dorian. She looked a bit distraught, like she'd had enough excitement for the night. If he took Glen, she'd have to go to the station also to answer some questions. Besides, knowing her sweet nature, she wouldn't want the guy thrown in jail. Or at least he didn't think she would.

Lynix held the citation in his hand, but before he handed it to the guy, he bent slightly and made eye contact with Dorian.

"Dee, get out the car," he said, trusting that she'd listen to him. "Though I'm sure Glen is going to slow down or risk going to jail, I don't want you riding with him. He clearly doesn't give a damn about your safety."

Glen sputtered, jerking back and forth as he looked from Dorian to Lynix and back again. "What the hell, Dorian? You know him? Did you text this guy to have me pulled over?" he snapped, anger seeping from him like steam from a geyser found in Yellowstone.

"No, I didn't, but I should've! Instead, it was just dumb luck that he's the one who caught you." She angrily started unfastening her seat belt, but Glen covered her hand with his, stopping her progress.

*Son of a...*

Fury shot through Lynix. He reached through the window but stopped himself at the last minute before he could throat punch the guy. "Mr. Smith, put your hands on the steering wheel where I can see them!" he demanded, barely hanging on to his temper.

Lynix wasn't sure if it was the lethalness in his tone or what, but the man quickly did as he was told. For the first time since getting pulled over, the guy actually looked scared.

"Dorian, please don't leave," Glen said, his tone softening. "I'm sorry for how things turned out this evening. But since I'm the one who picked you up, I should be the one to make sure you get home safely. Just stay in the car. I promise to slow down."

Dorian didn't respond. She hurried out of the car and slammed the door hard enough to rock the vehicle.

*Okay, maybe she would've preferred I haul his ass to jail.*

"Here." Lynix shoved the citation at Glen, and the man glared at him. "I suggest you get your license renewed tomorrow. If you're pulled over again before you do, you're going to jail. And when you get back into traffic, slow your ass down. Otherwise, plan on spending the night in lockup. Now get out of here."

Glen released a string of curses before waving the slip of paper around. "I'm fighting this, and I'm filing a complaint against you with Chicago PD! This was a set up."

"Do what you gotta do, man," Lynix said before the guy eased back into traffic.

That left Lynix with Dorian. He glanced at her and turned

off his body cam. She didn't say anything as he approached, but her leery eyes watched him as she fiddled with the purse strap in her hands. Surely, she wasn't nervous to be left with him, but it sure looked that way.

As he shortened the distance between them, a light breeze carried her incredible fragrance—vanilla and sandalwood—to his nose, and he almost groaned. Damn, she smelled good, and she looked even better. The dark-pink blouse that highlighted her perky breasts, and jeans that hugged her perfect curves, made him want to strip her bare and love on her naked body.

One day she'd be his, and he'd show her in more ways than one how a real man treated a woman.

"Are you sure you're okay?"

She swallowed hard, then nodded.

"All right, then. Come on, let's get you home." He placed his hand at the small of her back and guided her to his police cruiser. He opened the passenger door of the SUV and nodded for her to climb in.

"I don't have to sit in the back?" she asked, her voice quiet with a slight tremor.

"Not this time. Get in."

He had the discretion on when or if he allowed anyone to sit in the front seat. She wasn't in trouble or under arrest. Besides, there was no way he'd do that to a woman he was interested in, especially Dorian.

Once she was settled into the vehicle, Lynix took his time strolling around to the driver's side. There were things he wanted to say to her, like—*Why the heck did you go out with that guy instead of me?* However, that would just make him sound like a jealous prick, and he was neither.

He let dispatch know he was taking a short break, and then he turned down the volume of his police radio. For the first few minutes, he and Dorian rode in silence with her gaze steady on the passenger window. He felt like he should say something, but he honestly didn't know what to say.

Rarely was he ever at a loss for words. However, right now, he was stumped. Sure, there were things he wanted to say or ask, but it just didn't seem like the right time. His brain told him to keep his mouth shut despite his heart telling him to tell her how he felt about her going out with others.

He cared, and Lynix believed she was the one for him. But how was he going to show her that if she wouldn't give him a chance? This whole trying to get into a relationship thing was foreign to him. He didn't normally do relationships. For so long, he didn't trust women enough to put his heart on the line, but he wanted to do that with Dorian.

*Just be patient, and the opportunity will present itself,* he thought. His gut told him to wait for her to make the next move, despite how long it might take. One thing he had learned years ago after joining the police force was to trust his gut, and it never steered him wrong.

Dorian grumbled under her breath, and Lynix looked at her. "What's wrong?"

"I'm sorry, but can you take me to the B&B instead of my house? I left my car there."

"Sure." They weren't too far from the bed and breakfast, and he exited the highway. "Are you sure you're all right?" he asked again, knowing she was probably tired of him asking.

She sighed loudly and stared down at her lap before she cast him a quick glance. "I feel so stupid."

"Why?" Lynix asked, his tone gruffer than intended, and he gripped the steering wheel tighter, fearing what she was about to say. "Did that bastard do something to you?"

"No. He was somewhat of a jerk driving like an idiot the way he was, and his attitude during the date was hit or miss. Still, I don't think he's a bad guy. I just feel like an idiot for agreeing to go out with him. I'm not sure if Zion has ever told you, but over the years, my mother insists on playing matchmaker for us. Now that Zion and Nyla are off her radar, she's set her sights on getting me married so she can have more grandkids."

Lynix kept his mouth shut while she told him about the role her mother played in this past date and others. All he could think was, if Dorian would give him a shot, she wouldn't have to put up with any of that. He knew she was attracted to him because there was no way she'd kiss him the way she had if she wasn't. Yet, she wouldn't allow herself anything more with him.

His past whoring ways and being Zion's best friend wasn't doing him any favors. Even though Lynix had changed his ways and hadn't been out with a woman in months, Dorian still believed he was that same guy.

What the hell was it going to take? He was a patient man, but her rejection was something he wasn't used to. He needed her to take him seriously that he really had changed. Maybe he needed to switch up his approach and think outside the box to get her attention.

"I'm tired of my mother butting into my love life, and I know she means well, but I've had enough. I think I'm going to take a step back from dating for a while."

"What good is that going to do?" he asked, seriously wanting to know.

"I'm tired of going out with this guy and that guy, trying to get to know them. Dating has always been hard for me, but it's harder now. I know what I want, but I'm just not finding it."

"What do you want in a man?" he asked, genuinely curious though he believed he was the man for her.

She groaned and shook her head. "I can't believe I said as much as I have. I'm going to shut up now," she mumbled.

"Oh no you don't. You can't leave me hanging. Tell me what type of man you're looking for."

Once again, seconds ticked by without her responding. He wasn't sure if she just didn't want to tell him, or if she didn't know what she wanted.

"Dorian, you can talk to me. Though I want more with you, I do consider us friends. You can trust me. Besides, you can use me as practice in case your mother asks you what you want in a man."

She snorted and peered out the window. "She won't. She thinks she already knows."

"Well, tell me anyway because I'm curious."

"I want a nice guy who I have a lot in common with. Someone who has a good job, who is kind and trustworthy, a person who cares about what I want and need. He also needs to be fun and a little adventurous, but not reckless like Glen was tonight. I kept asking him to slow down because the way he was driving scared me," she admitted.

Lynix reached over and squeezed her hand. "You should've told him to pull over so you could get out. You guys were lucky. With the way he was driving, and at that speed, things could've gone sideways real quick. Instead of me pulling him over for moving violations, I could've been responding to a fatal accident."

He wasn't trying to scare her, but some of the horrifying shit he saw while patrolling the streets of Chicago was insane. It was like people didn't value life whether it was those who thought it okay to rob someone at gunpoint, or those who didn't think anything of beating up their spouse or worse. There were definitely things about the job he wouldn't miss.

"Anything else?" he asked, steering the conversation back to where they'd left off.

"I just... I'm just not meeting the type of guys who are right for me."

"Probably because the right man for you is sitting next to you," Lynix said, unable to hold the words in. So much for not pleading his case, but he couldn't help but give it another shot. "I'm the one for you, Dorian. I get why you're fighting your attraction to me, but I'm not the guy I used to be. I'm ready to settle down with one woman, and I think that woman can be you.

"As for your brother, if you and I ever date, we'll deal with him. I just need you to give me a chance to show you what I already know."

"What do you already know?"

"That we'd be perfect together."

She didn't respond, which was all right. Lynix didn't want to hear her reasons again for keeping her distance, and he wouldn't push. At least not right now. She'd eventually come around, and when she did, he'd be ready.

He neared the B&B and slowed. "Are you going inside?"

"No. If you could drop me near my truck, that would be great. I'm parked up there in front of that red car," she said, pointing at a spot half the block up.

Lynix wasn't ready to let her go, but he needed to finish his shift. He also didn't want to overwhelm her. When she finally came to him, and she would, he wanted it to be because she wanted to. Not because he pressured her into giving him a chance.

He stopped on the side of the car parked behind her. "Sit tight, and I'll get the door for you." When he opened the door, he extended his hand, and she placed hers in his grasp. Tugging lightly, he helped her out of the vehicle.

If she noticed, she didn't say anything when he didn't release her hand as they moved toward her jeep. The thing needed to be hauled off to a junk yard. From what he'd heard, it was almost twenty years old and barely ran. She needed something new and dependable. Yet, he kept the thought to himself since they'd already had that conversation.

Dorian unlocked the SUV with her key fob, and Lynix stopped her before she opened the door. He backed her against the vehicle and blocked her in with his hands resting on the roof on each side of her. They stood that way, with her staring at his chest, until she sighed loudly and finally looked at him.

"Thanks for the ride and the conversation."

"You're welcome. Any chance I can convince you to text me and let me know you got home safely? Or do I need to follow you home?" He still might do the latter, but he should get back to patrolling.

"I'll text you, and..." She swallowed. "I'm sorry I turned down your dinner invite."

When she didn't say anything more, he brushed the back of his fingers down her soft cheek, then placed a lingering kiss on her forehead. Though what he really wanted to do was taste her sweet lips again, he refrained. The next move had to be hers.

He eased away from her before he followed through on what he really wanted—another one of her body-stirring kisses —and headed to his cruiser.

"Have a good night, Dorian, and don't forget to text me."

# Chapter Nine

Dorian loved when she and her sisters got together, and now that Raven had married into the family, Dorian had four sisters. The way her sister-in-law fit in with the Priestlys, it was as if Raven had been a part of the family forever.

They all had just left the spa, and Dorian felt well pampered after receiving everything from a full-body massage to a French pedicure. It was amazing how taking a few hours out of the day to sit back and relax could make you feel as if you were riding on a fluffy cloud. Their monthly spa days were not only a treat for her body, but also her soul. It wasn't a cheap expense, but with Cree being part owner of the luxury spa, they were treated to a couple of services. Otherwise, Dorian knew she wouldn't be able to afford the lavish experience.

Now they were getting ready to have brunch at her sister, Essence's, favorite restaurants located inside a downtown hotel. Dorian hadn't been there before, but she had heard the food was scrumptious, and as a foodie, she loved trying new dishes.

While they waited at the hostess stand to be seated, she

glanced across the crowded restaurant. Hopefully, they'd get a table near the windows so she could check out the city views.

"Did you make a reservation?" Cree asked Essence as they all took a few steps back to make room for a small group of people who were getting ready to be seated.

"I did, but we're actually a little early," she said. "Let's sit on that settee over there or at least move farther away from the hostess stand."

They did as she suggested, choosing to remain standing instead of grabbing a seat.

"Essence, I'm loving your jumpsuit. Is it new?" Dorian asked.

Her sister didn't dress up often, but since she'd been losing a little weight, Dorian had noticed the subtle changes to her wardrobe.

"Thanks, Sis. Yes, I went shopping last weekend, and this was one of my purchases," Essence said as she adjusted the thin belt on the outfit.

The beige jumpsuit with a green and tan geometric pattern had short-sleeve batwings and wide pant legs that complemented her full-figure. It was bolder than what she normally wore, which was mostly scrubs since she was a nurse.

"I'm guessing our dear sister has a man because she's been dolled up the last few times I've seen her," Cree said with a slight smile and a knowing look.

"Nope. I dress for me and no one else." Essence might've denied their sister's claim, but the way she blushed and looked away made Dorian think a new man was in the picture.

"Essence?" the hostess called out, and they all stepped forward. The tall, rail-thin woman dressed in a stylish black and white dress offered them a smile. "You can follow me."

She took them through the maze of tables, and Dorian realized the restaurant was larger than she originally thought.

Clearly, she and her sisters weren't the only ones deciding to squeeze in brunch today. Almost every table and booth were taken, and tons of servers hustled about taking orders and delivering food.

"Is this okay?" the hostess asked when she stopped at a table next to the wall of windows.

"It's perfect," the sisters said in unison, then laughed.

As they took their seats, Dorian's gaze wandered to the spectacular view outside the huge windows. Though there were a lot of tall condominiums, apartments, and office buildings surrounding the hotel, the view was stunning. It was probably even more breathtaking at night. She could even see a little of Lake Michigan between the buildings.

"How'd you hear about this restaurant?" Raven asked Essence.

"One of the doctors at the hospital had a catered event here in the hotel, and the food was so good. Between that, the ambiance, and the incredible views, I came back again one day for lunch. Like the first time, the experience was great, and now I eat here at least once or twice a month."

"Well, so far this was a good choice. I'll have to bring your brother here one day," Raven said as she opened her menu. "If the food is as good as you say, we'll add it to the rotation."

Since they had several family members, including Dorian, willing to babysit the twins whenever they needed a break, Raven and Zion were able to get in a weekly date night.

The server came to the table, introduced himself, then took their drink orders.

"How are my niece and nephew doing?" Cree asked Raven. "I haven't seen them in a few weeks."

"*Girrrl*, they are growing so fast," she said of the five-month-old babies. "They are giggling, reaching for things to put in their mouth, and they're more active in playing with toys.

Yesterday, while Andrew was on his play mat, we caught him on his stomach, rocking forward trying to reach a toy that was out of his reach. I wouldn't be surprised if he starts crawling in another month or two."

"Wow, I know they're almost six months old, but isn't that kind of soon?" Nyla asked.

"Babies develop at their own pace, and some do start crawling at six or seven months," Essence offered.

She worked in the pediatric ward at the hospital and was wonderful with children. It had been hard for her as a teen mom, but now her son Tray, who had just turned eighteen, was headed to college in the fall. Dorian was curious to see how her sister would handle being an empty nester, especially since she'd been dubbed a helicopter mom.

When their drinks arrived at the table, and the server asked if they were ready to place their orders, only Nyla was ready. The rest of them still hadn't decided on what to eat and requested a few more minutes.

"I'll be back. I'm going to run to the restroom," Nyla said. "If the server comes to the table before I return, order me the skillet dish with thick bacon on the side."

After she left, conversation started up again, but this time they all perused the extensive menu while chatting. There were so many interesting items to choose from that Dorian was tempted to order more than one entree. She eventually settled on the stuffed poblano peppers and a side of pistachio carrots.

"You didn't say anything about your date from the other night," Cree said to her, and Dorian almost groaned.

The only person who knew details about the date, and how mad she was at her mother for the matchmaking, was Raven. Nyla used to be Dorian's main confidant since they were so close in age, but she was so busy with marriage and running her jazz club, they didn't talk as much. Dorian found herself chatting more with Raven.

"It was interesting. I shouldn't have gone out with him again since I knew I wasn't really feeling him. Except maybe as a friend, but after that night, he's history."

Dorian told them about shooting pool with Glen, and the more she thought about the night, the more she realized she should've ended the date sooner. She had vowed to herself, earlier in the year, that she was no longer dating just to be dating. That meant not going out with anyone who she couldn't see herself having a future with. No sense in wasting their time or hers, especially since she was ready to fall in love, get married, and have a few kids.

But now she was taking a step back regarding her dating life. It was mentally and emotionally exhausting getting to know men and weave through the BS that some of them dished out. Maybe she'd get lucky and her Mr. Right would just fall into her lap, which was highly unlikely. At any rate, she was done. All she had to do now was keep her mother off her back.

"Tell them the rest," Raven said, a twinkle in her eyes.

Her sister-in-law had been angry about the reckless driving part of the story. Especially since some teens, who were joyriding, had slammed into her car a few months ago. She and the twins had been rushed to the hospital, and her car had been totaled.

But when Dorian told Raven about Glen getting pulled over by officer Lynix Mathews, Raven had laughed for a solid minute. According to her, the incident was a sign that she should've been on a date with Lynix instead of *Bonehead Glen*.

Dorian trusted her sisters to keep her business to themselves, mainly away from their mother, but the last part of the date was almost too embarrassing to share. Still, she told them about Glen's driving, Lynix pulling him over, and then driving her back to the B&B to pick up her car. She also told them about how Lynix had been asking her lately why she kept turning him down.

Cree already knew of his interest, and Essence admitted she'd suspected something was up between them. Mainly because of their behavior during Zion and Raven's wedding reception. The more than usual bantering between them. Stolen glances at each other. She had also noted how Lynix kept hovering, which was something Dorian hadn't noticed.

"When Glen refused to pull over, you should've called the cops right then and there. Or hell, even pretended to call," Cree said, anger in her tone.

Dorian wasn't like her. She didn't speak up half as much as she should. She also tended to give people too many chances, as well as give them the benefit of the doubt. She also didn't like the idea of anyone getting into trouble because of her. Calling the cops on Glen could've landed him in jail for his driving shenanigans. Though he might've deserved that, she wouldn't have wanted to be the reason for it.

"You know, I get why you're hesitant to go out with Lynix. But if you're interested in him, which I know you are, maybe go out with him at least once," Essence said, which surprised Dorian. "It might be fun."

She and her oldest sister were the most alike of all of them. Like her, Essence was introverted, didn't like drama, and never dated the proverbial bad boy. Though she didn't date much, she typically gravitated to men who were considered a "nice guy" who were also clean cut and had professional jobs.

But maybe her sister was right. Maybe Dorian should at least spend some time with Lynix—away from her family. Normally, when they were in each other's presence, some of her family was around. Except for him being a babe magnet, there was so much she didn't know about him. Yet, there was so much about the man that appealed to her.

Like seeing his twin dimples that were sometimes barely visible because of the scruff on his cheeks. Then there was his sense of humor, his generosity, and she liked how attentive he was with her. And after the other night, she had to include the fact that he looked damn good in his police uniform. Despite being pissed at herself and at Glen, seeing Lynix had made her body hum with need. The man was big, bad, and intimidating on any given day, but in his uniform? He looked downright lethal... and yummy if she was being honest.

That, along with how sweet he was to her the other night had her thinking about him more. Her curiosity about him was piqued, but going on a date with him still gave her pause. Yet her defenses were weakening. Maybe they could hang out without dating. She wasn't sure if that would be enough for him, but right now, it was all she was willing to do.

Nyla rushed back to the table and dropped down in her seat with a huge grin on her face. "Dee, you are *never* going to believe who I just saw on the other side of the restaurant. Guess who."

Dorian rolled her eyes and shrugged. "Serious, Nyla? It could be anyone. I wouldn't even know where to start guessing. Just tell me."

"Lynix!" she whisper-shouted. "And you're never going to believe who he's in a meeting with—your old boss, Shauna, and your loser ex-boyfriend whose name shall not be mentioned."

"*What?*" Dorian said, the word barely audible. "Why on earth would he be meeting with them?"

Shauna had been Dorian's direct supervisor when she worked for Concept Marketing Agency. As for Dorian's ex, Rodney, the loser, had worked for the company as well. She and he had kept their budding relationship quiet, or so she'd thought. Ultimately, he had betrayed her in the worst way, and her work environment had become too toxic to remain at the company.

And now they were meeting with Lynix?

"I think I heard somewhere that Lynix's family recently took over ownership of this hotel and restaurant. Maybe your former coworkers are trying to drum up some business," Cree said, and learning his family owned the place surprised Dorian just as much as knowing he was there.

Nyla tapped her fingers on the tabletop. "I think you should go over there and see what's up. What if they are trying to get his family's business? You could stop him before he makes a mistake."

"She has a point," Cree added and picked up her strawberry mimosa and took a sip.

"Most importantly, you look *hot!*" Raven added, and the sisters chuckled. "Girl, this is the perfect opportunity for you to show your ex how good you look, while you swoop in and save your new man."

"Lynix is not my man, but I don't want him to get involved with those two," Dorian said. The agency as a whole did good work, but Shauna was a shark. As for Rodney, he was still trying to make a name for himself at the company, no matter how many bodies he had to walk over.

"How do you know it was a meeting?" Dorian asked, wondering if she should crash their meet up or just mind her business.

"By the way, your ex was talking with his hands and periodically pointing to the electronic tablet in front of him. He was definitely pitching some idea."

"I don't normally agree with Nyla," Cree said, ignoring the way Nyla glared at her. "But what could it hurt to stop by and say hi? Considering Lynix's behavior the last time I saw you two together, I'm sure he'd love to see you. Just go over and act like you have a right to be in his face."

Dorian shook her head. She wished she had half the confidence and badassness as Cree. As an entertainment lawyer and a former stripper, the woman always walked into a room and carried herself as if she owned the place.

If Shauna and Rodney really were trying to get his family's business, he should get a heads-up on who he was dealing with. Maybe Dorian could dig deep and tap into her inner Cree and somehow become a part of the meeting. Lynix might thank her later.

Dorian set her cloth napkin on the table. "Okay, Cree, tell me what to do."

# Chapter Ten

"I know you're interested in a marketing plan for just this hotel. However, I took the liberty of mapping out an additional campaign that would encompass all your family's hotels located in the Midwest."

Lynix wasn't opposed to hearing more, but his focus right now was on this place. They had just acquired the incredible hotel located in the Chicago loop, and Wes had big plans for it. Though the hotel's average occupancy rate was seventy-five percent, his brother wanted to get that percentage up to eight-five by the end of the year. While also increasing the number of events held in the facility.

Currently, there was very little social media presence, and they were heavily dependent on location which showcased tons of restaurants, attractions, and shopping. However, the hotel was competing with more well-known ones in the area.

"We even included this restaurant in the campaign," Rodney Webber, a representative from Concept Marketing Agency said. They were meeting inside the hotel's restaurant, a popular eatery even for those not staying at the hotel.

A couple of weeks ago, when Wes had asked Lynix to handle some business for him, Lynix had no idea it would involve marketing and advertising. Though he didn't mind the assignment, he had hoped to be doing something a little more interesting than meeting with several marketing agencies.

Still, he was excited about joining the family business, something he thought he'd never do. Working with Wes directly and their other brothers indirectly was a bonus. He would finally be putting his college degree to good use, and he was looking forward to the challenge.

He tuned back into Rodney's presentation, listening as the man drone on about research he'd done, the importance of brand awareness, and he touched upon strategies they'd used successfully in the past. When he pulled up the hotel's website, Lynix thought it looked good, but Rodney offered a few ideas on how to make it stand out more.

Lynix nodded as his gaze bounced from Rodney to the person he'd brought with him, his manager, Shauna Orman. It was hard to miss the way she watched Rodney. The expression in her eyes wasn't one of boss to employee, but more like lovers, which he found interesting.

He was trained to notice such things while other clients might not, and he couldn't help wondering why she tagged along. Maybe Rodney was in training or something, but he seemed to know what he was talking about. Or maybe she had come along with the intention of them getting a room at the hotel after the meeting.

Lynix shook the wayward thoughts free.

Focus dude. Focus.

He could already tell that sitting in meetings was going to be his least favorite part of this job. He thought having a casual discussion in the hotel's restaurant would make it more comfortable, but staying tuned in was proving to be difficult.

He glanced at the tablet that Rodney had turned his way and watched a short mockup clip of what a TV commercial would look like. When it was over, Lynix nodded. He liked how they had come prepared to show him more than what he'd asked for.

"That looks..." Lynix stopped when a vision in white appeared in his peripheral. At first, he thought he was seeing things, but nope, after blinking a few times, he assured himself he wasn't. It was Dorian, and she was heading his way with a gorgeous smile on her pretty face.

Damn, she was beautiful.

Her hair was piled on top of her head in a messy bun with a few long tendrils hanging down and framing her face. The little white dress with the deep V-neck she was wearing hung loose on her and stopped just above her knees. It was simple, tasteful, but seductive as hell. As were the wedge-heel sandals that added three to four inches to her height.

And those legs?

Good Lord.

The woman's long, shapely legs were what wet dreams were made of. He had always been a leg man, and hers sparked all types of impure thoughts to rush through his mind. But what really caught his attention was her smooth, sexy strut. She carried herself well, looking more like a runway model than his usual cute, sweet, innocent obsession.

Who was this nubile vixen, and what had she done with the woman he'd come to care for?

Lynix couldn't help but smile, and he slowly stood as she approached.

"Hey, sweetheart. This is—"

"Hey, yourself," she said, cutting him off and shocking the hell out of him when she cupped his face within her small hands and kissed him.

Not just any kiss, but a kiss that made his toes curl inside his loafers and caused the rest of his body to spark to life.

Hot damn. He wasn't sure what had gotten into her, but he was here for it.

His arm slid around her narrow waist, and he slammed her soft body against his. Her arms went around his neck, and she held on to him as he kissed her back. They might've been in a secluded corner of the restaurant, but there was no doubt they'd caught the attention of other customers.

When Dorian finally eased her mouth from his, he stood stunned until she gently wiped lipstick from his lips with the pad of her thumb. It was the sexiest thing he'd ever experienced. If there weren't so many people nearby, he would've swiped his arm across the table, clearing it of its contents. Then he'd stretch her out on it and have his way with her luscious body.

But there were people around. Besides, she might've been making a move on him, but he was sure she wouldn't appreciate him doing what he dreamed of doing.

He opened his mouth to tell her she could greet him like that anytime anywhere, but she spoke first, saying, "I know I'm early, but I couldn't wait to see you."

Okay, what the hell was going on?

Something was happening here, and Lynix wished he could read her mind, but he couldn't. However, he could follow her lead.

He cupped her cheek, and taking full advantage of whatever she was up to, he kissed her again. Loving how soft her lips were against his and how amazing she smelled. Hell, he could do this all day, but first, he wanted to figure out what she was up to. Because she was damn sure up to something.

When he lifted his head, her eyes were narrowed, and she

shot invisible daggers at him. Lynix couldn't help but grin. Oh, yeah. This was going to be fun.

A throat cleared, and he belatedly remembered he was in a meeting.

*Shit.*

Maybe he could shoo them away, then carry Dorian up to the hotel suite reserved for his family's use. Then again, who was he kidding? No way he could whisk her off and make mad, passionate love to her when she hadn't even agreed to go on a date with him yet.

Instead, he reached for her hand to make sure she didn't leave.

"Umm, sorry about that," he said to Rodney and Shauna. "I tend to get carried away when she's in my presence."

He pulled out the chair next to him for Dorian to join them. After reclaiming his seat, he draped his arm across the back of her chair and made introductions.

"We've already met," Dorian said, and Lynix straightened when he heard the edge in her tone.

"Really?"

He glanced from her, then to his guests, who fidgeted in their seats. For a minute, they looked everywhere but at him, especially Rodney. Interesting.

"How do you guys know each other?"

Dorian leaned in as close as their chairs would allow and placed her hand on Lynix's thigh as she looked at him. He stared back into her gorgeous brown eyes and knew whatever she was about to say, he wasn't going to like it.

"Remember the marketing agency I worked for before quitting and joining my parents at the B&B?"

*Hmm...* she hadn't told him anything about where she used to work, but he sensed things didn't end well. He tried recalling if Zion had ever said anything about her previous employment and came up blank. Still, he played along.

"Ahh yes," he said slowly as he looked at the two people sitting on the other side of the table. Then his attention zoned in on Rodney who looked the most uncomfortable.

What the hell had this bastard done to her? Dorian wasn't the type to make a scene, put on a show, or seek revenge. It wasn't in her nature. So whatever this guy had done to her must've cut deep, and suddenly whatever he'd done made Lynix want to snatch his ass up and seek his own form of revenge.

Instead of doing something crazy, he said, "I remember." Though he didn't, but he hoped Dorian would say more and enlighten him as to what had happened.

"That was a long time ago," Shauna hurried to say as she low-key glared at Dorian, and protectiveness slammed into Lynix. That one statement let him know this woman was a part of whatever took place.

"Actually, it was only a year ago," Dorian said. "These were the two involved in making my life a living hell at work. So much so, I ended up quitting and leaving the company. But you know what? That was in the past, and I'm over it."

"What's over is this damn meeting." Lynix stood, prepared to take her and leave, but Dorian, who was still seated, grabbed his hand and gently tugged, keeping him in place.

Rodney lifted his hands out in front of him. "Wait. That was a long time ago, but Dorian, I'm sorry if you felt I had anything to do with a hostile work environment." Then he turned to Lynix. "Mr. Mathews, we at Concept Marketing pride ourselves on being professional and meeting our clients' goals. We want your business and know we can provide you and your organization with the best marketing campaign. If you'd just give me a chance to finish my presentation, I'm sure you would agree," Rodney said in a rush.

The man didn't bother looking at his boss, but his gaze pleaded with Dorian as if she controlled the fate of the meeting. Well, as far as Lynix was concerned, she did. He would find out what they did to her, and no matter what it was, he had no intention of doing business with them.

Not only that, if whatever happened between them and Dorian was as bad as he suspected, he'd do everything in his power to make sure their agency suffered going forward.

"I'd love to hear the rest of the presentation," Dorian said with a sweet smile plastered on her tempting lips, but her tone said otherwise. "Please continue. Let's see what you've got."

Lynix stared at her a moment longer, then reclaimed his seat. His hellcat, that part of her she'd let him see outside of the jazz club weeks ago, was back. If he was honest, he loved this side of her. This bold, unflinching, take-charge side of her. The fierceness radiating off her reminded him of Cree. Dorian might've been more like her big sister than he first realized.

"Actually, this meeting is with Mr. Mathews," Shauna said, her fake smile in place. "It should only take us a few more minutes. If you don't mind leaving us, we can—"

"Oh, but she's the only reason I'm still sitting here. If she goes, I go," Lynix ground out, his patience waning. "Now, continue before I change my mind."

They had only ordered drinks at the start of the meeting, with Lynix planning to offer them lunch since they'd agreed to meet him there, but that wasn't happening. If it weren't for Dorian, he would've walked away the moment she mentioned quitting her job at their agency.

For the next thirty minutes, he sat there half listening to the rest of Rodney's presentation, with Shauna interjecting occasionally. Their ideas were good, but Lynix had already made his decision. WBM Enterprise wouldn't be using this agency. Which was why he had remained silent and let Dorian take over. He was impressed with the follow-up questions she asked, clearly showing her marketing knowledge. If she'd agree, he'd have her sit in on future meetings with other agencies.

"And that's it," Rodney said, looking relieved he'd gotten through his spiel. "Any other questions?"

Lynix peeked at Dorian.

She shook her head. "No. Not at this time. One of us will be in touch either way once WBM Enterprise," she said of Lynix's family's holding company, "makes their decision on which agency they'll be going with. *If* WBM does go with your agency, there's a good chance you'll be asked to create campaigns for several of their other subsidiary companies."

Lynix sat stunned and impressed. No doubt she had them shaking inside, or either fuming. She was letting them know that if... Nope not if—because he wasn't hiring them—but when they *didn't* get his business, they'd be losing out on more than just this project.

He stood and reached for Dorian's hand. "Thanks for the information. I'll be in touch in the next few weeks," Lynix said to Rodney and barely spared Shauna a glance.

"It was our pleasure," Rodney said, also standing and dropping a few bills on the table that would cover the cost of the drinks. Then he stuck out his hand.

Lynix hesitated, but as he stared into the man's eyes, he shook the guy's hand, giving it a firm squeeze and noting the way Rodney clinched his teeth.

"We look forward to hearing from you," Rodney said after Lynix released his hand. "Dorian, it was nice seeing you again." She only gave him and Shauna a slight nod, which spoke volumes.

Once they walked away, Lynix, still holding Dorian's hand, guided her toward the kitchen.

"I can explain," Dorian hurried to say, her voice low.

Lynix grinned down at her and brought the back of her hand to his lips and kissed it. "I would hope so. I figured you could explain everything over a late lunch with me."

"I—I actually was supposed to be having brunch with my sisters, but according to the text from Raven about twenty minutes ago, they started without me."

She glanced around him, and he followed her gaze to where her sisters sat at a table on the other side of the restaurant.

"Let's go tell them that you'll be dining with me."

Surprisingly, she didn't argue but did try apologizing for interrupting the meeting. She rambled while Lynix guided her along the perimeter of the restaurant instead of cutting across the room to get to her sisters' table.

"Sweetheart, don't apologize. You impressed the hell out of me back there. Not only with the way you greeted me, but also with the questions you asked Rodney about his proposal. But we'll save all that for conversation over lunch."

As they neared the table, Nyla spotted them first. Her gaze went to their joined hands, but then Dorian eased her hand from his grasp. That didn't stop a smile from spreading across Nyla's face, and she winked at him.

Lynix grinned, and though none of the sisters commented on the way he and Dorian had approached the table, he saw approval in their gazes. Even Cree wasn't glaring at him the way she'd done at Moody Days weeks ago. *Progress.*

It was good to know that, if Dorian did decide to give him a chance, he wouldn't have to wonder about approval from her sisters. Zion might be a different story, though Lynix would worry about that if or when the time came.

"I hope you ladies don't mind, but I'm stealing your sister for the rest of the day," he said.

"Wait," Dorian whisper-shouted and jammed her hands on her hips. "You said a late lunch. You didn't say anything about the rest of the day."

"Take her. Keep her as long as you want," Nyla said before anyone else could speak. "As a matter of fact, if you cover our meal, you can keep her for the rest of the weekend."

"Nyla!" Dorian ground out while everyone else laughed. "You don't get a say in who I—"

"Tell you what," Lynix hurried to jump in and placed his hand at the small of Dorian's back while his gaze went around the table. "Your meal is on me, and I'll see her home whenever she wants to leave."

"Deal," Nyla said and grabbed the small menu in the center of the table. "Now, let me see what type of desserts they have here."

# Chapter Eleven

I f anyone would've told Dorian that she'd be spending part of the day with Lynix Mathews, she wouldn't have believed them. Never had she done anything as brazen as walk up to a man and kiss him as if she had every right to do so. Thankfully, Lynix had played along despite being caught off guard. Had he not, that little stunt could've turned out to be one of the most embarrassing moments of her life.

For a person who claimed she wanted nothing to do with him, she had to admit she enjoyed every moment of pretending to be his woman.

The only snag in her charades was the hurt and anger she felt when she came face-to-face with Rodney and Shauna. Painful memories of how they'd treated her before she'd left the agency were forever sketched in her mind.

Seeing them again shook her more than she thought it would, but having Lynix by her side gave her the courage and confidence she'd needed. A calm she had never felt when it came to those two people. For that, she would be forever grateful.

When Cree had instructed her on what to do, Dorian had thought her crazy. She thought there was no way she could be that scandalous and bold. Yet, Dorian had been up for the challenge, determined to follow her sister's instructions exactly.

In hindsight, it might've been childish trying to show Rodney and Shauna that not only had she moved on, but she had hooked up with a man who respected her. A man who was a part of a wealthy family and had the authority to say yay or nay to a potentially huge contract that they wanted and probably needed. Seeing the looks on their faces, particularly when Lynix had been ready to leave before hearing them out, had been priceless.

"We'll get this up to the Harmony Suite shortly, Mr. Mathews, and just let me know if anything else is needed?"

Dorian's ears perked up. After leaving her sisters' table, Lynix had mentioned needing to speak to the manager of the restaurant. She had stepped back to give him a little space and had temporarily gotten lost in her thoughts.

Had she heard him correctly? The Harmony Suite? She assumed they'd be having lunch in private but not in a hotel suite.

"Thanks, Bob," Lynix said, and reached for her hand. He led her out of the restaurant and toward a bank of elevators.

"Harmony Suite?" she whispered when they were out of earshot of the manager. "Lynix, I don't think that's a good idea."

She had to take two or three steps to his single one to keep up with his long strides. When he realized she was practically running beside him, he slowed and grinned down at her.

"Why isn't that a good idea? Are you afraid you can't control yourself around me?"

She swatted his arm with her free hand. "Be serious."

She tried to pull out of his grasp, but he held on. "I'm dead serious. After that smoking hot kiss, I'm not sure what to think.

You might have more plans for me, and there's no way in hell I want to miss out if you do."

"Would you be serious?" She should've known that kiss would come back to bite her... even if she did enjoy it.

Lynix chuckled and squeezed her hand. "Okay, but seriously, the Harmony Suite is for my family to use whenever needed. Since it's empty and has incredible views, I thought it would be a good place for us to talk in private and get to know each other better while we eat."

Okay, that made sense, but she wasn't sure how comfortable she'd be with him in a room with a huge bed in it.

"My intentions are honorable, sweetheart, but I won't stop you if you want to ravish my mouth again. I have to say, you caught me off guard with that little show earlier, but I have no complaints. I enjoyed every moment, and I'm here for it if you want to do it again."

Her face grew hot at his words. She had hoped he wouldn't give her a hard time about that stunt, but it looked as if he planned to. At least he wasn't mad. No, it seemed he was more amused than anything.

They approached the elevators where several people were waiting, and she moved closer to him. She didn't know why her nerves were getting the best of her. Lynix wasn't the type of man to force himself on anyone. So she had nothing to worry about.

Releasing her hand, he pulled her against his body. Her heart skipped a beat, and unable to help it, she inhaled his masculine scent. It had a hint of spice and citrus, and she almost moaned. It was similar to something he'd worn in the past, but a little more pronounced today.

With a hand on her hip, she shivered against his touch as he leaned close to her ear and said, "It's just lunch and conversation. You can trust me."

Ha! He wasn't the one she was worried about. She wasn't sure she could trust herself alone with him.

Dorian had never been the type to pursue a man or make the first move. It just wasn't in her, but with Lynix she was tempted to step out of her shell. She finally understood why women gravitated to him. The man was irresistible and made her body sizzle by just being in his presence. She could feel herself weakening to the unfamiliar need he stirred within her.

She looked up at him and his gaze met hers, and she didn't miss the seriousness in his smoky-brown eyes. Too often he clowned around with her, either making her laugh or making her want to punch him, but this wasn't one of those times.

"I do trust you," she said just above a whisper.

When the elevator dinged, she and Lynix were the only ones to enter when the doors swooshed open. It made sense that most of the people waiting would be going down since the restaurant was on one of the top floors.

Holding her hand again, Lynix dug out a key card from his pants pocket and held it against the scanner below the numbers. Then pressed the button for the top floor. He explained the hotel had a presidential suite on that floor, but it was on the other side of the building away from the other six suites, one being the Harmony Suite. If the suites were anything like the rest of what she'd seen of the hotel, they were lavishly decorated.

The elevator doors slid open, and they stepped into the quietest hotel hallway Dorian had ever been in. The lush carpet was like cotton under her feet as they silently made their way down the long hallway. The room doors were generously spaced apart, giving her an idea of the size of the suites.

They stopped at the last door on the left, and after scanning his card, Lynix pushed the door open and gestured for her to enter. The moment Dorian stepped across the threshold, her mouth dropped open. In front of her were wall-to-wall, floor-to-ceiling windows that overlooked Lake Michigan.

"Wow," she said on a breath, unable to say much else. The view was like nothing she'd ever seen before. It was no wonder he had suggested they meet there. The open space offered unobstructed views between the rooms and was larger than her two-bedroom apartment. The walls were a deep gray with white trim and black and white accents. The paintings gracing the walls were eye-catching abstracts that added pops of color to the large space.

The kitchen was separate from the living room with a long island. That area wasn't huge, but it was modern with marble countertops and stainless-steel appliances.

Still checking out the space, Dorian strolled through the living room and around the cocktail table that sat between the two sofas facing each other. One wall held a huge television, and on the opposite side of the open floor plan was the dining area. The long table included six upholstered chairs but looked as if it could handle at least two more. Beyond that space was a room with the door opened, but from where she was standing, she couldn't see inside and assumed it was a bedroom.

Not wanting to think about them being so close to a room which probably had a huge bed that she and Lynix could test out, she glanced away. They were just there to talk. Nothing else.

"You like it?" Lynix asked from beside her.

"Are you kidding me? This is gorgeous, and I might never want to leave. Deciding to eat up here was a good choice." The moment the words were out of her mouth, her stomach rumbled as if punctuating the comment.

Lynix chuckled. "Food should be here shortly. Make yourself comfortable." He strolled into the kitchen. "What would you like to drink? We have everything from water to bourbon."

"A bottle of water, and if you have iced tea or lemonade, that would be great."

"I have all the above, and there's also a bottle of Arnold Palmer if you want a combination of lemonade and iced tea."

"That would be perfect."

Her attention went back to the windows as she moved closer to them. If she ever saved enough money, she'd get an apartment or buy a condo with a view like this one. A calmness engulfed her. She could already envision a reading nook near the windows where she'd probably sit for hours devouring a romance or just thinking about life.

What would it be like to feel as if she was living on top of the world? Because where she was standing, that's exactly how it felt. Her life was great but simple and uneventful, well, except for her date the other night and the meeting that she had just crashed. She'd definitely been out of her element with both, but if she had a place like this...

Dorian startled and jerked away when something touched her arm. Lynix. He stood beside her with drinks in hand and looked at her with amusement in his eyes.

The man was so fine, sometimes it was hard to look at him without drooling or wishing she could be wrapped up in his muscular arms. The olive-green button-down shirt he was wearing was beautiful against his cinnamon tone skin. He had rolled the sleeves neatly up to his elbows, and the way the garment hugged his biceps, it looked as if they were trying to burst free.

She always liked tall, built men who could carry her around if ever she needed. They also usually gave good bear hugs, which she had experienced with Lynix.

"Dorian? You okay?"

She blinked several times, realizing she'd been staring at him. "Oh, I'm sorry. Just thinking."

"What were you thinking about?" He held a drink out to her, and it was sweet how he had poured it into a glass.

"I was imagining what it would be like to live in this type of luxury."

"Well, if you ever want to experience that, let me know. My condo is a few blocks up, and I have a similar view." He nodded toward the sofa. "Let's have a seat."

Her eyebrows rose. "You live in a place with views like this?" She pointed her thumb at the window as he gently grasped her elbow and led her to the sofa.

"Yes," he said, and they both sat on the overstuffed furniture that seemed to wrap around her like a loving embrace. "You're more than welcome to come by, check it out, and stay as long as you want."

All Dorian could think about was how many women he'd probably invited to his place in the past, but she shook the thought free. No way would she allow her mind to go down that road.

As they sat next to each other, close enough to breathe the same air, Lynix told her about his grandfather leaving him a trust fund. He hadn't splurged on much, but she found it fascinating that he lived a life of luxury and could buy anything he wanted.

Just looking at him, he didn't come across as wealthy. Sure, he dressed nicely, and his clothes always looked of good quality, but he wasn't flashy. The only flashy thing she'd seen of him was his BMW, and even that, Dorian hadn't known about until a few weeks ago.

This was a reminder that he was way out of her league. He was financially stable, while she was just getting by. They might only be a few years apart, but she was positive her life experiences didn't come close to his. Yet, he insisted they were perfect for each other.

What could she possibly offer him when he seemed to have everything he could ever want or need?

But there was one area of his life that didn't make sense—him working for Chicago P.D. He definitely didn't need the money. So what was it about being a cop that kept him going to work every day?

Before she could pose the question, what sounded like a doorbell, rang. She glanced around, and then she heard it again.

"That's probably the food."

*Dang, the place even has a doorbell.*

As Lynix stood, he dug into the front pocket of his dress pants and pulled out a money clip. Dorian stood too, watching as two people strolled in, one pushing a serving cart piled with covered dishes. Enticing aromas filled the space, and Dorian's mouth watered as her stomach growled. She hadn't eaten since that morning, and right now, she felt as if she could eat everything that had been ordered.

The staff made quick work of setting up the food and more drinks on a side table near the dining area. They were efficient, and within minutes, Dorian and Lynix were fixing their plates.

When she had perused the menu earlier, she had struggled with what to order because she wanted to try several dishes. That was no longer a problem. Lynix had ordered a sample of everything on the menu, and it was as if Dorian had died and gone to food heaven. Everything from avocado toast to braised ribs was tempting her, and if that wasn't enough, petite size desserts were also included.

"Did you know I was a foodie?" Dorian asked.

Lynix flashed her a crooked grin. "Yes, I know a lot about you, and what I don't know, I'm looking forward to learning. So how about we start with you telling me what those bastards you used to work with did to you?"

# Chapter Twelve

Dorian cringed at Lynix's tone. She knew this moment was coming, and he had every right to know why she had kissed him in a crowded restaurant. Not only that, but she had also taken over his meeting, which she still couldn't believe she'd done.

Buying herself a little time, she shoved another bite of the braised ribs into her mouth. They were perfectly seasoned, tasted absolutely divine, and practically melted in her mouth. Normally, she'd be trying to determine what seasonings were used, but instead, she thought about what she could say to Lynix. Where did she even begin?

"Lynix, I know you said I don't need to apologize for crashing your meeting, but I do. It was unprofessional and childish if I'm being honest. I wanted to show Rodney and Shauna how I had moved on from the drama they'd created around me at the agency. I also wanted them to see I knew people who could be their potential clients, and that I could influence whether they got a contract."

Dorian moved potatoes around on her plate, embarrassed

she had to tell him the rest. Now she wished she hadn't put on that little show. Then she could keep her secrets, no matter how big or small, to herself.

Lynix placed his hand on her thigh under the table and squeezed. "Tell me about you and Rodney? I thought the man's eyes would pop out of his head when he saw you. When you said they ruined your work life at the agency, he looked as if he'd swallowed his tongue."

"*Rodney*," she said, the word tasting bitter on her tongue as she thought about how he'd made a fool of her. "He and I used to date. It was stupid of me to date my coworker."

Dorian could admit to not being the most experienced woman out there, but she'd always thought she was a good judge of character. Rodney had proven her wrong on so many levels. While she had dated during high school and college, it had never been anything too serious because she was focused on her studies, determined to get a college scholarship. She'd accomplished that goal but at the expense of not having much of a social life during those years.

Then came her first real job at Concept Marketing Agency where she had worked since college and enjoyed her job. She and Rodney had worked together for a few years before she started crushing on him, but she never intended to date him.

"Is he the reason you won't give me a chance?" Lynix asked, cutting into her thoughts.

"Yes, partly. Okay, mostly," she added and gave him a slight smile while shrugging her shoulders. "I had a crush on him for at least a year, and then he asked me out. I thought I had died and gone to heaven because he was considered the most eligible bachelor in our department. Actually, probably in the whole company.

"For him to ask *me* out had been a big deal, but I said no at first. I knew he was out of my league, and the whole dating a coworker was risky. Still, it had been nice to get asked out. He didn't give up, though. He hung out at my cubicle, making me laugh, paying me compliments, and basically giving me the attention I craved from a man. Needless to say, I finally gave in and became the envy of my co-workers."

Dorian stared down at her plate and moved some of the yellow rice around, giving her a reason not to look at Lynix as she contemplated her next words. She couldn't believe she was about to tell him one of the most embarrassing situations of her dating life. Him of all people.

He might've been interested in her before, but after this conversation he'd realize she wasn't worth the effort. She wouldn't know what to do with a man like him. A man as worldly and well off as him could get any woman he wanted. Heck, he already had, multiple times. He'd soon learn she wouldn't be a good fit for him.

"Rodney and I dated for six almost seven months, and I thought we were having a good time getting to know each other. But then he wanted to take our relationship to the next level..."

Her words trailed off, and she chanced a glance at Lynix. People like him would think that, after dating that long, all the levels would've been hit by then. However, Lynix didn't respond. His expression was patient and kind with no judgment. As a matter of fact, she was impressed with how he was letting her talk without much interruption.

*Good listener. Another point in the pro's column for him.*

"Basically, when I wasn't willing to *put out*, Rodney suddenly started canceling dates and ignoring my calls. He didn't officially break up with me, but his attitude toward me turned chilly. We had kept our relationship quiet at work. So I didn't think much of him not hanging out at my desk or us not going to lunch together. But there were no text messages, no phone calls, and there were no winks or smiles when we passed in the hallway.

"I eventually got the message and called myself all types of fools for dating a coworker. Something that will never happen again. My little impromptu show earlier was me trying to show Rodney how I was able to do a whole lot better than him. I'm sorry for pulling you into my pettiness, but more than that, I'm sorry for crashing your meeting. I hope I didn't embarrass you too much."

Dorian went back to eating, shoveling food into her mouth to keep from rambling. She liked Lynix. She liked him even more with how nice he'd been to her today, but maybe it was time to leave before more questions were asked.

"You didn't embarrass me at all," he said, rubbing the scruff on his chin as he watched her. "I'm just still wondering why you quit your job. Are you saying you quit because Rodney started ignoring you?"

Dorian's fork stopped inches from her mouth as dread seeped in. She already felt like a loser where Rodney was concerned. She didn't want to prove how much of one she was by answering more of Lynix's questions.

*You owe him.* The words blared through her mind, and she knew she did. You couldn't just infiltrate someone's business meeting without a full explanation of why you'd done it.

Dorian set her fork down and released a long breath. She wanted to curse the sudden tears that filled her eyes, but no way would she let them fall. She blinked them away, refusing to cry over how Rodney had treated her. She had shed too many tears for that parasite when he hadn't even been worth it.

"While Rodney and I were dating, he..." She nibbled her lower lip and glanced away for a second. When she felt like she could say this without bursting into tears, she looked at him. "Rodney, he umm..."

"So help me God, Dee..." Lynix's low growl and the angry mask that suddenly showed on his handsome face caught her off guard. "If you tell me that motherfucker physically hurt you, I'm leaving right now to hunt his ass down and—"

"No!" she said as shock slammed into her. When he started to stand, she grasped his wrist and held on tight. "Oh my God, Lynix. I am so sorry! I didn't mean for it to sound like he abused me in any way."

"Then what the hell happened?" he snapped, and as if catching himself, he released a breath, closed his eyes, and ran his hand over his mouth.

Dorian knew his anger wasn't directed at her, but that still didn't mean she didn't shrink against her seat. His temper seemed to flare out of nowhere. Normally, he was fairly laid-back. So this behavior was new.

"I'm the one who's sorry, Dee," he said and reached for her hand and held it. "I have a low tolerance for men who mistreat women. Especially those who think it's okay to put their hands on a woman with the intent of hurting them. Hell, I could tell you stories about what I've seen on patrol that would leave you having nightmares for weeks. And when you started to tear up..."

"I wasn't thinking. I guess I'm still embarrassed by the situation even though it's been over a year. I thought I had moved on, but seeing Rodney and Shauna today brought it all back. The hurt. The disappointment. The betrayal.

"Rodney didn't officially break up with me. Instead, he left me hanging while he was screwing around with Shauna. He cheated on me."

Lynix frowned. "He was hooking up with her while you two were dating?"

"Yes, well, according to Shauna." Dorian fiddled with the cloth napkin in her lap as memories churned inside her mind.

Now that she was saying everything aloud, it didn't sound like a big deal. Yet, she remembered being devastated.

"I get that people cheat or get cheated on and then move on. It's probably happened to more people than not. For me, though, that hurt cut deep. I was totally blindsided by their... union for lack of a better word. All I'd known was Rodney had been acting weird toward the end of our relationship, and then out of nowhere, Shauna started treating me like a leper. Like I had done something to her, and she was seeking revenge.

"She had never been the best boss, but at least she was fair. Apparently, she found out Rodney and I had been seeing each other. Then she took her anger and frustrations out on me at work. I had no idea he'd ever been involved with her but apparently, they'd dated.

"Anyway, she made my work-life hell. She started piling projects on me, even those which should've been team projects. Not only that, but none of the assignments or campaigns I turned in were good enough. She'd insist I redo them. Even projects that were done as per the client's requests.

"Lynix, she humiliated me during meetings to the point of me leaving the conference room in tears. There were days when I dreaded going to work. I eventually had to file a complaint with Human Resources."

"What happened then?"

"They gave her a slap on the wrist, but the harassment continued. Not only that, Shauna and Rodney started flaunting their relationship in front of me. She once thanked me for being a lousy lay where Rodney was concerned. I don't know what all he told her about our relationship, but I knew that part was a lie. Rodney and I never had sex."

"You two dated for almost a year and never had sex?"

Dorian shook her head. There'd been a time she'd been embarrassed to admit that but not anymore. She was so happy she hadn't fallen for his sweet talk and lies. Otherwise, after the way everything went down, she would've felt like a bigger fool.

"No, we didn't," she said to Lynix who seemed to be hanging on to her every word. "I liked Rodney. I even thought I was falling in love with him, but I just... It just never felt right, but I should've known if he wasn't getting it from me, he was getting it from someone else."

Dorian had felt like the stupidest person in the world, but that whole situation showed how inexperienced she'd been. It didn't matter that she had been in her early thirties, she hadn't dated much. It never crossed her mind that Rodney would cheat on her or with her, and that's what she told Lynix.

"He'd come over several times a week, and I'd cook for him. We'd watch a movie or go for a ride or sometimes take long walks along the lake. I thought we were having a good time getting to know one another. I had no clue he was involved with anyone else until shit hit the fan at work with Shauna."

"Before today, when was the last time you saw or talked to Rodney?"

"I heard from him about a week after I quit my job. He said he was sorry about how things went down. I asked him why he did it. Why he'd dated us both at the same time. He said he and Shauna had been taking a break before he asked me out, and then they patched things up.

"Rodney claimed he didn't know how to tell me, and then when our relationship wasn't going anywhere, he figured he'd move on." His words had hurt, but at that point, she hadn't cared about anything he'd had to say. "He also said I was really sweet, but he wanted to be with a woman who knew how to please a man."

"Son of..." Lynix growled, and Dorian lifted her hands for him to let her finish.

"I told him that when I find a *real* man it won't be a

problem with me pleasing him. And that was the last time I talked to him."

Lynix shook his head. "You should've sued the company or something," he mumbled as he picked at the rest of his food.

"Oh, Cree was livid when she found out and was ready to go after them with all her legal guns. And according to her, she still might. My sisters are the only ones who know the whole story about why I quit a job that I loved. Well, them and you now. Essence had offered a shoulder to cry on, and Nyla wanted to go old school and pour sugar into their gas tanks and key their cars."

Dorian adored her sisters who were always willing to throw down for her, but leaving the agency had been the best decision for her. The executives were close to the pulse of the organization, and she knew she hadn't been the only person to file a complaint about Shauna. They let her get away with treating staff like crap because she made the company a ton of money. She was always getting recognized for her stellar work and her timeliness on meeting campaign deadlines. No one cared that she couldn't accomplish those things on her own.

Dorian wondered what they'd think if she lost a potentially large contract. Though she had no intentions of telling Lynix what to do, she hoped he didn't go with their agency.

As if reading her mind, Lynix said, "Well, Concept Marketing won't be getting our business, and I'm not sure how I'll do it yet, but I'm going to make Rodney and Shauna regret the day they ever mistreated you."

Dorian's heart softened at the fierceness behind his words. It was sweet of him to take her experience with the company and their employees into consideration. Yet, she didn't want him to do anything he'd later regret, and that's what she told him.

"Also, you went beyond the call of duty when you played

along with my little charade today," Dorian assured him. "Seeing their stunned expressions when I walked in was reward enough."

She pushed her plate aside and propped her arms on the table. "Now, enough about me. Let's talk about you. Why were you even in a business meeting in the first place? I thought you weren't a part of the family business."

# Chapter Thirteen

Lynix understood Dorian wanting to change the subject, but every fiber in his body wanted to hunt Rodney and Shauna down and kick their asses. Dorian was one of the sweetest people he'd ever met, and the thought of them mistreating her didn't sit right with him. Especially when he had the power to do something about it.

He couldn't let them get away with pushing Dorian out of a job she loved. She might've moved on and accepted what led to her resigning, but he couldn't. He'd come up with some way of making them pay, but for now, he was going to enjoy their time together.

But first, there was something he'd been wanting to do for the last few minutes.

He wiped his mouth with the cloth napkin, laid it on the table, and stood. "Come here so I can give you a hug," he said, opening his arms to her.

Dorian stared wide-eyed at him, and then her eyes narrowed. "Why do you want to give me a hug?" she asked.

He chuckled. "Just come here for a minute."

He was relieved when she finally pushed her chair back, then walked into his open arms. Lynix held her close, enjoying the feel of her softness against him, and her fresh scent that met his nose. When her arms circled his waist, she buried her face against his neck and sighed.

This was nice. Dorian fit so perfectly in his arms that he never wanted to let her go.

"I needed this," she mumbled, her breath hot against his neck and her body relaxed into him.

Lynix placed a lingering kiss against her temple. "I'm glad, but this hug technically wasn't for you. It's for me," he said with a laugh. "Woman, you took ten years off my life when I thought Rodney had physically abused you. I needed this hug to help settle my nerves and keep me from doing something crazy like finding him so I can give him an old-fashioned beat down."

She snorted. "I don't know exactly what that entails but forget it. Forget him. Lynix, I didn't tell you the story so you could go off and fight my battles. That was a part of my past, and I don't want you doing anything that will get you in trouble. Neither one of them is worth it."

Still holding on to him, she lifted her head and met his gaze. "Thank you for being so great today. I appreciate you listening without judging me."

As he stared into her kind eyes, Lynix ran the back of his fingers down her soft cheek. "Dee, you can always talk to me and tell me anything, and I'll keep it to myself. I know that conversation wasn't easy, but I'm glad you trusted me enough to share what happened."

This was what he'd been wanting—them opening up to one another while getting to know each other better. He wanted Dorian to know she could trust him. Not just with her heart but everything.

Lynix just hadn't expected to feel some kind of way after

all she'd shared earlier. He had already sensed she didn't have much experience with men. Now, knowing for sure ignited a protectiveness inside of him. Not in a brotherly kind of way, either, but in a way a man felt when wanting to protect his woman.

Dorian might not be his yet, but that would change one day soon. He didn't know when or how, but like he told her before, he wasn't giving up. And now that she had lowered her guard some with him, it was only a matter of time when she'd see how he was different from what she first thought.

"Thanks for the hug," he said, giving her another squeeze. He wanted to kiss her incredible lips again, but he settled for a kiss against her silky hair before releasing her.

"It's funny you should ask about me meeting with that marketing agency," he said after they reclaimed their seats and got back to their meal. "I'm leaving Chicago P.D. in a couple of weeks, and I'll be officially joining WBM Enterprise, my family's business."

Lynix didn't realize just how excited he was about the change in his career until he was telling Dorian about his new title—Vice President of Operations. It had a nice ring to it, and it came with a significant pay increase and great benefits.

Once he left Chicago P.D., Lynix planned to take a week off before officially starting in his new position. He had only hosted the meeting today at Wes's request, but he wouldn't meet with anyone else until after he started the job. After that, Lynix would shadow Wes for a few weeks, or at least until he felt comfortable in the new role.

"When I graduated with my business degree, instead of working in an office at one of our businesses, I opted to join the police force."

"I'm impressed," Dorian said between bites. "I didn't even know you had a college degree."

"Hey, I'm not just another pretty face. I have brains too," he joked, and when she laughed, the lyrical sound made him want to keep her laughing.

This moment, of them eating a meal together and talking, felt perfect, and he wanted it to last forever. They had always gotten along well. They'd clowned with each other good-naturedly over the years, except for when he was egotistic and full of himself. Yet, even then, they were able to share some laughs.

Who would've thought they'd ever be able to have a serious conversation and learn things about each other they hadn't known?

"Okay, so you got your degree, but why didn't you want to work in the family business, especially with your brothers?"

"Because of my father. He's condescending, rude more often than not, and he's controlling. Since I'm the youngest of my three brothers, he thought he could control every aspect of my life, even when I became an adult. He's tried for years, in several ways, but when it came to where I'd work after graduation from college, I took control by joining the police force. At first, I had done it to piss off the old man, but once I started patrolling the streets of Chicago, I realized I enjoyed the job.

"Yes, there are days when I question humanity and wonder —what the hell is wrong with people. Then there are other days when I can't imagine not coming to someone's rescue or keeping people safe. Each day is different and there's an... energy, for lack of a better word, that you can't get from anywhere else."

"Yeah, that's what Zion used to say. He liked the adrenaline rush. At least he did before Raven and the babies came along."

Zion had been in the military for years, and when he'd gotten out, he had joined Chicago P.D. Which was how he and Lynix met, and they'd been best friends ever since.

Dorian stuffed a forkful of strawberry cheesecake into her mouth and moaned. "Oh, my goodness. This is *amazing*. The cheesecake I make is great, but this might come in a close second."

Not only did she cook and bake for the guests at her parents' B&B, but according to Zion, she also had a side hustle. She provided baked goods several times a week to a bakery near the B&B. She was one of the best cooks Lynix knew.

"You'll have to make your cheesecake for me so I can compare the two."

"Okay," she said.

Lynix reached over and, with the pad of his thumb, wiped off the smudge of strawberry sauce at the corner of her lower lip. He stuck his thumb into his mouth and licked it off before thinking about what he'd done.

"What?" He shrugged and laughed at the way Dorian's eyebrows shot up. "I wanted to see how it tasted."

She grinned. "And what did you think?"

"I think it tasted sweet like you. So of course it's delicious."

Dorian laughed. "Oh, you're *gooood*, Mr. Sweet Talker."

She scooped up another fork full of cake and instead of eating it, she held the utensil out to Lynix. He opened for her, and the moment the cake touched his tongue, he moaned.

She was right, it was amazing and practically melted in his mouth.

He chewed the strawberries as he watched her watch him. Man, she was beautiful. He loved how her hair was piled haphazardly but perfectly on top of her head in a bun. The style added to her sexiness, but it also tempted him to reach up and undo it so her hair could fall around her shoulders. Yeah, she'd probably punch him if he did, and the thought almost made him laugh out loud.

When his attention went back to her eyes, he caught her

just as her gaze darted to his mouth, lingered, and then met his eyes. Lynix knew what she wanted because he wanted the same thing.

He reached over and cupped her cheek. Then he leaned forward and boldly touched his lips to hers. When she didn't push him away, he deepened the connection. The kiss started sweet and gentle, the taste of strawberry exploding in his mouth. But as the kiss grew more intense, he slid his hand behind Dorian's head and held her in place as he savored her sweetness.

This was not what he had in mind when he invited her to the suite, but damn if he wasn't glad it happened. Tasting her again made his heart sing and his desire for her quadruple. No way could she deny this... this... whatever this was pulsing between them. Whatever this intense sensation thrumming inside of him was, he could honestly say he had never experienced it with anyone else.

This was what he wanted. Her. Nobody else. Just her.

Without warning, Dorian tore her mouth from his. "Whoa. Okay. Umm, you were saying," she said, her chest heaving as she returned her attention to the cake.

Hell, he was in too much of a kissing haze to remember anything before their lips touched. One thing he knew for sure was when they did get together, and they would, they were going to burn up the sheets.

Yeah, he was going there with his thoughts because there was nothing he wanted more than he wanted Dorian. Now that he'd had a taste of her again, he wanted more.

"You've always been well spoken and seem to always be in control," she said, her breaths still sounding a little uneven. "I have no doubt you're going to be great in your new role, but is working in the family business really what you want? What about your father? If you two don't get along, how are you going to work together?"

How could she think straight after that kiss? Lynix was still trying to stop his heart from hammering and get his body back under control. Maybe she hadn't been as affected as he'd been. Or maybe she was just better at hiding her feelings.

He poured a glass of water from the pitcher that the server had left, and he drank half the glass before he felt steady enough to jump back into the conversation.

"It's time," he said. "I get along great with my brothers, and since they are the ones running everything, I shouldn't have too many dealings with my father. At least I hope I won't. Besides, he's on another mission."

"Which is?"

"Getting me married. He thinks I need to quit screwing around and settle down. So, your mother isn't the only one trying to marry off her kids. My father always thought I was put on this earth to work his nerves." Lynix laughed, remembering plenty of times his father said as much. "I guess he thinks marrying me off will help get my head on straight so I can make something of my life."

Lynix considered telling her about how his dad had tried the whole arranged marriage thing years ago but decided to save that conversation for another time. Or never. Each time he thought of Marisela and what transpired in college, it felt as if someone had their hands on his neck, cutting off his air supply. There was no way in hell he'd ever consider marrying the woman, and nothing his father, or anyone else, could say would ever change his mind.

"There's no way he's as bad as my mother. The woman has a one-track mind."

Lynix wanted to tell her she was wrong about Virginia being worse than his dad, but he kept his mouth shut. He had been able to avoid his father for the last few weeks, but he was sure the old man wasn't done with him yet.

Years ago, when his father and Mr. Baldwin insisted he and Marisela would marry after college, Lynix had gone along with it. Why not? He and Marisela had grown up together, and he thought she was pretty, and she was easy. Which had been all he cared about at that age. It wasn't until he and Marisela went to college, the same school, did Lynix start thinking for himself. He also got to know Marisela and what he knew of her, he didn't like.

Years later, after breaking up with her, he understood why his father and Mr. Baldwin wanted them to get married. Or at least he was fairly sure he did. Mr. Baldwin's net worth was in the multimillions, and Marisela was his only child. Meaning everything would go to her upon his death. There was no doubt in Lynix's mind that if her father left her everything, she'd blow it within a year and wipe out her family's legacy and fortune.

It wouldn't be intentional, but the woman had no business savvy. Her father knew his little princess was a spoiled brat who even now, attracted the wrong type of people, especially men. Mr. Baldwin probably figured that, if he could find her a husband within a reputable family, then he wouldn't have to worry about her. So, setting her up with Lynix, and in turn his family, meant she'd be taken care of.

There was no doubt Lynix's father would go along with the plan. In doing so, it would make the Mathews even wealthier than they already were.

What Lynix didn't know was why the two old men were conspiring again. Maybe because he and Marisela were both still single. The problem with their potential plan was they didn't know what had happened after he and Marisela broke up in their freshmen year of college. And if Lynix had his way, they'd never find out. Even if he could somehow forgive

Marisela, it would be a cold day in hell before he'd ever consider marrying her.

"I'm not sure what I'm going to do about my mother," Dorian was saying as she cut into Lynix's thoughts. "When I tell her to stop fixing me up with these guys, she acts as if I'm joking."

"What do you mean?" Lynix pushed his plate away and sat back in his chair. The food had been tasty, but he couldn't eat another bite. "Does she force these guys on you?"

Dorian huffed out a breath and leaned back in her seat with her arms folded across her chest. The move brought his attention to the swells of her breasts peeking out of her low-cut dress. She might be petite, but she had curves in all the right places, and he looked forward to the day when he could see every delicious inch of her.

"Kinda. It's not like she doesn't care what I think, but sometimes, she gets into that *mom* mode, acting like she knows what's best. Then she doesn't listen. She hears me, but she waves my words off as if I'm still a kid incapable of making my own decisions."

Lynix rubbed his chin as he listened to her, and a hint of an idea swirled through his mind. Yeah, they were both old enough to say no to their parents, but sometimes, it took a little more than words to get the message across.

"*Hmm,*" he said as his thoughts took shape.

Dorian looked at him, her eyebrows downcast and forming a perfect V. "*Hmm,* what?"

"I have an idea that might benefit us both."

The idea wouldn't be exactly what he was looking to build with Dorian, but it could be a steppingstone to getting what he wanted—a chance to show her how good they could be together. He understood her wanting to protect her heart, especially after her fiasco date with Glen, and the refreshed memories of her time with Rodney. However, if she had a chance to spend some quality time with Lynix, without any pressure, she might see that dating him could lead to a happy-ever-after.

Lynix wouldn't call what they were doing now—having a late lunch and talking—a date, but so far, it was as close as he'd gotten.

"*O-kay*," Dorian said slowly, looking at him warily. "What's this idea, and why do I have a feeling I'm not going to like it?"

Lynix chuckled. "Actually, I think you might. It'll get your mother and my father off our backs, and we can have a little fun in the process."

"Okay, now you really have my interest piqued. Tell me what you're thinking," she said, leaning forward with her forearms on the table. "I'm listening."

Lynix matched her stance by leaning forward too. "What do you think about us pretending to be a couple?"

# Chapter Fourteen

Dorian sat looking at Lynix, waiting for him to say more. When he didn't, her eyebrows shot skywards. "Wait. *That's* your idea? That's all you came up with? I thought you would say something groundbreaking. Something like us getting a one-way ticket to the moon. Not for us to fake date."

He burst out laughing, and the hearty sound made her smile. She was enjoying her time with Lynix more than she expected to, and what surprised her most? How right it felt to be with him.

Ugh! But now that he was flashing that cocky grin of his, the one she had a love-hate relationship with, she wanted to wipe it off his mouth. How could that stupid smile tempt her to climb onto his lap and kiss him? She never had thoughts like this about any other man, not even Rodney who she'd dated for months.

But Lynix? Lynix made her want to act out of character and live a little on the wild side. She never had trouble or felt guilty about saying 'no' to a man or struggled to keep her hands to herself. Yet, this man was the exception.

Dorian wanted to kiss him, touch him, and she wanted to feel his hard body rubbed up against hers, and that was a first. She had never physically responded to any other man the way she did when it came to Lynix. And all they'd done was kiss a few times. He was so wrong for her. Yet, that didn't stop her from being drawn to him.

She had to be strong, though. Especially since she had decided to take a break from the opposite sex. She needed time to reevaluate what she wanted in a mate because clearly her picker was off. Besides, right now it felt like dating came with too much disappointment that would eventually turn into heartache.

As for Lynix's idea, she had hoped he had come up with a way to discourage her mother's meddling. Fake dating... him, though? No way. She wasn't that good of an actress despite what he might think.

"Hear me out," he said as if reading her mind, and then he stood and extended his hand to her. "First, let's move to the sofa where it's more comfortable."

Dorian let him help her up and escort her across the room. The moment she sat on the sofa, she had to agree with him. It was comfortable, and she was tempted to kick off her shoes and curl up on it. After eating so much, a nap would be great.

She wouldn't, though, because she wanted to hear more about Lynix's idea, even though she was fairly sure she wouldn't go along with it.

"I like the idea of a trip to the moon. Sounds like a life altering experience. However, pretending to be a couple would be easier."

Dorian shook her head. "I don't see how fake dating would help either of us."

But when the words left her mouth, she thought about what she'd just said.

*Fake dating.*

"Actually, I can see how it *might* help me with my mother, but she won't believe it unless she sees us together."

Lynix took a sip of the beer he'd been nursing during lunch. It was probably warm by now, but he didn't seem to care.

"Spending time with each other is part of the idea. So she would definitely see us together. I can easily swing by and pick you up from work sometime or send flowers to the B&B. We can make her believe we're a couple."

Dorian nodded slowly. The idea might just work... for her.

"What about you? How would any of this benefit you?"

"Actually, the more I think about it, the more I like the plan. My mother hosts an annual fundraiser gala. It's to raise money for a nonprofit her family started over thirty years ago to fight hunger and poverty. I'm expected to attend. If you were my pretend woman, you could be my date. Then I'd have the pleasure of escorting the most beautiful woman in the world to the event.

"I had considered going alone, but there will be women in attendance looking for a boy toy or their next husband, and I don't want the attention."

Dorian rolled her eyes and folded her arms across her chest. "Arrogant much?"

This reminded her of one of several reasons why they would never work as a couple. He thought too highly of himself... even if it did seem he could back it up.

"That's not me being arrogant," he insisted. "That's from experience. Me and my brothers attend every year, and in the past, we've gotten more attention from the opposite sex than any of us wanted. It doesn't help that my mother enjoys bragging on her sons. The thing is, this year two of my brothers have women, and the other won't be attending the event. That leaves just me. Even if you don't want us to pretend to date, can you help me out by being my date that evening?

"Oh, and besides you being my date for the gala, us fake dating would come in handy whenever I have dinner at my parents' house. It would be nice to take my girlfriend along with me." He rubbed the scruff on his chin and looked deep in thought. "Then again, that part might not be a good idea. I wouldn't want to subject you to my father."

"Lynix, he can't be that bad."

"He is, and I can already imagine him saying something to make me want to punch him on your behalf. Or he would look down on you because you don't come from what he would consider a 'connected' family. For him, it's all about where you come from, who your people are, and if you are well connected. How someone can help him get ahead is always at the forefront of his mind."

Dorian didn't miss the disgusted expression on Lynix's face. "So he's one of those pompous, rich dudes who thinks he's better than everyone else."

"Exactly."

"What about your mother?" Dorian asked.

"She's one of the sweetest people I know. She's loving, kind, loyal, and would do anything for almost anyone. She would adore you. You two have similar dispositions. She might be a sweetheart, but she's no pushover. Cross her and there will be hell to pay. She's a low-key badass."

Dorian laughed. "Is that how you see me?"

A warm glow flowed through her as she considered his words. He thought of her as a badass, which was one of the nicest things anyone had ever said to her. Her family considered her a pushover and thought she didn't have a backbone. Though they never said the last part, at least not to her face,

Dorian knew they thought it. Which she understood, since she didn't always stand up for herself, and she wasn't confrontational.

Lynix reached over and gently pushed a few strands of her hair from her face and tucked them behind her ear. He was such a big guy, but when he did stuff like that, showing how gentle he could be, she wondered what else she'd been wrong about when it came to him.

"You are a sweet badass," he said. "I've witnessed your hellcat side a number of times, and I liked it."

"Hellcat?" She sputtered a laugh. "Now that's something I've never been called before."

She secretly liked the idea of him thinking she wasn't just a nice people pleaser, which was how she reluctantly saw herself sometimes. That was probably why she had a hard time telling her mother to back off—in a way where she knew Dorian meant business.

"But anyway, getting back to my idea. I think we should give it a try. At least for a few months. If at any time you want to stop, just say the word. We can tell people you dumped me because we weren't compatible."

Dorian mulled over the idea. If her mother thought they were seeing each other, she would definitely back off, but for how long? More importantly, could she fake date Lynix without feelings getting in the way? Would anyone believe she could actually pull a man like him? Then again, he had been asking her out.

"Wait." Dorian glared at him. "This is a trick, isn't it? You're just trying to get me to go out with you."

His cool, calm expression remained firmly in place when he said, "I don't typically have to trick anyone to go out with me, Dorian, and I'm not going to start now. I do, however, like the idea of you being my woman even for a few months."

Dorian nibbled on her bottom lip as they regarded each other. Even if this was him being sly where she was concerned, the idea was still a win-win for her. She'd get a chance to spend time with a real man, an experienced man who seemed to know how to treat a woman. In the process, she would also get to see how the one-percenters lived—those whose net worth was over a million dollars. Then, when she was sure her mother was done matchmaking, she and Lynix could go their separate ways.

It sounded easy enough, but what if the plan backfired? What if she fell for his charming ass? But then, she thought of something else.

"The thought of lying to my mother..." Her words trailed off as she realized she wouldn't be just lying to her mother. They'd be lying to everyone, including his family. None of that sat well with her.

"Technically, we wouldn't be lying." Lynix ran the back of his fingers slowly down her cheek, and she leaned into his touch before realizing what she was doing. "We'll be hanging out and going a few places together. It'll just look like we're getting to know each other."

True, but this still felt like a bad idea.

She was a grown woman. She didn't play games, and she didn't want to start just to keep her mother out of her love life. But anyone who knew Virginia Priestly knew how pushy she could be, and Dorian was tired of it.

She glanced down at her dress, wiping invisible crumbs off her lap when she said, "What about kissing?"

When she looked at Lynix, his left eyebrow was lifted. "What about it? I already told you earlier that whenever you want to plant one on me, have at it."

She sighed and shook her head. "If I accepted the offer, we should probably stay clear of kissing—unless we're in front of others and trying to show we're a couple. Also, what about Zion? Even if we'd be fake dating, I don't know how he'd feel about any of it."

"Don't worry about Zion. I'll take care of him."

Dorian might not have much experience with men, but even she could recognize what Lynix was trying to do. Spend time with her in hopes that she'd date him for real. Granted, his idea would help her out of a jam, but would the situation be one of those times when she solves one problem only to create another? Probably.

After a long hesitation, instead of saying "no," like her brain was telling her to, she said, "Fine, we can give it a try but no kissing."

Lynix laughed. "Okay, if that's how you want it, but if at any time you change your mind, just do what you did in the restaurant, and I'll play along."

# Chapter Fifteen

Usually when Lynix made up his mind to do something, he didn't think twice. He trusted his judgment, and it rarely steered him wrong. However, the idea of meeting with Zion to share his intentions regarding Dorian gave him pause. Their friendship meant everything to him, and he hoped dating Dorian wouldn't put a wedge between them.

Zion was reasonable. He knew Lynix well enough to know he would never do anything to hurt Dorian. At least that's what Lynix told himself as he strolled into Roby's Pub, the local cop bar—a place he used to frequent often.

Times have changed. Since he no longer wanted to be known as the good-time guy who loved women, he didn't stop by the Pub often anymore. It was all part of his plan in cleaning up his reputation. So far he didn't miss it at all, especially now that he was making progress with Dorian.

Lynix moved around a couple of tables as he headed to the bar. With it being Sunday, the place wasn't too crowded. Normally, some of the guys would stop by after their shift during the week or on a Saturday. Sundays? Not so much. If any of them were there, it was mainly to watch sports. There was currently a baseball game on most of the televisions strategically placed throughout the space.

"What's up, man? Haven't seen you in a while," Percy, the bartender, said and set a drink napkin in front of Lynix when he took a seat at the end of the bar.

"Yeah, been busy. I'll have my usual and a glass of water." His usual included a bottle of Miller High Life with the top on and a basket of potato wedges along with a cheeseburger.

Lynix settled in, his gaze taking in the space. As for pubs, Roby's was fairly large. Most of the booths along the perimeter of the space were filled with customers. Only a few of the tables in the middle and near the bar were occupied. While most of the bar stools were taken. The back of the building held two pool tables as well as a dart board, and they all were in use.

"Here you go." Percy set the beer in front of Lynix. "Your food should be up in a minute."

"Hey, Lynix, baby. Where you been hiding?" asked Chelle, a woman he'd hung out with in the past.

Lynix tried not to groan. Chelle was relentless in her pursuit of him, which just made him keep her at a distance. She was cute with a pixie cut, light-brown skin, and an hourglass figure. She was nice enough, but he preferred to be the chaser. Not the other way around, and this woman was as thirsty as they came. It was also a turn off when a woman couldn't take a hint—even when he'd made himself clear he wasn't interested.

"What's up, Chelle?"

"You, baby." She leaned in, trying to kiss him on the cheek but Lynix pulled back before her lips made contact.

Maybe his reputation with the women around there made her think he was kidding when he told her he wasn't interested. Or maybe she thought she'd be the one to break his resolve.

Lynix didn't know, but what he did know was he wasn't letting any woman, especially this one, mess things up between him and Dorian. She might not be there to see him with Chelle, but it would be just his luck if Zion walked in at that moment.

Yeah, he needed to shut this down once and for all.

"Oh, so I can't even kiss you on the cheek?" She pouted.

"No," he said simply and took a big gulp of his beer. "I already told you. Whatever the hell you're trying to do here," he pointed between them, "ain't gonna happen. I'm sure there are plenty of men here who would be glad to spend some time with you. I'm not one of them."

She stomped away, mumbling something under her breath about him not being all that. Fine with him. Hopefully, she'd remember that the next time they bumped into each other.

Maybe he should've picked somewhere else to meet with Zion, especially since he wanted to talk about Dorian. The conversation might be premature, but Lynix wasn't taking any chances. He wanted Zion to know he was dating his sister, and he didn't want him to find out from someone else.

Lynix smiled to himself remembering how Dorian had called him out on his bullshit. She sensed his idea of fake dating was a ploy to spend time with her, and he was sure his denial of that hadn't fooled her. Yet the fact that she still agreed to give the idea a shot spoke volumes. She was just as curious about him as he was about her. They might technically be fake dating, but in his heart, he wasn't. His ultimate plan was to get her to fall in love with him because he was already crazy about her.

He checked his watch, surprised Zion hadn't arrived yet. Normally, he was always early for things, but since getting married, not so much. But his friend was happier than Lynix had ever seen him, and why wouldn't he be? He had a gorgeous wife, and the sweetest babies on this side of heaven. Sometimes, Lynix still couldn't believe Zion was a family man now. He'd once been just as much of a player as Lynix and had vowed to never settle down.

Clearly, there was something to the saying—never say never.

It was all good, though. With Zion having kids, Lynix became their godfather, a role he took very seriously. He wanted his own children one day, but in the meantime, he got plenty of practice with the twins, Andrew and Zanaya.

"Hey, man. Sorry I'm late," Zion said as he approached the bar.

Lynix stood, giving him some dap. "Not a problem. I started without you." He reclaimed his seat, and Zion sat on the stool next to him.

"Hooking up here was a good idea. It's been awhile," his friend said before ordering a beer and some food. "How was your week?" Zion asked.

"It was good. I've been putting in some crazy hours at work since a certain someone abandoned us," he joked, looking at Zion pointedly, and they laughed.

Zion had resigned a couple of months ago from Chicago P.D, opting to work for a personal security agency that they both used to contract with on occasion.

Small talk flowed between and as they ate, they caught up with each other's lives. Forty-five minutes later, Lynix realized they hadn't had any deep conversations since Zion got married. Sure, they'd seen each other often but hadn't really had a chance to talk in depth.

Back in the day, they'd come to Roby's after some of their shifts. Sometimes hanging at the Pub two or three times a week. Lynix missed this. He missed hanging out with his buddy and shooting the shit. Yes, he spent time with his brothers, but that was different. Too often their conversations turned to family issues—namely their father. But with Zion, they discussed life, the kids, and Zion even talked about what it was like to be married. Claiming he wished he and Raven would've met sooner.

"Okay, what's going on with you?" Zion murmured only loud enough for Lynix to hear.

"What do you mean?"

"I mean you've turned down a drink from a woman, a dance with another woman, and don't get me started with your two hookups. They've been circling, looking as if they want to stop over here but haven't. I know I've been out of the loop. So what did I miss?"

Lynix snorted, not surprised Zion had noticed.

"I told them a few months ago, shortly before you got married, I can't see them anymore. At first, they thought I was kidding, but I guess they finally got the message."

Zion's beer bottle stopped halfway to his mouth before looking at Lynix. "Why? What's changed?"

Lynix hadn't been sure how to bring up the subject of Dorian but now was as good a time as ever. "Okay, hear me out before you freak out," he said and pushed his plate aside. "Dorian and I are dating."

Zion stilled next to him, then set his beer on the bar. The two of them had never had a disagreement. At least not one that included fists flying. Lynix wasn't sure how this was going to play out, but he was ready.

When Zion didn't say anything, Lynix turned on the stool and looked at him. "What, nothing to say?"

"A year ago, I would've let my fists do the talking because I don't like the idea of my best friend dating one of my sisters. Especially a friend who's the *love 'em and leave 'em* type."

"Zion, I'm not that guy anymore," Lynix hurried to say.

"But I'm wiser and less of a hot head these days," Zion said as if Lynix hadn't spoken. "However, don't get it twisted. If you say the wrong thing while we're talking, I'm going to knock your ass out."

Lynix couldn't help it. He threw his head back and laughed. Not that he didn't think Zion wouldn't try to do it, but it was funny as hell that he thought he could. Lynix had him in size and fighting experience. You didn't grow up with three older brothers, who like to push you around, without learning how to fight.

So yeah, he had no doubt he could take on his friend, but Zion wouldn't go down easy, especially if he was fighting because of one of his sisters.

"Your fists won't be necessary. I'm crazy about Dorian. I would *never* hurt her."

Zion sighed loudly. "I know."

"You know?" Now Lynix was the one surprised.

"You weren't fooling anyone when you used to joke about her being *the future Mrs. Mathews.* Or when you'd say stupid shit like, *be sure to bring your beautiful sister to the party.* Or *I'm in love with your sister.* Or my least favorite—*Are you ready to accept that I'm going to marry her one day?*"

Lynix was laughing so hard at the way his friend imitated him, he had to stand up from the bar stool to keep from falling off it. On the one hand, he was glad Zion wasn't surprised. On the other hand, Lynix now wished he'd made a move on Dorian sooner.

With the heel of his hand, Lynix dabbed at the corners of his eyes where tears had gathered from his laughing. Then he sat back down.

"If you knew I was feeling her, why didn't you call me out on it?"

"Because I had hoped you'd get distracted by one of the other twenty women who'd been trying to get your attention over the years." Zion shook his head and went back to eating. "How long have you and Dorian been dating?"

"Since yesterday," Lynix said. There was no need in telling him that they were fake dating, because Lynix didn't see it that way. He also was confident that soon Dorian would see they were great together.

Zion's hands, holding the large hamburger, stopped inches from his mouth when he turned to look at Lynix. "*Yesterday?*"

Lynix nodded.

"Man, you must be losing your touch. It doesn't typically take you that long to convince an unsuspecting woman to fall for your charm."

Lynix chuckled and thought about how he and Dorian had spent most of the day together yesterday. She laid out the rules for how they'd move forward, including reiterating how there'd be no kissing and very little touching.

He wasn't concerned. He had no doubt she'd be changing her mind before it was all said and done.

"Your sister is the exception to the rule in every way possible. She told me *no* more times than I can count, but I guess I wore her down."

"Or she was secretly interested and tried to resist your charming ass," Zion said with a laugh.

Lynix smiled but didn't comment. There was no doubt Dorian was feeling him, but she didn't fully trust him or herself. Granted, there were enough reasons why she should tread lightly with him, especially knowing his reputation with women. But he sensed she didn't trust her judgment when it came to men.

With them dating, he would make sure she held all the power where the two of them were concerned. Lynix had no intentions of pushing her into anything she wasn't ready for. His plan was to follow her lead but make sure they both had fun in the process. That's how confident he felt that she'd come to her own conclusion about them being meant for each other.

His phone vibrated, and he dug the device out of the front pocket of his jeans and glanced at the screen.

*My mother's at it again. She brought a guy home from church.*

Lynix couldn't help but smile. Virginia had no clue that she was helping his cause.

Then he laughed aloud when Dorian sent another text with a ton of emojis, including a head exploding emoji as well as a crying one. Then in bold letters she typed, *HELP!*

"What's so funny?" Zion asked as he wiped his mouth.

Lynix started to blow off the question but decided to be honest. "Your sister. I guess your mother has been playing matchmaker, and it's making Dorian crazy."

"My mother has issues," Zion joked. "The woman is relentless, and I'm glad I'm no longer on her radar. My sisters have been hassled by her more than I ever had, thank goodness. I guess that means my mother doesn't know you and Dorian are dating."

Lynix shook his head. "Nah. Our relationship is new, and you're the first to know. We're still in the getting to know each other stage. Dorian's probably not ready to scream the news to the world that she and I are an item."

"Well, you guys might want to make your relationship known. Otherwise, my mother's never going to give Dorian any peace."

"Yeah, you're probably right."

Lynix didn't have time to stop by the B&B because he was headed to his brother, Thane's house, after he left the bar. He got together with him, Wes, and a couple of their friends monthly to play poker and tonight happened to be that night.

But he couldn't leave Dorian hanging. He needed to do something.

An idea popped into his head, and he found the telephone number he was looking for, but before he could make the call, Zion nudged his arm.

Lynix glanced at him.

"If you're serious about Dorian, you might have to find a different bar to hang out in." Zion nodded his head toward the entrance. Lynix moaned when he spotted a woman—Willow. A friend with benefits.

"I think you're right," he said when Willow spotted him and headed in their direction.

Lynix hadn't seen her since the beginning of the year and had honestly forgotten about her. She traveled for work more often than not, and that played out well for them both. They only saw each other a few times a year, with him sometimes going to wherever she was in the country. However, today he needed to let her know things had changed.

But before he dealt with Willow, he had to take care of Dorian's problem. He shot off a quick text to a contact who could help him get Virginia off Dorian's back—at least for today. Lynix only wished he could be there to see both their reactions.

Once that was done, he stood and dropped plenty of money on the bar to cover his and Zion's tab.

"Good seeing you, man. I'll be in touch."

Zion chuckled. "Yeah, go and handle your business."

Willow flashed him a beautiful toothpaste-white smile, and Lynix tried not to groan. It was moments like this he wished he had cleaned house, so to speak, years ago. Because if his past messed up his future, he was going to be pissed.

# Chapter Sixteen

"Dorian, I'm glad I took your mother up on the invitation. She's been telling me what an incredible cook you are, and now I see why she brags on you. These smothered pork chops are incredible."

"Thanks, Andre. I'm glad you're enjoying the meal."

Dorian moved back to the oven to pull out a tray of cookies but not without glaring at her mother first. This time, the woman had gone too far.

"I told you," Virginia said in that chipper tone she used when she knew she was in the wrong. She was leaning on the back of the chair across from where Andre was sitting. "My baby knows her way around the kitchen. I can't tell you how much our guests rave about the meals she prepares. She really should consider opening a restaurant or at least a bakery."

This wasn't the first time her mother had said that. From grade school age, Dorian had loved hanging in the kitchen with her sister, Essence, and their mother. Both women were amazing cooks, but neither were interested in cooking as a profession. They enjoyed feeding people, but they each claimed working in a restaurant would take away from the joy of preparing delicious meals.

Dorian felt the same way. Cooking at the B&B was as close as she'd ever want to get to working in a restaurant. There had been a time when she considered owning a bakery, though. Unfortunately, she had no interest in running a business and all that went with it, mainly the financial part. She hated anything that had to do with accounting.

Movement to her left caught Dorian's attention, and it was Virginia entering the oversize pantry. Good. Dorian slipped in behind her and closed the door. The room was in the back corner of the kitchen and out of sight from where the kitchen table was positioned. Meaning, Andre couldn't see them.

"Mom, I know what you're doing, and it's not going to work," Dorian said in a harsh whisper. "I told you, no more matchmaking."

Virginia had the nerve to look affronted, an innocent expression on her face. Her hand went to her chest. "Baby, what do you mean?"

"Mom! You know what I mean," Dorian whispered shouted. "You only invited him here to introduce us. How many times do I have to tell you I'm not interested? I'm not going out with anyone else you try to set me up with. Those days are over!"

"Oh, Dorian. Stop being so dramatic. I invited Andre here this evening because he hasn't had a home cooked meal since March, when his mother moved to Florida. And I knew we'd have plenty of leftovers after the guests ate." She shrugged. "I can't help it if he's showing an interest in you. But you have to admit, the young man is very handsome."

Dorian could admit that, but she didn't say it out loud. Andre was very nice looking. He had the prettiest greenish-brown eyes she'd ever seen and a kind smile. He was also tall, which she liked in a man, had a runner's build, and a deep voice that was as smooth as butter.

Still, she wasn't interested. Not just because she had a fake boyfriend, but mainly because she was done letting her mother run over her with her matchmaking schemes.

"I'm never going out with him. So if that's what you were thinking, think again. I'm done with your—"

"I know. I know. You say that now, but you'll change your mind when you get to know him. Now come on. It's rude to leave him out there alone." Her mother exited the room too quickly for Dorian to respond.

*Ugh! I can't with her!*

That's it! She'd been trying to hold off telling her about Lynix, mainly because she didn't want to lie. It didn't matter if Lynix insisted they weren't exactly lying about dating. Dorian disagreed. They were being deceptive no matter how it was worded. However, right now, she didn't care, especially if the plan worked.

She slipped off her apron and hung it on the hook inside the pantry. She only had a few more things to take care of, and then she'd be able to head home.

When she stepped back into the kitchen, she heard, "Niecy-poo, you have a delivery." And her Aunt GiGi strolled into the kitchen with the most beautiful flower arrangement Dorian had ever seen. "These are for you, sweetie."

"*Me?*" Dorian croaked as she stared openmouthed at the huge bouquet.

It was colorful and spectacular with red, yellow, and white roses, along with orange Lillies, purple chrysanthemums, and a sprinkle of greenery throughout.

Dorian didn't move. She cast a quick glance at Andre, praying he had nothing to do with the flowers. He glanced at the bouquet, studied them, then turned his gaze to her and smiled.

*Oh crap!* If he was behind this special delivery, she was going to scream.

Aunt GiGi plucked the card from the bouquet and handed it to her. "Hurry up. I want to know who they're from."

"Flower deliveries this time of night?" Virginia said as she moved closer. "Those are too beautiful to come from a grocery store. They had to have come from a florist, but this time of night? On a Sunday? No way."

Those were Dorian's thoughts exactly, but maybe Andre had purchased them earlier and had a friend drop them off. She pulled the small card from the envelope and sighed before reading the note.

*Dee, thanks for making my day yesterday. Can't wait to see you soon. Love, Lynix.*

Dorian's mouth dropped open, and then she squealed before catching herself. She covered her mouth but burst out laughing.

*Oh my goodness!* This was almost as good as him showing up in person. She had only texted him because she needed to vent. She had no idea that he was going to actually do something about the problem with her mother. And as she looked at the high-end flower arrangement again, she knew he had to have spent a pretty penny for it.

God, she was going to owe him big for this, and the timing couldn't have been more perfect.

"Give me that." Aunt GiGi snatched the card from Dorian's hand before she could protest and read the note. "Lynix?" her aunt whispered, and a frown marred her pretty face as if trying to figure out who it could be.

Dorian could tell the moment that realization dawned because her eyes grew big, and her mouth formed a perfect O.

"No. Way!" her aunt shrieked, then cracked up.

"Will one of you tell me what's going on? Who are the flowers from?" Virginia asked, trying to take the card from her sister, but Aunt GiGi kept it out of reach.

"They're from Lynix," Dorian said, trying to keep the giddiness out of her tone. No sense in acting like a man hadn't ever sent her anything before, even if it was true.

"Lynix who? Wait," Virginia's eyes narrowed, "Zion's friend, Lynix?"

Aunt GiGi was still laughing. "Soooo, Niecy-poo, how'd you make his day yesterday? Inquiring minds want to know."

"Why is he sending you flowers?" Virginia asked with her hands on her rounded hips as she looked at Dorian pointedly.

"Because we're dating."

Her mother gasped, and Aunt GiGi cackled loud enough to be heard on all three floors of the building.

"Now that's what I'm talking about! Got you a real man," her Aunt GiGi high-fived her, and Dorian laughed with her.

Giddiness was full-blown inside of her, and she couldn't wait to thank Lynix for coming through for her. She had told him no kissing during this little farce, but she might have to break her own rule the next time she saw him. He deserved a big wet one for putting the shocked expression on her mother's face.

"What? How?" Virginia stuttered. "When did this happen? How long has this been going on, and why him? Isn't he too old for you?"

It wasn't that Virginia didn't like Lynix. She did, but she still saw Dorian as her little girl, and Lynix was all man. It didn't matter if they were only a couple of years apart. When her mother saw him, she saw an alpha male who was comfortable in his skin with the ability to corrupt any female in his wake.

Or at least that's how Dorian assumed her mother felt.

"We recently started dating exclusively," Dorian said, no longer caring if it was a lie. If it got her mother to back off, it would be well worth it.

"But what about Andre?" Virginia said innocently, and Andre started coughing and hitting his chest with the side of his fist as if food had gone down wrong.

"Excuse me?" he croaked between his coughing fits. "I umm, we aren't—"

"Don't mind my mother," Dorian said and approached him, gently patting him on the back as he continued coughing. She was so embarrassed. "Virginia doesn't know what she's talking about. Here, drink some water."

Dorian handed him his glass, then scowled at her mother. The woman thought nothing of humiliating her, and Dorian couldn't understand why she couldn't see what she was doing. How could she not comprehend these little stunts were getting old, and they were embarrassing?

Going along with Lynix's plan had been a good decision. It was the only way to get free of her mom.

Dorian grabbed the bouquet from the counter and excused herself from the room. She needed to find a quiet place to call Lynix, and as she strolled down the hallway to the front of the house, she decided the living room would be perfect.

A short while later, she entered the brightly decorated space with its tall ceiling, butter-yellow walls, and elegant white crown molding. Thankfully, no one was in there. Setting the bouquet on the coffee table in front of the sofa, Dorian pulled her cell phone from her back pocket.

She called Lynix, then paced the length of the large space, her feet silent on the oriental rug that covered the hardwood floor. Her heart was practically beating out of her chest, and

Dorian wasn't sure if it was from being angry at her mother or anxious to talk to Lynix. Maybe a little of both.

When the call picked up, she stopped moving. There was loud talking and laughing coming through the phone line before Lynix said, "Hey, sweetheart. Everything okay?"

With those few simple words, Dorian's heart rate eased, and she melted a little inside. She loved his deep, calming voice, and the concern she heard seemed genuine.

"Everything is perfect thanks to you," she said, deciding not to vent to him about how her mother was trying to push her onto another unsuspecting man. "The flowers are stunning, Lynix. Thank you so much for your thoughtfulness."

"Anything for you," he said, his voice dropping an octave, and she no longer heard talking in the background. But then she remembered—poker night with his brothers.

"Shoot. I forgot you were playing poker tonight. I'm not going to hold you long."

"It's not a problem. We were taking a break to replenish our snacks," he said with a chuckle. "Anyway, I'm glad you received the bouquet. Hopefully, they did the trick."

Dorian dropped down on the sofa and leaned forward to sniff the flowers, then touched a delicate petal on one of the white roses. "Yes, they are perfect in every way." She would go into detail, about how the delivery played out, the next time she saw him. "I love flowers, and no one has ever sent me any before now." She hadn't planned to admit to that and cringed when the words left her mouth.

It was bad enough he knew about how things ended with Rodney. If she kept telling Lynix everything, he was going to think she was beyond pitiful.

"Seriously?" he said, shock dripping from that one word. "I guess I'm going to have to make up for the assholes who didn't send you flowers. Actually, I'm going to make sure I give you experiences that will make you forget about the losers. You're special, Dee, and it's about damn time someone treated you as such."

Dorian was too surprised to respond. It was sad to admit, but with the few men she'd dated, she couldn't say she'd ever really felt special. Yep, that was just sad. Now, here Lynix comes, her fake boyfriend, promising to change that. She had no doubt that hanging out with him was going to be very different from what she was used to with other men. And he called her Dee. She secretly loved when he used her nickname. A nickname only used by her family.

Instead of telling him that he didn't have to prove anything to her or go to any trouble for her, she said, "I'm looking forward to our time together. Are you free one day this week?" she asked. "I'd like to cook dinner for you."

There was a slight pause before he said, "I would *never* say no to that. I'm on second shift for the next three days, but how about Thursday night?"

"Works for me. I'll see you then."

"Oh, sweetie, you're going to see me before then. There's no way I can go that many days without spending time with *my woman*." He chuckled, and she smiled at the joke. "Text me when you make it home tonight."

"Okay."

By the time the call ended, Dorian was grinning like an idiot. Pretending to have a boyfriend for a few months was going to be fun. She just had to make sure she didn't fall for said boyfriend.

# Chapter Seventeen

Lynix's cell phone alarm blared from somewhere to his left, and he groaned as he patted the top of the night-stand, trying to silence the device. When his hand didn't immediately make contact, he lifted his head and searched the tabletop through half-opened lids until he found the phone.

He hit the snooze button, then dropped his head back down on the pillow and closed his eyes. It felt like he had just climbed into bed minutes ago. When in reality he'd been asleep for three hours—not nearly enough after working a twelve-hour shift.

All he wanted to do right now was roll over and return to a deep sleep. Another five or six hours would be perfect.

He couldn't. He needed to get up and get dressed because Dorian agreed to come over to watch a sunrise with him from his rooftop deck. In hindsight, he should've planned this for a day when they both were off work. Unfortunately, their sched-ules weren't lining up. Her days typically started super early, and he was working second shift this week.

But this was just temporary. In another two weeks, he'd have more control of his work schedule, and he'd plan around her days. She typically worked split shifts at the B&B. Maybe he'd be able to steal her away for lunch or something.

In the meantime, Lynix would figure something out. If left up to Dorian, they'd only get together whenever they had to put on a show for their parents. That wasn't enough for Lynix, even if they were supposed to be pretending to be a couple. He had a small amount of time during this so-called fake relationship for her to see he wasn't a man whore. That he had changed, and they belonged together. He planned to use every opportunity to bring that message to the forefront.

Releasing a noisy yawn, he reached over and turned off the alarm before it could go off. It was time to get up because if he lay there any longer, he'd risked falling back to sleep.

He sat up and placed his bare feet on the thick carpet before walking naked into the ensuite. Dorian would be there in forty-five minutes, and he had a few things to get together before she arrived.

He smiled thinking about how she had responded when he suggested they hook up early this morning.

*"You're kidding, right? You want me to intentionally get up at three a.m. on my day off?"* she had said, and though they'd been on the telephone, Lynix could almost picture the cute frown on her face.

It took some convincing, but when he described the experience of seeing a sunrise over Lake Michigan from his rooftop deck, she conceded. He had even offered to pick her up from home, not liking the idea of her roaming the streets that time of morning. Of course, she shot down the offer, claiming she usually started work at five in the morning at the B&B. Making it common for her to be out and about that time of day.

Once showered, comfortably dressed, and feeling more

awake, Lynix re-entered his bedroom and picked up his cell phone. He told Dorian to text him when she was on her way, and he was glad to see she had.

*Be there in fifteen minutes.*

Lynix shoved the cell into the pocket of his jogging pants and headed to the kitchen to start the coffee. He wasn't much of a cook, so he'd planned to have a light breakfast prepared for Dorian, but she told him that, if he provided the coffee, she'd take care of breakfast.

One thing he knew about her was she liked flavored coffee while he normally took his strong and black. Since this morning was all about her, he brewed a hazelnut-mocha blend that he had bought yesterday. Within minutes, the enticing aroma filled the kitchen, and he inhaled deeply.

"Hopefully, it's strong," he murmured under his breath as he poured the dark liquid into two travel mugs. Then he went to the guest room closet and grabbed a lightweight blanket. They probably wouldn't need it since the temperature was in the mid-seventies when he arrived home a few hours ago, but just in case.

Lynix returned to the front of the penthouse and made sure everything was presentable. He had a housekeeper who came twice a month to clean and do his laundry, but this past week had been her week off. Still, the place looked all right.

It was going to be weird having a woman in his home who wasn't his mother or housekeeper. But he was having a lot of firsts when it came to Dorian. She was the only woman he'd been interested in enough to welcome into his home. She wasn't just a hookup like the others and warranted to be treated differently.

Sad to say, he'd met his share of crazy women who had stalker-like tendencies and learned early on to keep them at a distance. So he never brought them to his house, and they had no clue to his net worth.

It was safer that way. It didn't matter if he was a cop. Some women didn't care. Hurt their feelings and be prepared to face their wrath.

That had happened to him once when he lived in an apartment near Hyde Park. He invited a woman back to his place, with the understanding that they were just hooking up, only to have her key his truck when weeks later he stopped seeing her.

Lesson learned. That had been many years ago and the last time he welcomed a woman into his personal space.

His cell phone chimed. He had a special ringtone for the building's concierge, and it let him know Dorian was on her way up. Lynix had already added her to the list of people allowed to come up to his penthouse without an escort.

A few minutes later, a soft knock sounded at his door.

Excitement swirled inside of him, and Lynix's pulse amped up. He chuckled at his reaction, feeling like a kid getting ready to go on his first date. Dorian had that effect on him, though. He had already been crazy about her, and since their lunch at the hotel, his feelings for her had multiplied. They talked daily, even if it was only for a couple of minutes. When they weren't talking, they texted.

Granted, he was the one who usually initiated the interaction, but he could feel her guards lowering with each passing day. It was only a matter of time when she'd officially be his. For now, though, he'd keep letting her think they were fake dating.

Lynix opened the door and grinned when he saw her leaning against the doorjamb, looking as tired as he felt. Her hair was pulled up in a messy ponytail with a few tendrils framing her pretty face that was free of makeup. Her long-sleeve fitted T-shirt hugged her perky breasts and flat abs, and the white shorts stopped mid thigh, revealing beautiful, toned legs. On her feet were a pair of yellow Chucks that matched her shirt.

Dorian was so damn adorable. It was no wonder her family was protective of her. Her petite frame and girl-next-door features made her appear vulnerable and tugged on his protective instincts. Which was probably just the caveman in him because he knew she was tougher than she looked.

His gaze traveled back up her feminine curves and his body stirred. Damn, just the sight of the woman did something to him. Forget watching a sunrise. What he really wanted to do was sweep her into his arms, carry her to his huge bed, and familiarize himself with every inch of her.

If only...

He wanted way more from this woman than a quick rump between the sheets. He wanted forever, and one wrong move could destroy his chances if he weren't careful.

"Are you going to keep staring at me, or are you going to let me in?" Dorian said, snapping him out of his thoughts. She held up a basket of something that smelled sweet and savory. "I brought breakfast."

"Then by all means, come on in."

Lynix opened the door wider, and Dorian stepped across the threshold but didn't move farther into the house. She did, however, glance around the open floor plan that gave a view of the kitchen, living room and dining room.

"You have a beautiful home, Lynix," she said and took a tentative step forward.

"Thank you. Make yourself at home."

As if pulled by a magnetic force, she practically floated into the kitchen, only stopping when she reached the long, marbled countertop. She glided her hand over it and smiled. "I love this. Did you pick the finishes?"

"No, everything in the kitchen came that way, except I had all the walls painted. The yellow they had was a little too bright for me." The space wasn't super big, but what it lacked in size, it made up with style and high-end appliances.

Dorian set the basket of goodies on the counter that separated the kitchen from the dining area as she took in the space. One night, while talking to her on the phone, he had described the three-bedroom, three-bathroom penthouse, promising to show it to her one day soon.

"Feel free to take a tour, but we only have about fifteen minutes before the sun rises. Actually, maybe not even that long. Let's head out to the deck. You can look around inside afterwards."

She turned to the wall of windows in the living room and her mouth dropped open. Lynix smiled. That was everyone's response at first sight, including his, and it had been the selling point for him.

"Wow! This was not what I was expecting when you mentioned your rooftop deck. I thought we'd have to climb up some winding stairs to get to it, but this is incredible."

After grabbing the basket she'd brought with her, as well as the coffees and blanket, Lynix followed her across the room. "Here, hold this for a minute." He handed her one of the travel mugs, then slid the glass doors open.

"Okay, now you're just showing off," Dorian said, and they laughed. "Indoor, outdoor. Love it!"

The majority of the glass wall opened to the outdoors, but he rarely kept it open in the summer. Not while running the air conditioner. He'd make an exception today.

When they stepped outside, they set the coffees and the basket on the small table, and the blanket on one of the loungers. Normally, this area was shaded by a retractable

143

awning, but since the sun wasn't out, the entire deck was opened to the elements.

Dorian stood by the clear-glass railing that overlooked the lake, seeming deep in thought as she gazed out. Lynix moved up behind her and bracketed her in with his arms on each side of her, his front to her back, and his hands gripping the railing.

Her subtle floral scent wafted to his nose, and though he was tempted, he refrained from burying his nose against her long, graceful neck for a better whiff. He was going to have to keep reminding himself to follow her lead and let her set the pace. Which wasn't going to be easy since he was used to going after what he wanted.

It might not be easy, but he already knew Dorian would be worth the effort and the wait.

When she glanced back at him, he thought she'd push him away or ask him to move. She did neither. Instead, she smiled at him, and Lynix was pretty sure his heart cracked open a little wider for her. Each time they shared the same space, his desire for her intensified.

Yeah, taking his time getting to know her before luring her into his bed was going to be his greatest test to date. His mind was in line with his plans, but his traitorous body wanted her more than he wanted his next breath. Who wouldn't? The woman's luscious lips and her incredible body were tempting as hell.

Her attention went back to the lake as the sun started its ascent. "Oh, my goodness. Isn't it beautiful?" she whispered.

"Yes, it is," he said, his attention on her, though she was referring to the rising sun. But nothing compared to her beauty.

She glanced at him, then elbowed him in the gut, forcing a laugh from him.

"I'm talking about the sunrise, and you're not even looking."

"Oh, sweetheart, I'm looking at the prettiest thing on this side of heaven."

She blushed and hid a smile before returning her gaze to the view. "You're supposed to be watching the sunrise, not looking at me."

He'd seen the sunrise a thousand times and granted, it was always remarkable. However, he had never experienced it while being hugged up against her curvy ass. Now that... was priceless.

He glanced out over the water just as the sun's rays painted the sky in a burst of red, orange, and yellow streaks, creating a majestic picture. Lynix loved this time of morning. Watching the sunrise in all its glory always made him reflective. Witnessing and experiencing such beauty and tranquility as the sun slowly climbed into the sky with such ease and grace.

On a wistful sigh, Dorian turned within his arms and faced him. They were standing so close, all Lynix had to do was lower his head a few inches and his lips would be lined up perfectly with hers.

God, it had been days since he'd tasted her, and he longed to...

"That was magnificent," she said, smiling up at him and making his heart crack open even more for her. "Thank you for inviting me over to watch it with you."

"It was my pleasure. Feel free to come over anytime, morning, noon, or night. You're always welcomed here."

A warm breeze blew loose strands of her hair around her face, and he lightly ran a finger across her forehead and pushed them away from her eyes. He swept them behind her ear before meeting her eyes again.

"For a big guy, you can be quite gentle," Dorian murmured as she gazed up at him, and Lynix chuckled.

"Only when I want to be, like when I'm with you."

Lynix let the back of his fingers glide down her soft cheek, and her eyes drifted closed at his touch. He loved touching her, and the desire to touch other parts of her body grew more intense each time they were together.

But patience would soon get them both what they truly wanted. He wanted her, and she'd said she wanted a man she could trust and depend on. Someone she could have fun with, and he already knew he could be that for her and more.

"Come on. Let's have some coffee and whatever treats you brought with you." Lynix guided her over to the loungers where they'd set everything.

"Scoot over," he said, nudging Dorian's leg when she claimed one of the loungers. She was sitting in the center of it, which left no space for him to slide in next to her.

"Why? You can sit over there." She pointed at the identical lounger on the other side of the short table. "This one isn't big enough for both of us."

"Yeah, it is, move over. I want to sit next to you while we eat breakfast and enjoy the view."

She hesitated, nibbling on her lower lip as if considering his request but didn't move.

"Woman, you can either move over, or I can just pick you up and..."

"*Fine.*" She scooted to the other side of the seat and glared at him. "Are you happy, now? You big bully!"

Lynix threw his head back and laughed. He could already tell dating her was going to be a blast, and this was only the beginning for them.

# Chapter Eighteen

**D**orian loved watching as Lynix enjoyed the breakfast she'd prepared. Like him, she should be devouring the empanadas and homemade spicy honey dipping sauce, as well as the strong hazelnut-mocha coffee he'd made. Instead, she couldn't think straight with him being hugged up on her right side. The big, solid, bear of a man was so close that he was wreaking havoc on her senses.

He was right, the lounger was big enough for the both of them. However, he was hogging up the space, and his masculine, woodsy scent made her want to snuggle against him. Well, that and the cool breeze brushing against her heated skin.

Still, knowing he was a ladies' man, she shouldn't want to be hugged up to him. If anything, that should make her want to keep her distance, but it didn't. Spending time with him like this was allowing her to see other sides to him.

Lynix might be a babe magnet and a little gruff at times, but he was also sweet, kind, and thoughtful. Which probably had a lot to do with why women gravitated to him. For her though, it was the small things he did that made her want to know him better. Like when he'd given her a ride home after her fiasco of a date with Glen. Or when he sent her flowers the other day at the B&B.

And even this morning his thoughtfulness showed in more ways than one. She loved how he had arranged for her SUV to be valeted to one of his underground parking spots. She could've parked on the street, but no he made it convenient for her to drop the car off and come inside.

How sweet was that?

Now that she thought about it, Lynix was also extremely generous with his time and even his wealth. Who offers to give you their car, a top-of-the-line BMW, because your car is on its last wheels? Lynix. He'd done that for her.

There was more to him than she originally thought.

Dorian glanced out at the lake, still awed by the view and the sounds that came with a new day. Birds chirping, sea gulls squawking, and the lapping of waves crashing against the shore was starting to relax her. What a perfect way to start the day.

Watching the sunrise with Lynix had been dreamy and jaw-droppingly beautiful. It was like one of those moments that should be experienced with the one you loved. Not the one you were secretly lusting after like she was doing lately.

"I can hear the gears inside your brain working hard. What's on your mind?" Lynix asked, and Dorian smiled as she brought the mug of coffee to her lips.

No way would she tell him how her feelings for him were starting to shift. Lynix would pounce, and she'd be defenseless to say no to him. Even though thoughts of him had taken up permanent residence in her mind, she had to remember that this wasn't real.

Lynix nudged her. "You know you have skills in the kitchen when you can make a little hand pie taste this good. These empanadas are delicious."

"I'm glad you like them."

The chorizo, potato, egg, and cheese hand pie with peppers and spices were easy to make. It helped that she assembled them last night. Then all she had to do this morning was let them bake while she got dressed.

"I should've asked if you were allergic to anything. Are you?"

"Only green vegetables."

Dorian jerked her head to look at him. "All green vegetables? Seriously?"

He chuckled. "Nah, I just don't really like them, but I force myself to eat them because they're supposed to be good for you."

She smiled and set down her coffee. "Just like a little kid."

He shrugged. "What can I say? I'm a big kid at heart, but to answer your question, I'm allergic to mangoes. I also might have an intolerance to walnuts since they make me cough."

"Interesting. What about other nuts?"

He shook his head. "Not that I can tell, but I don't eat any of them too often. What about you? Any allergies?"

"None that I know of, and considering how I love to cook and eat, I'm glad I don't have any."

"Good to know. Now, going back to my original question. What's on your mind?"

Dorian grinned. She had hoped he had forgotten. Apparently not. Good thing there was something else on her mind that was a safe topic.

"Remember how I'm supposed to cook dinner for you Thursday?"

Lynix groaned. "Come on! You can't cancel on me. I was looking forward to having dinner with you."

"I'm not exactly canceling. Just tweaking the plans a little.

How do you feel about having dinner with me and our godbabies?"

When he didn't respond, she glanced at him and laughed when she caught him frowning. Okay, having dinner together would've been a nice, relaxing way to spend an evening. Having dinner while babysitting five-month-old twins? Not so much.

"It'll be fun," she insisted. "Zion has to travel to New York for work, and he wants to take Raven with him. My parents would keep the kids, but they're going to Lake Geneva for a long weekend to celebrate their friends' fiftieth wedding anniversary. Essence will be staying with the babies, but she has to work overnight Thursday. So I volunteered to watch them until she gets off work Friday."

"And where do I come in?" Lynix asked, humor in his tone.

"You will come over and babysit with me. In doing so, you'll earn an incredibly delicious home cooked meal that will have you licking your lips."

He laughed. "That sounds great and all, but I'd rather lick your lips."

Dorian's mouth dropped open, but she quickly closed it as goosebumps scattered over her skin. Wow. She hadn't expected him to say that. Her gaze immediately went to his lips, remembering how good they felt against hers each time they kissed.

"Umm, okay," she said slowly as she tried to come up with a response. "I guess we can add that to the list of things to do that night."

Her words sounded as unsure as she felt in that moment, knowing she shouldn't be encouraging Lynix. Yet, the idea of licking lips, possibly leading to tongue aerobics, sounded exciting.

He chuckled and slid his arm around her back, then pulled her against his side. "Why wait?"

The man moved so fast, his mouth covered hers before she could respond, and Dorian immediately tasted the spicy honey sauce on his tongue. Delicious.

She moaned into his mouth as their intense lip-lock went from five to sixty in a heartbeat. His masterful tongue explored the inner recesses of her mouth as the kiss sent spirals of ecstasy powering through her.

Goodness, the man could kiss, and with his long arm wrapped around her and his large hand cupping her butt cheek, her senses were on overload. Yeah, the heady sensations that he was creating inside of her were mind-boggling.

How? How could one little kiss make her want to throw all common sense out the window and allow Lynix to have his way with her? She couldn't explain it, and right now, she didn't want to. She just wanted more of him.

The panty-melting kiss intensified, and Dorian wasn't sure if she moved or if Lynix lifted her. One minute she was sitting beside him, and the next, she was straddling his lap. And what a lap it was. The way she was positioned on top of him, she could feel his hardness between her thighs and one of her many questions about him was answered.

Yes, his package was as big as she'd imagined. Of course it was. The man was huge everywhere else, why wouldn't he be big down there too?

Her hand gripped the back of his head, holding him in place as their tongues continued tangling. She was surprised by her eager response to him, but she shouldn't be. It was this way each time they shared a kiss, but this one... this one somehow felt more fervent. Like she couldn't get enough of him.

That might've also had something to do with the way he'd skillfully slid his hand under her T-shirt and unsnapped her bra. She moaned and shivered at the feel of his hand on her bare skin. Then it was as if her body had a mind of its own. As he squeezed and fondled one of her nipples, she couldn't stop her hips from rotating on top of him, grinding against his erection that was poking her.

They were treading into dangerous territory, and she should stop this before it went too far. But it felt too good. Too right.

Warmth spread through her body, and the throbbing pulse between her thighs was almost too much. This... all of this was like nothing she had ever felt with a man, and Dorian wanted to feel more of him. Maybe if she...

*Oh my God. What am I doing?*

She jerked back. Chest heaving, mind whirling, she placed her hand on her mouth and couldn't look at Lynix. She'd messed up. She tried to scurry off his lap, but he held her in place.

"I'm sorry. Let me up," she mumbled, still trying to pull away, but Lynix held on to her.

What the heck had gotten into her? This was fake. They were not a couple, and they sure as hell shouldn't have been dry humping each other.

"Dee, slow down and listen to me," he said, his voice gravelly, yet calm as his chest heaved and he fastened her bra with practice ease.

Still breathing hard, she shook her head. "Lynix, I'm sorry. That shouldn't have happened. I didn't mean to..."

"*Shhh*, sweetheart. Just stop," he whispered, and suddenly she deflated and fell against his hard chest.

Lynix's heart was pounding loudly against her ear, and she was glad to know she wasn't the only one worked up.

"Why are you apologizing?" he asked as he rubbed her back. "You didn't do anything that I didn't want us to do. I should be the one apologizing. I broke your *no kissing* rule."

Dorian snort laughed. "Like you were really planning to stick to that rule."

A laugh rumbled inside his chest, the sound soothing against her ear.

"I was going to try. At least for a while," he said, still laughing.

Releasing a long breath, Dorian settled into him as he held her in the safety of his big, strong arms, and her eyes drifted closed.

This was nice. She was still straddling his lap, and though he was still semi-erect and pressed against her, it didn't freak her out. If anything, it made her want to grind against him again. Instead, she remained still and soaked up the comfort that came with the way Lynix held her.

He placed a kiss on top of her head. "I'm not going to lie, Dee. If you hadn't stopped us, I don't know if I could've. You feel too perfect in my arms, and that kiss..." He shook his head, and his words drifted off.

"You're so tempting," she mumbled, hating to admit she'd lost control. Something she had never done with a man before, but Lynix wasn't just any man. He was different from anyone she'd ever met. "Maybe when we're alone together, we stick with our rules for this arrangement."

"Umm, you mean *your* rules? Because if it were left up to me, we'd do whatever came naturally. And sweetheart, that kiss and the way you were grinding on top of me was definitely natural."

Dorian didn't respond. He was right. It had felt natural. Actually, everything about her alone times with Lynix felt perfect, and that was a problem. A big problem.

# Chapter Nineteen

Standing in her brother and sister-in-law's kitchen, Dorian unloaded the groceries she brought with her. Hopefully, she hadn't forgotten anything, but considering how well stocked their refrigerator was, she should be fine.

Finally, she'd get to cook for Lynix. Though she would've preferred to be at her apartment, where she knew where everything was, it probably wouldn't have been a good idea. At least at her brother's house, babysitting the twins, there'd be less temptation for her and Lynix to pick up where they'd left off at his place the other day.

She trembled at the memory of them kissing, moaning, and grinding against each other. The moment had been hot, and the feelings ignited—scorching. At least until they came to their senses. If they—or she—was going to survive this charade they were putting on for their families, she was going to have to catch herself before she got carried away with him like that again.

"What's that?"

Dorian startled at the sound of Zion's voice and whipped around to find him standing just inside the kitchen. She held up the large, covered container that she was getting ready to place inside the refrigerator.

"Sirloin steaks that I have marinating. Lynix is stopping by to spend time with the babies, and I promised to cook dinner for him."

She quickly turned away from her brother. Lynix might've talked to him about them *dating,* but Dorian hadn't. She knew there'd be questions, and she needed to be convincing when responding.

The main issue she had with Lynix's plan of fake dating was deceiving their families. Lynix didn't seem concerned about the deception when it came to his parents, who she'd be meeting next weekend. They agreed to only pretend to date for a couple of months, but the guilt of lying to everyone was gnawing on her nerves.

Zion leaned his hip against the counter and folded his arms across his chest. "How's it going with you and Lynix?"

Dorian set the last item on the counter and started folding her reusable bags. "It's going well. I know I've given him a hard time over the years, but he's actually a nice guy."

Zion grunted. "That's one way to describe him."

Dorian finally gave him her attention. "Does that mean you don't think it's a good idea for us to date?"

Zion hadn't met many of her dates over the years. He'd ask questions, or she'd share information about them, but he didn't often give an opinion. Except with Rodney. He didn't like him the moment they met. Claimed he looked shady, and in hindsight, Dorian should've listened. Her brother didn't dislike many people, and she could've saved herself from heartache had she'd seen what he'd seen. Except she'd been excited to be in a relationship and excited to say she had a boyfriend.

"To be honest, you guys might be good for each other," her brother said, surprising her. "Lynix is ready to settle down and needs someone like you who can ground him, and I think he can bring you out of your shell. Not only that, but he's also protective, trustworthy, and you'll never want for anything. That's all a big brother can ask for."

Dorian laughed. "You do realize you're my little brother, right?" He was two years younger than her, but he had always been protective of her and their sisters despite being the baby in the family.

He waved her off and chuckled. "That's beside the point. Anyway, I know Lynix has a past, but he's cleaned up his act, and I've seen the changes in him. I think he's ready for a serious relationship."

Wow. Okay, this whole conversation was unexpected, and Dorian wasn't sure what to do with the information. She'd been keeping Lynix at a distance because of his reputation and because he was Zion's best friend. There'd been a time when she didn't think her brother would approve of her going out with any of his friends, let alone Lynix.

But if she was honest, those weren't the only reasons why she'd been slow to give Lynix a chance. He scared her. She knew he would never hurt her intentionally, but what if things turned out the same as they had with Rodney? What if she clammed up the way she'd done with her ex when it was time to be intimate? Who's to say it wouldn't happen with Lynix?

As soon as the last thought penetrated her mind, she recalled the other day on his deck. His kisses and touches turned her on more than she cared to admit. They made her want more of him.

Who knows, maybe she was different with Lynix. Maybe their pretend relationship and spending time with him would help boost her confidence.

Time would tell.

"I'm glad you're okay with us being together," she said to Zion. "We're not serious right now. We're still in the getting to know you stage."

Zion nodded while he watched her intensely.

"What?" she snapped when he continued to stare. "Why are you looking at me like that?"

He shrugged. "No reason. Just be careful. Lynix is a great guy, but he's umm..."

"Experienced," she finished for him and started grabbing bowls and pots that she'd need to fix dinner. "I know. He's... a lot of man," she said and snorted.

She couldn't believe she had just told her brother that, but she didn't know how else to describe Lynix. There were times when she was around him that she felt like a sheltered kid pretending to be an adult. When in reality, they were only a couple of years apart, but Lynix seemed more accomplished and worldly compared to her. Which was why she thought he was out of her league.

Instead of saying any of that to her brother, she said, "We're just hanging out. Don't worry."

"I'm not worried. Lynix already knows I'll kick his ass if he hurts you."

Dorian sighed. "Zion, I don't need you to fight my battles. I can take care of myself. I'm not some little girl who doesn't know what she's doing."

"Maybe so, but I warned him anyway," he said and turned to leave without a backwards glance.

While Dorian started dinner, Zion and Raven finished last-minute tasks before it was time for them to leave, but she couldn't stop thinking about the conversation with Zion.

What would he think if he knew she and Lynix were pretending to be a couple? Their little charade had clearly fooled him and her mother, but would it work on Lynix's parents? She'd find out when they attended his mother's gala Saturday night.

*How do I get myself into this stuff?*

Thirty minutes later, Dorian was alone with the babies and Onyx, the family dog—a boxer. She glanced at the three of them and smiled. They were so cute. She had moved the babies to the edge of the kitchen where she could keep an eye on them. They seemed content in the bouncers that Lynix had bought them a month ago.

Dorian chuckled as she watched Onyx go from one baby to the other, sniffing them one minute, then nudging them the next, as if to say, *y'all good?* It was adorable how attentive he was to them. And once he was satisfied they were okay, he lay on the floor between them.

Glancing at the clock on the microwave, she realized Lynix would be there shortly. She had hoped to have most of dinner prepared by the time he arrived.

Excitement swirled inside of her at the thought of cooking for him. In the big scheme of things, it was a simple gesture. Yet, she secretly wanted to impress him with her culinary skills. Seemed he'd been coming through for her over the last few weeks, and she wanted to do something nice for him.

Onyx leaped up and started barking just as the doorbell rang.

"Dang, I thought I had more time."

Dorian hurried to the hallway mirror to make sure she looked okay. She ran her fingers through her hair which hung in waves around her shoulders. No matter how many times she told herself that she wasn't trying to impress Lynix, she knew she was lying. Fake boyfriend or not, she wanted to look nice... for him.

"Okay, good enough," she murmured to herself in the mirror, then rushed to the door and opened it.

"Hey, beautiful," Lynix said, looking like a tasty treat in the black polo shirt that hugged his pecks and biceps. Black pants covered his long legs that seemed to go on forever.

His dark gaze did a slow crawl down her body, and the appreciation she saw in his eyes as he took in her yellow sundress, sent warmth rushing through her body.

Whew! This man and his fiery gazes.

"I know I'm not supposed to kiss you, but I can't help it." He stepped forward and placed a lingering kiss on her lips before strolling across the threshold. But not before her internal temperature skyrocketed.

All he'd done was kiss her, and there wasn't even any tongue action. Yet, her insides were on fire.

"These are for you." He handed her a crystal vase with an exquisite bouquet of pink lilies, and Dorian inhaled their incredible fragrance while closing and locking the door.

"Lynix, these are breathtaking. Thank you."

"My pleasure," he said, and chuckled when Onyx swiped at his leg and barked, determined to get his attention.

"What's up, boy?"

Lynix bent down, giving Onyx some love with a rub down. When he was finished playing with the dog, she watched as he rinsed his hands and moved to where the babies were sitting.

Dorian set the vase in the center of the kitchen counter and smiled when she turned to the twins. Even at five months, they were crazy about their godfather, especially Zanaya. She started fussing, flailing her arms, and moving around in the bouncer as if trying to get Lynix to look at her while he talked to Andrew.

"What's going on, baby girl?"

Lynix somehow managed to get both babies out of the

bouncers and was holding one in each arm. When he suddenly turned to her and smiled, Dorian's breath caught, and her heart slammed against her chest. The picture the three of them made together had her ovaries leaping to attention.

This man. This sweet, kind, and generous man. A man who adored his godbabies and was good with them. It was too much. *He* was too much, and she hoped like hell she wasn't *for real* falling for how perfect of a man he really was.

# Chapter Twenty

The evening was going better than Dorian had planned, except dinner was a little late. She was putting the finishing touches on the meal while Lynix hung out in the nursery with the kids. They'd been fussy, but between her and Lynix, they'd manage to entertain the babies until it was time to put them to bed. Andrew had already fallen asleep a few minutes ago, and Zanaya was on her way.

Dorian had known Lynix was good with them, but he was proving to be more experienced with them than she originally thought. According to him, Zion had taught him how to make bottles, change diapers, and distinguish one cry from another.

Yep, impressive.

She carried their dinner into the dining room where they were going to eat, but it wasn't until she set down the asparagus and French bread did she realize what she was doing.

"This is too romantic," she mumbled. The last thing she wanted to do was stoke the fire that had been building inside of her ever since Lynix walked into the house.

Nope. They needed to eat in the kitchen.

She hurried and cleared the table, then set all the food up on the kitchen counter, with the flower vase in the middle. Next came Lynix's favorite red wine, a Malbec, that she placed next to the two wine glasses. After grabbing two bottles of water to add to the spread, she stepped back to look at everything, making sure she hadn't forgotten anything.

"Looks good."

All that was missing was Lynix.

Instead of hollering for him, she started out of the kitchen, but before she took two steps, her cell phone rang. Pulling it from the pocket of her dress, Dorian glanced at the screen but didn't recognize the number.

"Hello," she answered in case it was Zion or Raven.

"Hey, Dorian. How you doing?"

Her eyebrows furrowed as she tried to identify the voice. "I'm fine. Who is this?"

The man chuckled. "Wow. You move on to bigger and better and forget all about me."

"Rodney?" she said in surprise. "Why are you calling me?" Before seeing him at the hotel, she hadn't heard from him in over a year.

"I was thinking about you and figured I'd give you a quick call. Did I catch you at a bad time?"

"Seriously? I haven't heard from you in forever, and all of a sudden you're thinking about me?"

He sighed loudly. "Just because I haven't called doesn't mean I don't think about you. I guess I just... Well, it was good seeing you the other week, and I wanted to say you looked great and happy."

Staring down at the granite countertop, Dorian reflected on his words. She hadn't really thought about it, but she was happy. When she left her marketing job, she'd been devastated and concerned about next steps in her life. She had considered looking for work at a different agency, but before she could start job hunting, her mother asked if she would help out at the bed and breakfast.

Dorian enjoyed being able to cook and bake whatever she wanted and whenever she wanted to. She also liked spending time with the guests who came from all over the world and had great stories to share. Then there was the flexibility and the freedom that came with the position. That type of peace was priceless.

"I am happy," she finally said to Rodney.

"It showed. I guess dating a millionaire could do that for you," he said, and Dorian didn't miss the sarcasm in his tone. "The Mathews are well known in the business world. How'd you even meet one of them? Let alone date one of them."

Anger stirred inside of Dorian and intensified as she absorbed his words. "Is that why you're calling me? To find out about my love life?"

Rodney huffed. "Love life? Baby, I doubt you even have one. Unless you've made a one-hundred-and-eighty-degree turn, you're not giving Mathews any loving the same way you didn't give me any."

Dorian's anger spiked, and if Rodney had been standing in front of her, she would've slapped him.

"Surely, you're not comparing yourself to Lynix Mathews," she snarled. "He's more of a man than you'll *ever* be. Actually, there's no comparison. Did it ever occur to you that I didn't have sex with you because I wasn't that into you?"

"No, that never occurred to me. I figured you were too much of a Pollyanna to give it up to anyone. Hell, your legs are closed so tightly, air probably can't even get between them. While we were together, I had even considered maybe you played for the other team and didn't like men. Because it was clear you wouldn't know what to do with a man even if one came with instructions."

Dorian gasped.

Rodney cursed.

"I'm sorry," he said quickly. "That was way out of line. I didn't mean it."

Hurt bubbled inside of Dorian, and she bit down on her bottom lip as she blinked back tears. No way was she letting his hurtful words bring her down. At least that's what she told herself, but a rogue tear slipped down her cheek before she quickly swiped it away.

"I'm sorry, Dorian. I'm an idiot and didn't mean any of that."

She wasn't dumb enough to think he had said all that and didn't mean it. Her mother often said what's in your heart eventually comes out of your mouth. Good or bad, he spoke what he thought of her, and it pierced deep.

She placed her hand over her mouth, struggling to keep herself together. She couldn't let this jerk ruin her evening. After breathing in and out a couple of times, she was able to say, "What do you want, Rodney? Because we both know you didn't call to see how I was doing."

After a long hesitation he said, "Damn, Dorian. I really am sorry, and I was calling to see how you're doing."

"Well, now you know. Goodbye," she said and started to disconnect the call but heard, "*Wait!*"

"Dorian, don't hang up yet. I also called for another reason. I wanted to ask a favor."

Dorian released a humorless laugh. "You've got a lot of nerve. You insult me with your hurtful words, and then you want to ask for a favor? A year ago, you didn't give a damn about my feelings and discarded me like I was nothing! And a few minutes ago, you basically did it again by saying all those hurtful things. So whatever favor you need, my answer is *hell no!*"

"Come on, Dorian. We both know you're not the type to hold grudges, and you're not mean-spirited. Technically, the favor isn't for me, it's for Concept Marketing. You love and admire this agency and what it's done for its clients. Despite my stupidity and insensitivity, I'm just asking for you to put in a good word for our—"

"Like I said, *no!* Oh, and Rodney? Let this be the last time you call me. Otherwise, you'll be hearing from Lynix."

She disconnected the call as more tears slid down her cheeks, but she quickly wiped them away. Resting her hands on the edge of the counter, she lowered her head and took a few cleansing breaths as she struggled to get her emotions under control.

What had she ever seen in Rodney? Had he always been a jerk? Were there signs she had ignored? Probably.

She shook her head. *God, I'm so stupid. I should've...*

"Dee?"

Dorian swung around, shocked to see Lynix in the kitchen. How long had he been standing there? How much had he heard?

"So I need to give Rodney a call, huh?"

Oh crap!

# Chapter Twenty-One

Lynix struggled to keep his anger in check. After putting the babies down and hanging out with Onyx, who made himself comfortable on his dog bed outside of the nursery, Lynix returned to the kitchen. He stopped short when he heard Dorian on the phone.

At first, he started to walk away and give her some privacy. That was until he realized she was talking to Rodney, and when she'd raised her voice, it took herculean strength not to rush in and snatch the phone from her. Whatever her ex had said to her had cut deep for her to snap on him.

One thing Lynix knew for sure was that Rodney was going to regret the day he ever met him. From the one-sided conversation he'd heard, Lynix wanted to hunt the bastard down. He wanted to pay him a personal visit and shove his fist into the man's face for upsetting Dorian.

When Lynix had made his presence known, and she whirled around to face him, the tears in her eyes were like taking a punch to the kidneys. For that, Rodney was going to pay.

"Come here," he said as he moved farther into the kitchen and was glad that she walked into his arms without arguing.

She held on tightly, sniffling every few seconds. They stood that way for several long minutes before he felt her relax. When he thought she might be ready to talk, he kissed the top of her head and slowly released her.

"What was that all about?" he asked, watching her closely.

"Nothing," she said, trying to put a lightness in her tone, but her voice cracked before she cleared her throat. "Rodney is not worth our time. Let's eat before the food gets cold."

"Dorian, what did he say?"

"Lynix..."

"Dee."

She sighed loudly. "He wanted me to put in a good word with you for Concept Marketing, but I told him no. You can pick whatever company you want to work with, but I'm staying out of it."

She diverted her gaze and smoothed down her yellow sundress. The fitted dress was cinched at the waist and stopped above her knees, showing off her legs—which he loved. What he also liked was how the outfit fit like a second skin, highlighting her petite but curvaceous body.

The color was beautiful on her, and she looked like a ray of sunshine when there weren't tears in her eyes.

Lynix reached out and lifted her chin with the pad of his finger, forcing her to look at him.

"What else did he say? And before you consider lying, don't," he said harsher than intended and reined in his anger. "I'll know if you lie because you have a tell."

She narrowed her eyes at him, and he smiled.

"What kind of tell?"

"I'm not saying because you'll try to hide it, and I won't know if you're being honest with me."

She didn't really have a solid tell, but he noticed that, when she was debating on something, she nibbled her lower lip, and her eyes moved back and forth.

Her shoulders slumped. "Before he asked me for that favor, he said some not so nice things about me. And before you ask, I'm not telling you." She glanced away, but he got in her line of sight, forcing her to return her attention to him.

"What if I want you to tell me?"

She shook her head, and more tears filled her eyes.

*Shit.* This was bad.

"Dorian, sweetheart, you're killing me here. Talk to me. You know you can tell me anything. What. Did. He. Say?"

She took so long to respond, Lynix thought she wouldn't tell him, but then she recounted the conversation. He had heard her side of it, but now hearing Rodney's side, Lynix really was going to make the man regret meeting him. Not only were the words mean-spirited, but as far as Lynix was concerned, Rodney had been calling on behalf of the agency. Dorian might not be the client, but he was, and she was his.

It was taking all Lynix's self-control not to blow up, but he had to be careful what he said next. This was about building Dorian up, telling and showing her that Rodney's words had no merit. He had to play this right and not say something that would make her feel worse or make her cry more.

"He's a piece of shit," she mumbled, shocking Lynix, and he couldn't stop himself from laughing. "I am such a fool. I hate I ever dated that jerk." She suddenly looked worn out, like she might collapse from exhaustion.

Lynix reached for her hand. "Come with me." He guided her to the living room, and after he sat on the sofa, he pulled her onto his lap.

"This might not be a good idea," she mumbled but didn't try to get out of his hold.

Lynix leaned back, and she fell against his chest.

"I'm glad you went out with Rodney," he said, and she jerked her head up and glared at him.

"Why would you say that?"

Lynix brought her hand to his mouth and kissed the inside of her scented wrist. "Because it's true. I'm glad you dated the asshole. That way, you'll have something to compare him to. I know we're pretending to be in a relationship," he said, the lie sounding bitter on his tongue because he was one hundred percent in. She was his even if she didn't realize it yet. "But Dee, I'm going to show you that there is nothing wrong with you, and Rodney is a fool for ever letting you go."

Lynix might've promised to keep his mouth and hands to himself tonight, but she needed some reassurance. She needed to experience just how damn irresistible she was to him. If he couldn't have all of her yet, he was going to at least kiss the hell out of her.

He leaned her back slightly and cradled her in his arms before his mouth covered hers. Pure sweetness. His lips moved over hers, devouring their softness and loving the way Dorian kissed him back with a fervor that rivaled the kiss from the other day.

The kiss might've started tender and light, but he pulled her closer and deepened the connection. His little hellcat, with the erotic sounds she was making with every lap of their tongues, was making it impossible for him to think straight. She felt so damn good in his arms but having her rubbed up against his erection was wreaking havoc on his entire body.

He wanted her. He wanted her more than he'd ever wanted another woman in his life, and it was killing him knowing he should slow things down.

Dorian suddenly pulled away, catching him off guard, but then she repositioned herself and was now straddling him.

Lynix cursed under his breath. His brain screamed this was a bad idea, but his dick, which was as hard as stone, was saying something totally different. Yeah, this was happening. He only had so much control, and when it came to this woman, he basically had none.

Dorian gasped when he stood with her in his arms and carried her to the guest room. Onyx ran to the door, but Lynix closed it, not needing an audience. The door to the nursery was closed, and thankfully, Dorian had already put one of the baby monitors in the guestroom. They'd be able to listen out for the twins.

He laid her on the bed and climbed on next to her, pulling her body against his.

*Don't rush this,* he thought. She was sometimes skittish around him but not tonight. She hadn't said anything about no kissing or touching, and he planned to take full advantage.

Lowering his head, he scattered kisses along her jawline, down her long, graceful neck, and then to her shoulder. Her perfume was intoxicating as his lips grazed the pulsing hollow at the base of her neck.

As he moved his mouth along her scented skin, Lynix's hand slid down her side and slowly eased her dress up. When his hand made contact with her soft, smooth, thigh, he groaned. He might've wanted to go slow, but he couldn't wait to see and feel every inch of her gorgeous body.

Dorian's small hand cupped his cheek and slowed his exploration. He lifted his head and moved back to her sweet lips. Nipping at the lower one, then the top one before covering her mouth with his. Her arms went around his neck, and the kiss grew more demanding as her curvy body rubbed against him.

He was getting harder with each passing second and had a

burning desire, and an aching need to kiss and touch her everywhere.

Yep, his woman was too irresistible.

He cradled her close as he continued kissing while his hand cupped her firm ass, and he squeezed, kneading her soft flesh. She would soon learn this so-called fake relationship was as real as it got for him. No way was he letting her go. It was too late— he was a goner. She owned his heart whether she knew it or not.

As he continued loving on her mouth, he took advantage of her short dress being bunched around her upper thighs. It gave him easy access to what lay beneath. His hand explored her body until he reached the apex between her thighs.

Yessss, he was right where he wanted to be.

When he cupped her mound, Dorian moaned and started rotating her hips. Lynix knew what she wanted, and he was just the man to get things started. Her lace panties were already soaked, and when he slid a finger between her slick folds, he was the one moaning.

"Damn, I love that you're wet for me."

And she was tight, which he also loved and slid another digit inside of her.

Dorian ripped her mouth from his and whimpered. Her nails dug into his arms when he began stroking her nice and slow at first. As he increased the pace, she rode his hand hard, her movements getting jerkier as she bucked against him.

"Lynix," she whispered and followed it with a groan.

"You like that?"

"Yes. Yes," she said, her voice growing louder as her hips bucked faster against him. Suddenly a scream ripped from her as she lost control. Lynix quickly covered her mouth with his, absorbing another scream before she woke the babies.

Her chest heaved, and when he was sure there wouldn't be

any more screaming, he slowly eased his lips from hers and slid his fingers from between her thighs.

Damn, that was hot. He was tempted to make her scream again, but he had to remind himself that he was supposed to be going slow with her. The last thing he wanted was to do anything with her that she'd later regret. Still, there was nothing wrong with giving her a little pleasure as long as he didn't get too carried away. And by carried away he meant no intercourse. Not until she realized there was nothing fake about their relationship.

Until then, he'd enjoy pleasing her and watching as she fell apart in his arms.

He smiled down at her, taking in her glistening skin and bow-shaped lips that looked well kissed. She was so beautiful. He wanted more than anything to be buried balls deep inside of her, but he had a plan, and now he needed to stick to it.

"You smell so damn good," he murmured, squeezing her butt as he nuzzled her neck. He didn't know what type of perfume she was wearing, but he planned on buying her a case of it.

"Lynix," Dorian rasped her chest still heaving.

He lifted his head to look at her. "Yeah, sweetness?"

"I need..." She cleared her throat, looking a bit nervous. "I— I need more. I want... more."

A slow smile spread across Lynix's face until he was full on grinning. "Good, because I'm here to give you what you need and whatever you want."

# Chapter Twenty-Two

Dorian didn't know exactly what she wanted. All she knew was her body was humming from the pleasure that Lynix had just bestowed on her, and she craved more. Never in her life had she been this aroused while also feeling as if she was going to spontaneously combust.

After she had admitted to wanting more, Lynix had her out of her dress within seconds, leaving her in nothing but her yellow lace bra and panties. She had squirmed under his perusal, his passion-filled gaze ratcheting up her need for him.

How was it possible that she was this turned on? All they'd done was some kissing and heavy petting. Which was more than she'd ever planned to engage in with him. But so far, she had no regrets. Her body yearned for his mouth, his touch, and his attention on her.

So what if they were pretending to be a couple? People did this type of stuff all the time with less of a connection, right? Surely, she could enjoy a little intimacy without feelings getting in the way. Lynix had admitted as much when he casually mentioned his past hookups.

Hopefully, she could be just as casual with him while they got to know each other physically. She also hoped she could give him as much pleasure as he'd given her.

"I knew you had an incredible body, but this? Damn, baby. You're breathtaking."

He lowered his head, and his lips seared a path down the side of her neck, over her shoulders, and he kept going. When he reached her breasts, he didn't even pause at the front closure of her bra. With a flick of his wrist, the bra was unhooked and her breasts spilled out.

Lynix cupped them both, pushing them together as he ran the pad of his thumb over her taut nipples. She was a solid "B" cup, but the way he teased and admired her girls was like a meat eater admiring a T-bone steak.

"Yeah, definitely breathtaking," he said gruffly before gently biting down, then sucking a nipple into his mouth.

Dorian hissed and slammed her eyes shut as she squirmed beneath him. The licking, sucking, and teasing he was doing was almost too much, and then he did the same with her other breast.

Desire charged through her body like a live wire igniting every nerve within her, and her heartbeat picked up speed. So much so, it felt as if her heart would pound right out of her chest.

He moved lower.

The man's mouth and lips were wicked as he explored his way down her body, stopping occasionally to nip at her skin. Then he reached her hips, and the sweet torture of his kisses continued while he made quick work of sliding her panties down her legs.

This was happening.

This was really happening, her brain screamed.

Her body trembled with anticipation as Lynix mumbled

something while peppering kisses just below her belly button and continued a downward path. Dorian squeaked when he slid his arms beneath her knees and lifted her slightly before his face was buried between her thighs.

The light scruff from his full beard brushed against the inside of her thighs seconds before his tongue made contact with her small bundle of nerves.

*Oh. My. God!*

She practically lurched off the bed, her body twisting and turning, struggling against the intense sensations charging through her.

"Ly—Lynix," she stuttered, her breath catching in her throat.

He held on to her, keeping her in place while simultaneously inflicting the most feral type of pleasure with his mouth and tongue that she'd ever endured. And she was loving every breath-stealing minute of his ministrations.

But she couldn't lie still. She had no control of her body. The intensity from what he was doing to her felt too good. She whimpered and fisted the bedding within her hands as sensations plowed through her, swirling around like a flying saucer. Her hips moved on their own accord, thrusted against his face, harder and faster.

It was too much.

She couldn't breathe.

"Lynix," she moaned as the pressure built, and then she lost it. She screamed his name as a hot tide of passion rocketed through her leaving her boneless and gasping for air.

Tears leaked from the corners of her eyes, but she wasn't crying. Hell, she wasn't sure what was going on. Her body trembled and her chest heaved while she struggled to get breath into her lungs.

Her energy was shot. Her mind was spinning. And she

couldn't move even if she wanted to. So many emotions spun inside of her, feelings she couldn't put a name to. That... all of that had been wild.

What had he done to her?

What had he done to her body?

"Dee?"

Dorian could hear Onyx whimpering at the door until Lynix said something to the dog. Then she could feel Lynix's hand on her thighs, but she still couldn't move. She was barely able to think and forget about breathing. Her chest was still heaving.

"Sweetheart, are you okay?" Lynix's words sounded closer, and she didn't miss the concern in his voice. His hand was on the side of her neck for a second before moving it to her cheek. "Dee? You gotta talk to me, babe. You okay?"

Her eyes finally eased open and met his troubled ones.

"Woman, you scared the hell out of me. Are you alright?" His voice was gentler this time, but he still looked concerned as he lightly brushed his fingers over her cheek.

"I—I'm..." She released a long breath. "That was... that was a lot," she admitted, unable to come up with a more accurate description of how he had rocked her world.

Lynix huffed out a breath, and his broad shoulders relaxed. As he lay beside her on the bed, he chuckled and gathered her limp body into his arms.

"It sounded like you were hyperventilating, which caught me off guard. You kind of freaked me out there for a minute," he whispered, then kissed her.

It was weird tasting herself on his lips, but it was another new experience with him.

"I freaked *you* out?" she said, still feeling a little breathless. "I'm the one whose world was flipped upside down. I've never felt anything like that before in my life," she admitted quietly, and the moment the words were out of her mouth, Lynix stiffened next to her.

Silence fell between them and long seconds ticked by before he lifted up and looked down at her.

Dorian frowned. What? He was looking at her as if seeing her for the first time. Then his eyes searched hers like he was trying to figure something out. But what?

"Lynix?"

Hearing his name snapped him to attention, and he sat on the edge of the bed with his back to her.

*Okaaay.* She was at a loss here. What had she said to spark this type of reaction? She tried to mentally search her mind, but if she was honest, she was still a little out of it. Still trying to pull herself together after experiencing the most intense orgasm of her life.

Lynix stirred, and her eyes snapped to him as he released a long breath before glancing over his shoulder at her. "What did you mean when you said you never felt anything like that before?" he asked.

His voice was calm and controlled, but he was still searching her eyes for something, maybe answers she didn't seem to have.

"Dee?" he prompted.

Then it dawned on her. Embarrassment sent heat rushing through her body, and her face felt like it was on fire.

He doesn't know. She thought he knew. How could he not know?

*Because I didn't actually tell him.*

Dorian scurried to move away from him, practically tumbling out of the bed in the process, but she caught herself. Barely. She stumbled to her feet and snatched her dress off the floor.

God, she must be the most pitiful woman on the face of the earth.

Instead of putting on the dress, she used it to cover herself and rushed to the door.

Lynix's large hand rested against the face of the door, keeping it closed, but she couldn't look at him. She didn't want to see the disappointment or the pity in his eyes.

She swallowed hard and started to move away from him, but he caught her around the waist.

"Don't," she said and pushed him away, still using the dress to keep her nakedness hidden. "Just don't."

"You're a virgin?" he asked, his voice gentle but carrying a bit of shock. "Sweetheart, why didn't you tell me?"

Dorian nibbled on her lower lip, looking everywhere but at him as she tried to keep her emotions in check. She felt, rather than saw, him inch closer. He was easing toward her as if she was some scared animal who might bolt at any second.

Actually, that was exactly how she felt.

"Look at me, Dee," he said when he got closer, but he didn't touch her.

After a slight hesitation, she did as he asked, and the tenderness in his gaze almost made her burst into tears. Instead, a few tears trickled down her cheek.

"I'm so embarrassed. I thought you had figured out that I'm —I'm... I haven't been with anyone intimately before."

"Don't cry, sweetheart. I hate seeing you cry." He pulled her into his arms, and Dorian deflated against him as he held her tightly. He placed a kiss near her temple. "You have nothing to be embarrassed about. I'm sorry about how I reacted. I was surprised."

She eased away from him, feeling a little self-conscious with no clothes on while he was fully clothed. Not bothering with underwear, she hurried and slipped into the dress.

"I assumed you knew, especially after I said I hadn't had sex with Rodney while we dated."

"I figured you hadn't been with a lot of men, but I didn't know you were a virgin. Otherwise, I wouldn't have..." His voice trailed off, and Dorian folded her arms across her chest.

"Otherwise, what happened tonight wouldn't have happened," she finished for him.

"Oh, no. It would've happened, but I would've been more careful with you. I would've made sure we had a conversation before any of that happened."

"I didn't need a conversation. Nothing happened that I didn't want to happen, and since we're on the subject, I've made a decision."

"Okay," he said slowly. "If you're thinking about pulling out of our fake dating agreement, don't. Nothing has changed. I want us to continue moving forward. Besides, I still need your help in keeping my father off my back. Basically, you're stuck with me as your fake boyfriend," he said.

"Good, because I'm not done with you either." Dorian lifted her chin higher and dug deep for an extra dose of courage for what she was about to request of him. "I want you to be my first."

Lynix stood frozen.

He didn't move. He didn't speak. He just stood there, his eyebrows lifted skyward and his mouth slightly ajar. The shocked expression on his handsome face was like that of someone who'd just been told they owed the IRS a million dollars.

Great. That's just great. She'd clearly said the wrong thing. Maybe she should've waited to spring that on him. What if he wasn't interested since they were only fake dating? It was one thing to pursue her like he'd done before they'd come up with their agreement, but it was another to take her virginity.

Maybe he didn't do virgins, preferring someone more experienced. But just because she'd never had sex didn't mean she was a prude. She read a ton of romance novels, watched porn, and even had a battery-operated boyfriend. Granted, her self-induced orgasms hadn't come close to what she had experienced with Lynix, but still, she wasn't a prude.

"Never mind. Forget I said anything," she mumbled and rushed to the door just as she heard one of the babies crying and Onyx whining.

Perfect Timing.

# Chapter Twenty-Three

"**D**ammit. I'm an idiot!" Lynix ground out and punched the air so hard he felt a twinge in his right shoulder but ignored it.

He ran his hand over his head and down to the back of his neck as he expelled a long breath. How had things come to a screeching halt so fast? The last thirty or forty minutes with Dorian had been downright amazing, better than anything he could've planned for the evening. But then, out of nowhere, she sprung the virgin confession on him.

Talk about throwing a curve ball. He'd been caught off guard by her admission and then sat there like a dufus not knowing what to say.

And if that hadn't been enough, she'd blown him away with her request.

*I want you to be my first.*

The words blared through his mind as he dropped down on the bed, then fell back and stared at the white ceiling. He could've handled that better, but the woman had a way of throwing him off his game.

He was thrilled she wanted him to be her first, but that was a lot of pressure to put on a guy. His first time with a girl, Marisela, hadn't meant much to his fifteen-year-old horny body. But it had given him bragging rights with his even hornier buddies.

But Dorian?

She was special, and she deserved for her first time to be just as special. The thought of her saving herself for so many years and then asking him to be her first... It should be an honor. Hell, it was an honor, one he wouldn't take lightly.

First, he had to wrap his brain around everything. Sure, he'd known she wasn't as experienced as some of the women he'd been with, but a virgin? Mind. Blown. Now a few things made more sense.

"It's okay, sweet baby. TT Dorian has you." Dorian's soothing voice came through the baby monitor that Lynix had forgotten about. He'd heard Zanaya crying but had been distracted.

"*Shhh*, it's okay. We need to be quiet so we don't wake your brother." Zanaya quieted as Dorian continued talking softly to her. "Were me and Uncle Lynix too loud? Did we wake you up? Sorry about that, but you need to learn how to sleep as sound as your brother."

Lynix closed his eyes, picturing Dorian sitting in the rocker holding his goddaughter. She was a natural with them, and he could totally see her with kids of her own.

"I think I messed up with your godfather tonight," Dorian continued. Lynix's eyes popped open, and he propped himself up on his elbows.

He should probably turn off the baby monitor since Dorian didn't realize she had an audience, but he wanted to know what she was thinking. The last thing he wanted was for her to have any regrets when it came to him.

"He's such a nice guy, and he made me feel things tonight that I've never felt with anyone. Ever. And I enjoyed every moment."

Lynix relaxed, glad he hadn't totally blown it with her.

"I've told myself a hundred times," she continued, "he's out of my league, and tonight proved that. What would he want with a virgin when there are so many beautiful, sexy, experienced women out there? Have you seen him? He can have any woman he wants. Yet, he's doing me a favor by pretending to be my boyfriend."

If only she knew. She was the one doing him a favor. Yes, he was glad to help get her mother to back off, but in turn, he was getting so much more. He was getting the opportunity to show Dorian a different side of him. Yes, she'd be helping him out by being his plus-one at the gala and showing his father that he had a woman, but it was so much more than that.

"I might've messed up our pretend relationship," she was saying to the baby.

Lynix could almost picture her looking defeated. He'd seen the expression the first time she'd told him what had transpired between her and Rodney. Which reminded him—Lynix dug his cell phone from his pocket—he needed a direct phone number for the owner of Concept Marketing Agency.

Once he shot off a quick text to Wes, he shoved his cell phone back into his pocket and stood. He needed to fix the mess between him and Dorian. He couldn't have her thinking he'd ever want any other woman but her.

And she thought she was out of her league? That's crazy. He might have more money and connections than her, but that was it. If anything, it was the other way around. Dorian was too good for him, and for a while, he feared that if they got together he'd corrupt her in some way. Steal her innocence—though at the time, he hadn't known she was a virgin—but he thought he'd somehow taint her moral purity. Everything about the woman was good and pure and so different from who he was, and he didn't want her to change. Not because of him.

As for her being a virgin, untouched by another man? Even better. He needed to make it clear that he'd be honored to be her first. He just didn't want it to happen yet. Not until he knew she was ready to move past this pretend shit that his stupid ass had talked her into.

Lynix left the guest room, and when he made his way to the nursery, he stopped in the doorway. Onyx lifted his head and looked at him, then laid his head back down on his paws.

Dorian hadn't noticed him yet, giving him a chance to watch her for a moment as she sat in the rocking chair with Zanaya. It was a beautiful sight, and in that moment, he could imagine her rocking their baby.

Lynix wasn't sure if he'd made a sound, but she glanced up and gave a small smile.

"She's almost asleep," she whispered.

He moved quietly into the room and knelt next to the rocker. He could wait and talk to her after Zanaya was back in bed, but he couldn't have Dorian thinking he didn't want her. That he didn't want to be her first.

Her attention went back to the baby whose eyes were drifting closed.

"Listen to me," Lynix whispered, and Dorian looked at him. "I want you more than I have ever wanted another woman. The fact that you're a virgin, and you want me to be your first, is an honor. But it also makes me want to know for certain that you're sure."

"I am," she said quickly. "I know we're just hanging out, pretending and stuff, but I still want to...you know, with you." She blushed and lowered her gaze.

"Look at me," he said gently, and she did.

How could he tell her that he wasn't taking her virginity until he knew she was in love with him? He was sure of his feelings for her—he loved her—but the feelings weren't mutual... yet.

Instead of saying any of that, he said, "I'm going to make sure your first time is perfect. That you're not only sure you want me, but you're ready for what we're going to share. I don't want you to have any regrets."

"I won't. I know I won't, and it won't change our friendship. I promise."

Lynix nodded. He was disappointed she was still seeing him as a friend, but deep down, he knew she felt something more between them. Otherwise, she wouldn't have let him touch her so intimately earlier. He knew she cared about him and more importantly, she trusted him.

He could work with that.

"How about I leave you to put Zanaya back to sleep, and I'll go heat up the food?"

"That's a great idea because I'm starving." Dorian glanced down at the baby in her arms who was drifting off. "I'll be in there shortly."

"Okay." Lynix placed a lingering kiss on her lips before leaving the room with Onyx following him into the kitchen.

After giving the dog a treat, Lynix glanced at the food on the counter, and his stomach rumbled. He'd worked up an appetite and couldn't wait to dive in. Instead of putting the dishes in the microwave one at a time, he turned on the oven. He figured he could heat everything at once, and then by the time Dorian came in there, the food would still be warm.

While he waited, Lynix sat at the table and scrolled through his emails, checked his voicemail, and skimmed through text messages that he'd missed from earlier. When he saw Wes had texted him back, he read the message.

*I don't know the owner of Concept Marketing, but I'll get my assistant on it. You'll have contact info by the end of the day tomorrow. BTW, you need an assistant.*

Lynix snorted. Yeah, he was going to need more than an assistant. He was going to need a complete brain overhaul to go from a cop mentality to a businessman. He just hoped the learning curve wouldn't be too hard.

Onyx, who'd been laying at his feet, scrambled up and started barking. That was when Lynix smelled something burning. Then the smoke detector blared.

He leaped from the seat and hurried to the oven. When he opened the door, smoke billowed out. What the hell?

A peek at the stove's control panel made him realize what he'd done wrong. The oven was on the broiler setting.

"Oh, this is just great," he ground out and turned off the stove. Then he searched desperately for something he could use to get rid of the smoke. Which in turn would stop the ear-piercing noise.

A dishtowel would work.

He spotted one at the end of the counter and started waving it back and forth beneath the smoke detector. "Every-thing's okay," he called out to Dorian, wanting to assure her that he had it all under control, but seconds later, she rushed into the kitchen.

She looked around frantically. "What happened?"

"Umm, I might've burned dinner," he said, still waving the dish towel until the shrieking noise stopped.

"Really, Lynix? All you had to do was put the food in the microwave."

"You see, what had happened was, I put everything in the oven. I figured if I turned it down low, the food would slowly warm up and still be warm by the time you came in here." He told her how he accidentally pushed the broiler button.

Dorian shook her head and laughed. "So much for a delicious, lick-your-lips home cooked meal. Well, I think there are takeout menus in one of these drawers. Get to calling, buddy, because I'm starving. Oh, and before you even think about it, I don't want pizza or burgers."

Lynix chuckled and looped his arm around her before she could leave the kitchen. He pulled her against his body and kissed her lips.

"Thanks for one of the most soul-stirring, entertaining, and enlightening nights I've had in a while. I can't think of any place else I'd rather be than here with you."

*I love you* was on the tip of his tongue as he stared into her pretty brown eyes, but it was too soon to admit that to her. They were still in a weird place. Somewhere between fake dating and friends getting to know each other intimately.

He might not have ever been in love before, but Lynix knew deep in his heart he was in love with Dorian Priestly.

Now he just had to wait for her to feel the same about him.

# Chapter Twenty-Four

**D**orian stared at herself in the full-length mirror not believing her eyes. They were at a high-end boutique, a place where she wouldn't typically shop, but Cree insisted. The store was currently closed to the public, but the owner, Jada Jenkins-Anderson, was in town and had the store manager open for them.

Jada walked around Dorian, looking at the outfit with a critical eye. "We might need to take it in at the waist, but other than that, it fits perfectly. What do you think?"

"I think I don't recognize myself." The jumpsuit was gorgeous and way too expensive, but Dorian kept those thoughts to herself, and instead said, "It's definitely a keeper."

"Good. We'll add it to the 'yay' pile," Jada said, and went to a rollaway rack where other items were hanging. Some had already been at the store, while others she'd brought with her from Cincinnati where she lived with her husband and son.

Still staring in the mirror in awe of how she looked, Dorian ran her hand down the sides of the white, off the shoulder jumpsuit that was as sexy as something Cree would wear but had a delicateness to it that was totally Dorian's style. She didn't have a ton of disposable income, but for this outfit and the two she'd tried on before this one, she'd splurge.

"There are a few more garments Cree asked me to pull for you to try on. Then we'll get to the evening gowns."

Dorian shook her head, already concerned by the price tags. The other day, Cree had said she'd help her out, but Dorian didn't want to be financially indebted to her sister. At least not this much.

"I'd better stop at this jumpsuit, the black cocktail dress, and that yellow and white two-piece set," Dorian explained. "As for an evening gown," she glanced at Cree who was sitting on a settee watching her, "can I borrow one of yours?"

"Girl, please. I'm at least four inches taller than you and bigger in the waist. You need your own gown, maybe even two since Lynix is paying."

Dorian straightened. "What?"

"I talked to him, and before you get all bent out of shape, he offered up his black card. He said he knew you wouldn't take his money, which was why he reached out to me."

"He's right. I'm not taking his money. It's not like that between us," Dorian said, and Cree's left eyebrow went up.

"Then how exactly is it?" her sister asked in her no-bullshit-lawyer-tone that she had perfected. "Surely you know the man is crazy about you, and I sense the feelings are mutual."

"I—I..." Dorian sputtered, "Our relationship is too new for him to be buying me clothes."

Their relationship might've been new, but her feelings for Lynix had intensified, and it was frustrating. They needed to keep their arrangement casual to ensure her stupid heart didn't get broken, but she feared it might be too late. Lynix wasn't cooperating. He had somehow wormed his way into her system, and she couldn't seem to get him out.

Something had shifted between them since that night at Zion's house. She felt it and she was fairly sure Lynix did too. Otherwise, he wouldn't be finding every opportunity to spend time with her. She'd seen him every day, and that wasn't helping the situation. When she'd tell him that they didn't need to spend so much time together, he'd insist they had to practice being a couple. That if they didn't, his father would see right through their charade.

In the meantime, Lynix was wreaking havoc on her self-control. They hadn't discussed their intimate night at Zion's house, but she thought about it every day and wondered when they'd go all the way. Lynix didn't seem to be in a hurry, but she was a little anxious.

That might be why each time she saw him or heard his name or his voice, her heart did this wild fluttering thing. She couldn't make it stop, and what scared her the most, she wasn't sure she wanted to. She loved how the man made her feel. Whether he was kissing her, touching her, or making her laugh, she loved it all.

And at this rate, if she wasn't careful, she was bound to get her heart broken when they went their separate ways.

"I don't want Lynix to think I'm using him for his money," she finally said to Cree.

Her sister shrugged. "Hey, you might not want to ask for what you want or need, but I'm not above asking a man for money. Especially if the man is wealthy and wants to give me the world. And for the record, your man's exact words were, *I don't care what it costs. Make sure she gets whatever she wants. I'm planning to give her the world.*"

Dorian stood speechless. "He said that?"

Her sister nodded. "Those were his exact words, and I, for one, plan to let him. On your behalf, of course."

Jada laughed and high-fived Cree before looking at Dorian. "My kind of man. I think my husband said something similar when he was trying to woo me."

Cree had mentioned Jada's husband was a sports commentator and a former NFL running back and Hall of Famer.

"And like your sister," Jada continued, "I've never had a problem asking for what I want and accepting that my man enjoys spoiling me. Dorian, it sounds like you need to get used to it too."

Dorian's gaze volleyed between Cree and Jada. They were clearly cut from the same mold when it came to style, self-confidence, and their view on men.

While Cree was tall and had an hourglass figure that men drooled over, Jada was petite like Dorian. But unlike Dorian, the woman looked like money. From her silk two-piece pant set to her bejeweled high heel sandals, she looked like a million bucks. And that didn't even include her jewelry. She was wearing enough diamonds to warrant a bodyguard.

Dorian returned her attention to the mirror. She wasn't like them, but maybe they were right. Maybe she shouldn't turn down Lynix's gifts. She could totally imagine him saying the words about giving her the world because that's how generous he was. But it just didn't feel right to allow him to fund this shopping spree when she wasn't his for real woman.

"Stop overthinking and take what he's offering," Cree said, snapping Dorian out of her thoughts. "Besides, I'm sure he's going to love seeing you in these outfits, and you are on this shopping spree because of him. You don't want to look like a pauper when you meet his parents."

True.

"Okay, fine. Let's hurry this up." She turned to Jada. "What else you got?"

For the next hour, Dorian tried on one outfit after another. Most she liked, others she didn't, mainly because she didn't feel comfortable in some of the skimpier pieces. When she started trying on the evening gowns, she immediately felt like Cinderella, and it was as if Cree and Jada were her fairy godmothers.

Jada even included underwear and lingerie, which Dorian fell in love with. She didn't splurge on much, but underwear was an exception. From the first time she started making her own money, she always bought matching bra and panty sets. And as she got older, her underwear got sexier.

Thinking about that, she recalled the flaming hot expression in Lynix's eyes when he'd seen her in the yellow lace set. If they ever went to the next level, she wanted to see that expression again.

Once Dorian was done trying on clothes, Jada handed everything off to the store manager. Except she gave Dorian the bags that held the underwear and lingerie. Everything else would be delivered to her apartment later that day.

Dorian was slipping back into her shoes when Jada excused herself and left the dressing room area to take a call.

"Here." Cree handed Dorian a small shopping bag.

"What is it?"

"A little something for when you need it."

Dorian moved the tissue paper out of the way and when she dug in, she pulled out a box of condoms. There was also lubricant, and she burst out laughing when she saw the pack of cigarettes and a lighter. She laughed even harder when she realized they were candy cigarettes, and the lighter was actually a flashlight.

"Really, Cree?" she said, still laughing as she shoved every-thing back into the bag.

"I wasn't sure if you needed those things, but I figured it couldn't hurt to be on the safe side, especially if you haven't secured other means of birth control. Trust me, you don't want to end up pregnant before you're ready for that type of respon-sibility."

Cree left the dressing room area before Dorian could unpack everything that was said. First, she wondered how her sister knew she might still be a virgin. But even more, what was that all about, not wanting to end up pregnant before you're ready? Did Cree have some experience with that?

Dorian grabbed her bags and hurried to catch up with her. She wanted answers, but when she made it to the sales floor, she almost ran into the back of Cree. Her sister stood frozen in place, and when Dorian glanced around her, she saw two huge men who hadn't been there earlier.

One, a handsome, well-built white guy who looked like he should be on the cover of a fitness magazine. Wide shoulders, thick biceps, flat abs, and thick thighs made him a poster boy for all things big and rugged. It was suddenly clear that he was Jada's husband when he wrapped his arms around her and kissed her.

But the other man... The gorgeous, giant, black man who looked like he could bench press a ten-story building, only had eyes for Cree. By the way they were looking at each other in shock, it was safe to say they had history there.

"Cree?" the man finally said. "What are you—"

"Go to hell!" she snapped and stormed out the building.

The man growled, like literally growled and said, "Some things never change." Then he ran after her.

When Dorian glanced at Jada and her husband, the two shrugged. Apparently, they were as clueless about the situation as she was. So she said her thank yous and goodbyes and hurried out of the store. She had driven herself but hoped to catch up with Cree.

No such luck. Her sister was nowhere in sight, and neither was her mystery man.

*Hmm...* Dorian couldn't wait to get the scoop on that story.

# Chapter Twenty-Five

"Lynix is going to lose his mind when he sees you in that dress," Cree said, and Dorian smiled as she took one last look in the full-length mirror hanging on the inside of her bathroom door.

Dorian laughed. She didn't want her fake boyfriend to lose his mind, but she did want him to take notice. She wanted him to see what his money bought, and she couldn't have been more satisfied with the choice.

An all-white fundraiser gala would be a first for her, and the dress was perfect for the occasion. The strapless, satin, high split, mermaid dress hugged her body and flowed to the floor revealing her right leg. The four-inch high-heel sandals added to the elegance of the gown.

She turned slightly and glanced over her shoulder into the mirror so she could see the back, and she couldn't help grinning. Oh, yeah, he was definitely going to lose his mind when he saw how most of her back was showing.

After a few minutes, Dorian stepped out of the bathroom

and into her bedroom and found her mother standing in the doorway with a sour expression on her face.

"I don't like that dress," she said. "It shows too much skin, and I'm tempted to snatch it off you and sew up that split."

Dorian knew she shouldn't, but she couldn't help laughing, and she laughed even harder when Cree joined in.

"Mom, you've made your feelings known about the dress," Cree said, shaking her head as she approached Dorian. "I think she looks beautiful."

"Of course, you would because some of the dresses I've seen you in should be outlawed. I'm going to make coffee."

She turned to leave, and Dorian called out after her. "You don't need coffee because you guys aren't staying!" She wasn't sure if their mother heard her, but then Dorian looked at her sister. "Why'd you even bring her?"

"Like I had a choice. You're the one who told her about attending the gala. Then she called, told me to pick her up, and bring her over."

Dorian huffed. "Well, can you leave before Lynix gets here?"

Cree sat in the small, upholstered chair near the window and crossed her long legs. "Nope. He's the main reason she wanted to come. I don't think she likes you and Lynix dating."

"What makes you think that?"

"Because she said she didn't." They both laughed before Cree sobered. "Well, she didn't actually come out and say it like that, but I think she's worried about you, as usual. She still sees you as her little girl and is having trouble letting go. Just get married, have a few kids, and she'll be fine."

"Ha! Sure she will," Dorian said and ran her hand down her stomach, trying to calm her nerves. Lynix would be there soon, and though she couldn't wait to see him, she was nervous about meeting his family.

She adjusted the dress and sat on the bed. Hearing Cree mention kids made Dorian think about their time at the boutique the other day.

"Your updo is cute, but it looks like you might need a few more hair pins," Cree said. She stood and grabbed a couple that were on the dresser and walked over.

"Are you ever going to tell me what happened at the boutique the other day? Who was the mystery man?" Dorian asked. She'd been trying to get info out of her sister since that day, but Cree's lips were sealed.

"Leave it alone, Dee."

"But you be all up in my business. I deserve to know a little of yours. Besides, it's not like I'm going to blab to anyone. Whatever we discuss stops right here. So who was he? I'm assuming he plays football or basketball because the guy was huge. Is he an ex-boyfriend? Friend with benefits? Former client with benefits? What?"

As an entertainment lawyer, she represented entertainers as well as professional athletes. Him being a former client wasn't a stretch.

Cree didn't respond as she stuck another hairpin into Dorian's hair and not too gently.

Dorian flinched. "Ouch! Cree! If you don't want to tell me, then don't, but don't take your frustrations out on my head."

"You keep talking, and I'm going to knock you upside the head. Or better yet, maybe I should get Mom in here and let her finish it up for you."

"Please don't," Dorian murmured. "I'd rather you convince her to leave. I don't want her to embarrass me in front of Lynix."

"Girl, she lives to embarrass us. Just suck it up and deal with it."

After the words left Cree's mouth, a knock sounded on the apartment door, and Dorian's pulse spiked.

"I'll get it," their mother called out.

"No!" Dorian and Cree said at the same time.

Dorian didn't want her mother anywhere near Lynix. She hurried to stand up, but it was too late. She could hear Lynix's deep voice as he greeted her mother.

"Gawd! I just can't with her," Dorian grumbled and looked at her sister. "Please take her and go. *Please,* and I promise I won't ask anything else of you."

Cree laughed and grabbed her oversized purse from the chair she'd been sitting in. "Fine. I'll get her and go but let me give you a couple of tips for tonight."

Dorian would willingly accept any advice her sister had to give on attending the gala. Cree had mentioned she'd attended the same fundraiser several times over the years and spoke highly of the event. Some of the people in attendance? Not so much.

"You walk into that ballroom like you own that bitch," Cree said, and Dorian laughed at the fierceness in her tone. "As for Lynix's parents, I've only met them in passing, but I heard Mr. Mathews is a real piece of work. Don't let him intimidate you if he tries. Just because they have a shitload of money don't make them better than you. Remember that. And because there will be some pampered princesses in attendance, stay close to your man. Don't be afraid to get a little catty if you must."

Dorian snorted. "I don't do catty."

"Maybe not before you started dating Lynix, but now? Get your cattiness on, girl. I wouldn't be surprised if some of his exes or women who want to date him are there tonight. I'll tell you like I told you at the hotel the other week, channel me and yo mama, and you'll do fine."

Dorian laughed and shook her head. She wasn't sure what

to expect of the evening, but she hoped it didn't come to that. Cree and their mother weren't to be played with. You step to them wrong, and they'll give you a tongue lashing to beat all tongue lashes. Especially Cree. Virginia was the same, except she could curse you out without using a curse word.

"Got it," Dorian said and saluted her sister.

"Okay, now, chin up and shoulders back. You might as well start acting like the sexy woman you are," Cree said and strolled out the bedroom as if she owned the whole world.

Dorian grinned. "Man, when I grow up, I want to be just like her," she mumbled.

* * *

Lynix was laughing at something Mrs. Priestly said when Cree came into view. The apartment wasn't huge—two bedrooms, two bathrooms—but it was bright and cheery just like Dorian.

"Cree," he said in greeting as she strolled into the living room, which was a part of an open floor plan.

Instead of saying hi or hello or what's up, she pointed a hot pink, manicured nail at him and narrowed her eyes. He grinned, unable to help himself.

"Don't forget what I told you that day at Moody Days. I'm watching you," she said and turned to her mother. "Grab your stuff, Mom. We're out of here."

Lynix didn't hear anything else they said because the magnificent vision in white, standing in the hallway, stole his breath.

Hot damn. Talk about a transformation. Dorian was pretty enough to grab a man's attention on any given day. But tonight? The way she was looking in that white evening gown, she could bring a grown man to his knees.

The day of her shopping spree, she had called to thank him.

She also told him that if she spent too much to let her know, and she'd pay him back. Lynix had laughed at the absurdity of the conversation. The woman clearly didn't understand he'd do anything for her, and he didn't give a damn what the cost of the clothes added up to. If her other outfits were anything like this one, it was money well spent.

"Wow," was all he could seem to get out of his mouth, and when she smiled at him, Lynix reflexively grabbed his chest. "You are absolutely the most beautiful woman I have ever laid eyes on," he said, meaning every word as he walked toward her.

He handed her the single white rose that he'd been holding, then slid his arm around her and pulled her against his chest.

"Hi," he whispered.

Her smile grew even brighter if that were possible. "Hi, yourself, handsome."

And then he kissed her. He didn't care if they had an audience, and he sure as hell wasn't trying to play up a role for her mother. All he could think about was how he'd been waiting all day to get a taste of this incredible woman.

"Okay, you two. We're leaving now," Mrs. Priestly said loud enough for people down the street to hear her. But Lynix was half listening, unable to pull his mouth from Dorian's. "And Dee, remember your home training. Don't be out in these streets acting like you…"

"Oh, for the love of God, Mom! Would you stop? Leave her alone and let's go," Cree grumbled.

Lynix and Dorian pulled apart and laughed before hearing the door slam shut.

"Your mother is a trip," he said.

Dorian shook her head as she wiped lipstick from his lip with the pad of her thumb.

"You don't know the half of it. I'm afraid to admit it, but she probably would've purchased a ticket to the event if I'd told her about it sooner. All so she could be my chaperone."

Lynix smiled, and as if they had magnets on their lips, he was drawn back to Dorian's mouth and kissed her again. Her sweet lips were becoming addictive, but he guessed there were worse addictions to have.

When he'd gotten his fill, he lifted his head and looked at his beautiful woman. "Are you ready for this?" he asked.

Though he wanted the world to know she was his, he was a little concerned about taking her around some of the people who'd be in attendance. For the most part, guests would be on their best behavior, but he wasn't looking forward to introducing her to his father.

"Yes, I'm ready, and I promise not to embarrass you."

Lynix cupped her cheeks and stared into her gorgeous eyes. "Sweetheart, you could never embarrass me. If anything, you're going to be the highlight of this event and of my night. All right? Now, let's do this."

# Chapter Twenty-Six

Dorian felt like she was living a fairy tale as Lynix helped her out of the limousine. He was being so attentive tonight, like a knight and shining armor, and she felt like a princess for the first time in her life.

As they fell in line with numerous guests who were also arriving, she took in the huge, stately, mansion, surprised the event was being held there. She had assumed it would be at a hotel with a large ballroom, but Lynix mentioned the owner had offered the use of the building, as well as the catering, free of charge. It was his way of supporting the organization so the majority of the funds raised would go to the nonprofit.

When they entered the building, Lynix was greeted immediately by several people. It was clear he and his family were well respected in the community. Stories were told, photos were taken, and there were so many introductions, Dorian was sure she wouldn't remember anyone's name. It took them almost thirty minutes to get from the entrance to the ballroom.

"What do you think?" Lynix asked when they entered.

"It's bigger than I expected."

It was the size of one that you'd see in a hotel and the decorators had done an outstanding job. They'd gone with a mostly white color scheme with pops of emerald green and royal blue. It was an interesting combination, but it worked.

"My mother must've been looking out for us. She's on her way over," Lynix said near Dorian's ear, and nodded his head toward an older woman who was making her way to them. She was dressed in a white evening gown, looking regal like a Nubian queen.

Before she could reach them, she was stopped a few times by guests.

Dorian would've known it was her by her smile alone. It was the same as Lynix's.

"You guys made it," the woman said, embracing Lynix before turning to Dorian.

"You must be Dorian," she said, squeezing both of Dorian's hands before wrapping her into a tight hug. "It's so nice to finally meet you. Lynix has spoken very highly of you, and I have to say, you're even prettier than he described."

"Thank you," Dorian said and blushed.

"And your dress is absolutely stunning," the woman continued.

"Mom, you didn't even give me a chance to introduce her," Lynix grumbled.

"Oh, I'm sorry, honey," the older woman said with a laugh. "I was excited to see her."

"Anyway, Dee, this is my mother, Bridget Mathews."

"It's a pleasure to meet you, Mrs. Mathews."

"The feeling is mutual and please, call me Bridget. I'm so glad you were able to attend tonight. We'll be sitting down to dinner shortly, and..."

As Bridget rattled off the plans for the evening, Dorian felt Lynix go still next to her. When she glanced at him, she found him watching two older men who were heading their way. The tall one on the left had to be his father. He looked like an older version of Lynix.

"Oh, that's my husband," Bridget said just as the men reached them. "Honey, this is Dorian Priestly, Lynix's girlfriend."

The man didn't smile but extended his hand. "Nice to meet you, I'm Weston Mathews III." Then he gestured to the other guy. "This is a friend of the family, Karsten Baldwin."

The man nodded at her, but before she could say anything to either, Lynix reached for her hand.

"There's my brother, Thane." Lynix escorted her away without acknowledging his father or the family's friend.

"Lynix, what is wrong with you? That was rude," she said, walking fast to keep up with his long stride.

"Sorry, sweetheart. We have to sit at a table with my father. I figured we'd wait until then before he starts his interrogation. Had we stood there any longer, he would've started in on you. I don't want to subject you to any more of his superior attitude than necessary."

Dorian wondered if his father was really that bad or if it was Lynix letting his dislike of the man cloud his judgment. But for the next few minutes, she forgot about his dad as she enjoyed conversation with his brothers, as well as their women.

Soon everyone in attendance was directed to their assigned tables and dinner was served. Dorian loved chatting with Lynix's family, specifically his mother, brothers, and their dates. Mr. Mathews didn't say much and neither did Lynix, but between the great music the band was playing and the delicious food, she was having a good time.

It wasn't until Bridget left the table did Mr. Mathews start lobbing questions at Dorian. He claimed it was to get to know her better, but it felt more like he was trying to show her that she didn't belong.

"Wait a minute, the B&B your parents own is in Lincoln Park? Is it the Greystone that had a big write up in Architectural Digest last year?" Thane's date asked from the other side of the table.

"It is," Dorian said proudly and talked about the Italian architectural style and the interior.

"Do you do anything else besides help out at your parents' B&B?" Mr. Mathews asked.

"Actually, Dorian also has her own small business," Lynix said, telling those at the table about her baking business that she had on the side.

Dorian smiled at him and how proud he sounded when he told everyone that he was thinking about secretly signing her up for one of the baking shows on HGTV. Claiming she could out cook and bake anyone on any of those shows.

Questions came at her from left and right, his brothers asking about her family, the business, and whether she'd bake for them sometime.

"Can't imagine any of those little jobs being enough to live off of," Mr. Mathews interjected. "Is that why you're with my son? So he can be your sugar daddy?"

"Be careful, Dad," Lynix said, his tone lethal enough to make everyone at the table stop talking. "I won't have you disrespecting my woman."

"What?" The elder Mathews shrugged, trying to look innocent while Dorian's heart dropped. "I'm sure I'm not the only one at the table thinking the same thing. Just because she walks in here in a designer dress and diamonds dripping from her ears, doesn't make her one of us."

"Dad!" the brothers barked just as Lynix jerked out of his seat.

Dorian gasped as everything seemed to play out in slow motion. Lynix charging toward his father, and his brothers practically leaping over the table to stop him.

"What is going on over here?" Bridget hissed, seeming to come out of nowhere. She'd been circulating throughout the room, talking to those in attendance, and had been gone for a while.

Dorian was glad to see they'd only caught the attention of the tables closest to them. No one else seemed to notice the rise in tension. Most people appeared to be having a good time talking, laughing, and some were even on the dance floor.

She stood and reached for Lynix's hand. "Dance with me?" She stated it as a question but didn't wait for an answer as she pulled him toward the dance floor.

She ignored him when he suggested they leave the gala. His father was a jerk, but it warmed her heart knowing Lynix was willing to fight for her honor. The line between fake dating and what felt like a real relationship was blurring for her and, apparently, him too.

Once they reached the middle of the dance floor, Lynix relaxed and pulled her close. Dorian was thankful the band was playing a slow song because in his arms was exactly where she wanted to be. And one nice thing about her ridiculous high-heel shoes was they made her taller. It was easier to wrap her arms around his neck.

"Are you okay?" she asked.

He frowned and tightened his hold on her. "I should be asking you that. I'm sorry about my dad. He was way out of line. When we finish dancing, we're out of here."

"We can't leave yet. Your mother would be disappointed if we left early."

"She'd understand."

"No, I want us to stay a little longer," Dorian insisted.

"Well, if we do, we're finding someplace else to sit. There's no way in hell we're sitting at the table with my father," Lynix said gruffly. Then he lowered his head and kissed her sweetly.

God, she loved when he kissed her. He could be intimidating with others, but he was always gentle with her. Making her feel special, like she was the most important person in the world.

That's why she could no longer fight her feelings for him. It was no use. She loved him. Somehow, she had fallen in love with Lynix Mathews and had no clue how she was going to tell him.

An hour and a half later, after dessert, drinks, speeches, and more dancing, Dorian was ready to call it a night and get out of her shoes. She was glad Lynix was also ready to leave. He had told her that had it not been for her, he would've left already.

As they headed to the other side of the ballroom, they stopped periodically for Lynix to greet people he hadn't seen earlier in the evening. Considering he didn't start working for the family business until recently, he knew quite a few of the family's business associates.

They had just passed the dance floor when Lynix started laughing, and Dorian glanced up to find him grinning from ear to ear. She followed his line of vision and spotted a guy approaching, wearing the same silly grin as Lynix's.

"Dude! They just let anybody up in here," the man said with a laugh before he and Lynix greeted each other with one of those man hugs that included a handshake and pounding each other on the back.

After introductions, Dorian took a step away to let them catch up with one another. She glanced around the ballroom, impressed with the sheer number of people who had attended. Though some had already left, there were still plenty of folks in the room.

Dorian's gaze landed on a tall, thin woman who was heading their way wearing a gorgeous white and silver evening gown. She was one of the most beautiful people in attendance and considering her seductive walk, and the attention she was getting from a few men, she knew it.

"All right, sweetheart, sorry about that," Lynix said and placed his hand at the small of her back and kissed her. "I haven't seen that guy in years. Not since he moved back East to be closer to—"

"Well, well, well. What do we have here?"

Lynix stiffened, and Dorian turned slightly and came face-to-face with the lady she'd been admiring a few seconds ago. Now that she was closer, the woman's dress was even more spectacular than she realized. It hadn't been silver she saw, but diamonds on the garment. The outfit looked like it cost a fortune, and standing next to the classy-looking woman, Dorian suddenly felt like a kid playing dress up.

*You walk into that ballroom like you own that bitch.* Cree's words blared through her mind, and Dorian straightened her shoulders. Despite the way Mr. Mathews had treated her earlier, she didn't need to feel inferior. She belonged there just like anyone else.

"So, Lynix, which escort service did you get this one from?" the woman asked. "I would think with your type of money you could afford a better quality woman. Is she even old enough to drink?"

Dorian's hackles went up. "Excuse me?" she said, shocked by the nerve of this woman. "I don't know who you are, but you clearly have me mixed up with someone else."

"Let's go, Dee," Lynix growled.

The anger pouring off him was palpable, and if looks could kill, this woman would be dead. Dorian had never seen him like this before.

They tried to move past the woman, but she jumped in front of them.

"What? Leaving so soon? Lynix, I haven't had the chance to introduce myself to your little friend here."

"Marisela, so help me. If you don't move your ass out the way..."

"Oh, I get it. You haven't told her yet, have you?"

Unease crawled through Dorian as her gaze bounced from one to the other. There was some type of private conversation going on between them that she wasn't privy to.

What was even more unnerving was how stone-faced Lynix had turned, and how his jaw was clamped tight enough to break his teeth. There was also fire in his eyes, and it looked like he might attack at any moment.

"I guess you didn't tell her about our engagement," Marisela taunted. Then she looked at Dorian and wiggled her fingers out in front of her. Sure enough, there was a huge diamond on her ring finger. "Our marriage has been arranged by our fathers for years. So don't get too comfortable. I'd hate for your little delusional heart to get hurt."

Engaged?

Arranged marriage?

Delusional?

Dorian tried not to react, tried to remain cool and calm despite the questions racing through her mind. She knew Lynix. There had to be an explanation, but he wasn't saying anything. He just stood rigid with his breathing sounding ragged.

She wasn't sure what was going on, but it was having a weird effect on him. She needed to do something or say something. He'd come to her rescue too many times to count over the last few weeks. Now it was her turn to help him, to shake loose whatever mental hold this woman had on him.

"Ahh, I get it," Dorian hurried to say and smiled up at Lynix, hoping he'd snap out of it. "This is the woman you were telling me about, isn't it? The one who couldn't take no for an answer."

Shock showed in his eyes but disappeared so fast Dorian wondered if she'd imagined it. But then he blinked several times, and his expression softened. The tender way he looked at her made her heart squeeze.

He was back. Whatever daze he'd been in had dissipated.

When Dorian returned her attention to Marisela, the woman looked as if she wanted to spit bullets. Dorian was waiting for her to say something else, but once again there was some type of silent communication going on between her and Lynix.

But then, without taking his eyes off the woman, Lynix reached for Dorian's hand and interlocked their fingers.

"Marisela, let me introduce you to my future wife, Dorian Priestly."

# Chapter Twenty-Seven

Lynix was pretty sure he fell more in love with Dorian on the way back to his penthouse after leaving the gala. Not only didn't she say anything about him claiming her as his future wife, but she also didn't inundate him with questions that she deserved answers to. He promised her that, if she could wait until they got to his place, he would explain everything.

Still holding on to her hand since leaving the gala, he opened the door to the penthouse and escorted her in. If she thought it weird that he refused to release her, she hadn't said. He hadn't even let her go while they rode back in the limousine. Deep down, he feared that if he did she might disappear from his life. A life that he couldn't imagine without her in it.

He was so proud of how she'd handled the run-in with Marisela, but he hated he hadn't given her a heads-up about the woman. For a while, he assumed Marisela wouldn't be attending the gala because his mother had told him that she was out of the country. But then out of nowhere, she showed up, catching him off guard.

Like usual, being near her made him feel as if he was suffo-cating. Like someone had their large hands wrapped around his neck, squeezing the life out of him. Tonight was no different, except Dorian was there. She was his peace. His calm.

After she put Marisela in her place and then looked into his eyes, Lynix saw his future. He knew without a doubt that Dorian was the woman he wanted to spend the rest of his life with. He just hadn't planned on announcing it to her and Marisela in the way he'd done.

"Do you mind if I take off my shoes?" Dorian asked.

Lynix glanced down at her sandals that showed off pink toenails and wondered how she'd managed to survive in the heels for this long.

"Of course, sweetheart," he said, his voice sounding hoarse. "Make yourself at home. Actually, I have something for you."

He swept her into his arms, and she gasped, holding on to him while he carried her down the hall.

"Where are we going, and why are you carrying me?" she asked, resting her head on his shoulder. That simple move showed just how much she trusted him.

"We're going to my bedroom, and I'm carrying you so you don't have to take another step in those killer heels. There's a little something in the room I think you'll be happy to see."

When he reached the last door on the right, he strolled in and set her on the bed. Her gaze went immediately to the huge white box with a red bow sitting next to her. He hadn't been sure she'd come home with him, but he had hoped.

"That's for you. Open it."

She took a cursory glance around the large bedroom. She had seen it the first time she'd come over, and though she hadn't said, it was probably too masculine for her taste. If her apartment was any indication, she loved bright-colored walls, but his were a deep gray. But if things between them turned out the way he wanted, she'd have full rein on redecorating the space.

Dorian removed the lid from the box and burst out laughing as she pulled out fluffy yellow Big Bird slippers. "These are hilarious," she said.

"There's more," he nodded to the box for her to keep digging.

She pulled out several sets of lounging pajamas, a robe, and thick socks. He had included those in case she wasn't a house shoes person. With some help from Cree and her friend, Jada, he had also purchased a few additional clothing items to leave at his penthouse... just in case.

Maybe he was being too presumptuous thinking she'd soon be spending more time at his place, but once again, he was hoping.

"Oh, Lynix. This is so thoughtful, and I see a theme."

He smiled. "Yeah, I've picked up on the fact that yellow is your favorite color. I figured whenever you come over, you can make yourself at home. What better way to do that than with comfortable clothes?"

She strolled toward him smiling and hugged him. "You are too good to me."

"Nah, sweetheart, you've got it all wrong." He bent down and kissed her lips. "You're too good for me, and I think tonight proved that."

"Lynix..."

"I know you have questions, and you deserve answers, but let's change clothes, get comfortable, and then we can talk."

"Okay."

Twenty minutes later, after a quick shower and changing into a T-shirt and basketball shorts, Lynix poured himself a drink. He rarely drank hard liquor, but the conversation they needed to have would require something stronger than beer.

He had just poured three fingers of whiskey when Dorian strolled into the kitchen. Her shower-fresh scent wafted through the air, and she was wearing one of the short pajama sets. On her feet were a pair of thick socks.

Her hair was in a loose ponytail at her nape, and her face was scrubbed free of makeup. She looked completely at home, and Lynix loved it.

"Would you like something to eat or drink?" he asked.

"I'm not hungry, but a glass of red wine would be great."

"Okay, have a seat in the living room, and I'll bring it to you."

How was he going to tell her about Marisela? How was he going to tell her about the most humiliating and scariest night of his life? What would she think? Would she look at him differently? Would he even be able to get through the story?

He wasn't sure, but because he didn't want any secrets between them as they moved forward in their relationship, he needed to explain about Marisela.

"Here you go," Lynix said, handing her the wine.

"Thank you."

He settled next to her and sipped his drink. "Thank you for being patient with me," he said. "Before I tell you about Marisela, I want to apologize for what happened tonight. For lack of a better way to describe who she is to me, she's a complication from my past life."

He took a big swig of his drink before setting the glass on the table. A little liquid courage was just what he needed. "I have to tell you about a past that I thought I had buried and moved on from, but each time I see Marisela, I'm taken back to a dark place in my mind." He told her how it feels like he can't breathe whenever he sees her or is near her. "This is extremely hard to talk about, Dee."

Dorian reached for his hand. "Lynix, you have come

through for me so much in the last few weeks. I never thought you, the man who used to drive me nuts with your arrogance and banter, would become so important to me." She smiled, and he laughed. "You can trust me," she said, using his words that he'd said to her that day at the hotel. "Whatever we discuss here will stay between us."

Lynix nodded and brought the back of her hand to his lips. "I know and thank you. I'm glad you're here."

She took a sip from her wine glass and set it on the table next to his glass. Then she ran her palm over the stubble on his jaw and smiled. "There's no other place I'd rather be than here with you."

He needed to hear that. He'd known their feelings for each other had changed, and her words confirmed it. She might not have told him she loved him, but Lynix felt it in his heart. She was his.

He sat back, and pulled her against his side, her head resting on his chest. Maybe if he held on to her while sharing his truth, it'll be easier to tell her everything.

"My dad's friend, Mr. Baldwin, is Marisela's father. Her mother died when she was a little girl, and he raised her alone."

"Oh," Dorian said. "That had to be hard for both of them. I wonder if that's why Marisela is so mean."

Lynix grunted but didn't comment. He was sure her father did the best he could with her, but she was a horrible person. He thought by now she would've grown out of her mean-girl tendencies, but after her behavior tonight, it was safe to say she hadn't.

"When I was younger, maybe fourteen or fifteen, my father and Mr. Baldwin made an agreement. They wanted me to marry Marisela after we graduated college."

Dorian bolted up and shrugged out of his hold. "Wait. She

was telling the truth? You were married... or what, engaged to that... that woman?"

"No," Lynix said in a rush. "We are not engaged, married, or anything. There is nothing between her and I except bad memories," he said emphatically.

Dorian shook her head. "Then I don't understand."

After pulling her back into his arms, Lynix told her about how he and Marisela had known each other forever. They might've lived in different households, but their families spent a ton of time together, including holidays and vacations.

"When our fathers insisted we marry, it hadn't been a big deal. We were always together and had even attended the same private schools. Besides that, we were young and naive. At that age, we did whatever our parents said to do."

"An arranged marriage, though?" Dorian said. "I thought stuff like that only happened in books or in movies or in other cultures."

"It happens more often than you think. Some parents do it to ensure acceptable partners for their kids. Partners who have the same family values, cultural norms, or even societal standings.

"I don't know for sure, but I suspect in our case, Mr. Baldwin was thinking of Marisela's future for when he's no longer around. The man is worth an obscene amount of money, and Marisela is his only child. Everything would probably go to her upon his death, and I have no doubt she'd blow it within a year.

"You've met her. She doesn't use good judgment—in anything—and she's a spoiled brat. From what I used to know of her, she has no moral compass and attracts the wrong type of people, especially men. Mr. Baldwin knows to be concerned about her. He was probably trying to set her up in a reputable family where she'd be taken care of after he's gone. And my father has always wanted us to hook up with daughters from his circle of wealthy friends."

Dorian nodded. "That's probably why he questioned my intentions with you. He doesn't want you with someone who doesn't have money or the same social standings. For the record, I don't want your money, Lynix. I hope you know me well enough to know that, no matter what happens between us, your money means nothing to me."

Anger stirred inside of him as he recalled the way his father had treated Dorian. "My father was being a bastard, but for the record, I know the type of person you are. You might not be after my money, but there is nothing I wouldn't do for you. As far as I'm concerned, what's mine is yours."

"Lynix," she said in what he knew was her warning tone.

He didn't want to hear her say anything about their relationship being fake. He knew better. Just because she hadn't admitted to loving him, didn't mean she didn't. He could see it in the way she looked at him and the way she treated him. He could feel it whenever they were together.

Dorian's eyes widened as if just thinking of something. "I was wondering why you introduced me to Marisela as your future wife. It was to get her to let go of the idea that she'd one day be Mrs. Lynix Mathews, right?"

"No, I said that to her because it's true. Dorian, you're the only woman I ever plan to marry, and before you freak out, I'm just letting my intentions be known."

When she started to speak, he stopped her by lifting his hands and shaking his head. He didn't want to hear her protests, assuming that was what she was about to do.

"Anyway, I broke things off with Marisela during our freshmen year of college."

Lynix explained how he began to come into his own and started really thinking for himself. He was at the stage of deciding what he wanted to do with his life, and it didn't include Marisela. He saw how mean she was to some people, and he told Dorian something his mother often said.

*However people treat others, that's how they'll eventually treat you. Good or bad.*

"She would also say when people show you who they are, believe them. That's not to say folks can't change for the better, but what I saw in Marisela, I didn't like.

"Needless to say, our fathers didn't take the news of our breakup well. My dad even threatened to disown me if I backed out of the agreement, but I didn't care. I couldn't marry her, and there was nothing he could say that would change my mind."

"What did Marisela say when you broke up with her?"

Lynix sighed and laid his head back against the sofa. "At first, she was in denial, saying we were just going through a rough patch. When she realized I was serious, she was livid, calling me every degrading name you can imagine. Her behavior toward me validated my decision to move on from her."

Still holding Dorian close, Lynix pinched the bridge of his nose with his free hand, trying to think of a way to tell her the rest. Apparently, he was taking too long to continue, because she sat forward. When she did, he lifted his head to look at her. The compassion in her beautiful eyes almost did him in. She continued to amaze him—showing him what type of person she was—sweet, sensitive, loving.

Deciding to pursue her might end up being the best decision of his life.

"At the gala, when you made the comment about Marisela not being willing to accept no for an answer, you were dead on. I was shocked by your words."

"Really? I only said that because I didn't know what else to say. I could tell something was wrong because you looked as if you were going to explode or kill her. I couldn't let her get away with making you feel like that. Besides, she looks like the type to expect to get whatever she wants."

Lynix nodded. "You read her correctly. When I broke up with her, she wouldn't take no for an answer. She even went as far as drugging me... and then attempted to rape me."

# Chapter Twenty-Eight

"Oh, sweet Jesus," Dorian whispered, the words falling from her lips before she covered her mouth with her hands. "H—how?" Was all she could get out, and it didn't seem appropriate to ask for details about something so heinous.

No wonder he'd had a reaction when coming face-to-face with Marisela. Dorian didn't even know the details, but she couldn't imagine what seeing her again must've been like for him.

"I know what you're thinking," he said, his body tense and a small bead of sweat broke out on his forehead.

Then he stood, leaving her on the sofa, and she watched him pace the room.

"You're wondering how someone her size got the jump on me."

"You said she drugged you."

Noting he was getting more agitated as he walked back and forth, Dorian stood and slowly approached him. He stopped when she neared, watched her, and then his shoulders relaxed.

"Is it easier for you to talk about it while you're moving? Or would it be better for us to sit down?"

He released a long breath and ran his hand over his low haircut. "There is nothing about this story that's easy to talk about, Dee. I haven't spoken of the incident in years, and besides me and Marisela, only my brother Omari and my old college roommate, Jake, know what happened."

"Your parents..." she started, but he shook his head.

"No, they don't know. It was one of the most humiliating times in my life. I wished no one knew, and the only reason I'm discussing it now is because I don't want any secrets between us."

Dorian's heart squeezed at his admission, only making her fall for him even more. "I don't want that either, but I also don't like to see you hurting," she said. She moved closer, trying to gauge whether it was a good idea to hug him. If he didn't need one, she sure did.

As if sensing her dilemma, he opened his arms to her, and she walked into them. They stood holding each other for what seemed like forever but was only a minute or two before he slowly released her.

"Let's have a seat," she said, pointing to the sofa.

"I'll give you the short version of what happened," he said, leaning forward with his legs spread apart and his elbows on his muscular thighs. "Weeks after breaking things off with Marisela, I attended a party with some buddies, and I ran into her.

"Before that, she'd been calling and stopping by—basically not handling the breakup well, and I did everything to ignore her. I didn't accept any of her calls and whenever she dropped by my room, I'd have my roommate tell her I wasn't there.

"Eventually, she backed off, and I figured she had finally moved on. When I saw her at the party, she said as much. Told me it was my loss and I'd given up on a good thing. Then she suggested we toast to being rid of each other. We did, and one drink led to three, which was my limit, but I started feeling lightheaded after that last one.

"I was a big guy even back then and could hold my liquor, but my head was spinning, and I basically felt like shit. I figured maybe I was dehydrated, so I drank a few bottles of water that seemed to help. Still, I knew something was wrong.

"I couldn't find my friends, so I went outside for some air hoping it would help."

"Did it?" Dorian asked, gently rubbing his back, hoping to provide some comfort.

"A little, but I still felt out of it. I sat on a stoop with my eyes closed and my head in my hands. I don't know how long I was out there when I thought I heard Marisela asking someone to help get her fiancé back to the dorms. She could always talk people into doing her bidding for her. When we were kids, I thought it was cool because I often benefited from whatever she acquired."

Lynix cursed under his breath and rubbed his beard methodically with the back of his hand. Seconds ticked by, and Dorian waited patiently, wanting to hear the rest. Or as much as he'd share. When she laid her head against his shoulder, he continued.

"My memory is still spotty regarding how I got back to the dorms, but I vaguely remember telling Marisela she couldn't stay. Then I closed my room door and passed out on top of the bed. The rest of the night was a blur... until I watched the video the next day."

"Oh, my God! What?" Dorian snapped. "That witch video-taped you?"

\* \* \*

Lynix never thought he'd have to tell this story again, and if it were anyone other than Dorian sitting next to him, he wouldn't. He loved her so much, but telling her about the attempted rape was hard to do.

"No, the video came from Jake," Lynix continued. "My roommate was a techie who used to take electronics apart and tweak them to make them better. He was also a computer science major who loved gadgets.

"Anyway, someone's dorm room had recently gotten broken into, and Jake thought it a good idea to have a hidden camera set up in our room in hopes of catching the perp. Assuming they'd try to break into our room. It was motion activated and had some other wild features.

"The night of the party, Jake was studying somewhere in the building and got an alert on his phone that someone had entered our room. It was me. Once he saw me crash onto the bed, he didn't think much of it, especially after a party."

Lynix swallowed hard. "A few minutes later, Jake received another alert but didn't check the feed that time. Not right away at least. When he did finally look at the live footage, Marisela was in the room... on top of me."

Dorian moved closer, still rubbing his back as he tried to force the rest of the words out.

"Jake almost ignored what he was seeing, but what gave him pause was I wasn't moving, and my wrists and ankles were tied to the bed posts."

"Oh. My. God." Dorian whimpered next to him, and he could feel her trembling. Lynix wanted to hold her, comfort her, but if he didn't keep going, she wouldn't hear the rest.

"The video included sound and showed Marisela on her cell phone, telling someone that she might've spiked my drink too much. That she was having trouble getting me aroused. That's when Jake came running. He burst through the door, catching her off guard, and yanked her off me. All of it was captured on tape from when she reentered the room, struggled to get me undressed and tied up, to Jake getting her out of there."

Dorian lifted her head. "Wait. He didn't call the cops?"

Lynix grunted. "No. He was too busy freaking out."

In watching the video, Lynix saw his friend cover him up, then frantically trying to wake him.

"I couldn't tell by watching the video, but Jake said I told him, *call Omari. No parents. No cops.* He said it was like I knew what was happening, but I struggled to move and fell in and out of consciousness."

"What did Jake do?" Dorian asked, swiping at her tears.

Lynix sat back and pulled her against his body, holding her close. "He called Omari, told him what he saw, told him about the video, and told him what I said to do. My brother told him to call 911 and to not mention the video or Marisela.

"Keep in mind, we all came from influential families who kept personal shit in-house. With four boys, my dad was always warning us to stay out of trouble. That we represented the family, and that we all had too much to lose if we made wrong choices. That our decisions not only affected us, but also the family and the family business. Basically, he didn't want any negative press to touch us.

"So Omari told Jake to make the ties disappear, say nothing about the video, and to tell anyone who asked what happened that he'd found me barely breathing and called 911. He also told Jake if anyone asked about my parents to tell them that Omari was my guardian."

"Wow. Is your brother a lawyer?"

"At the time, he was in his last year of his undergrad, majoring in political science. He has a law degree now, but he doesn't practice law."

"I just don't understand. Why would Marisela do something like this? Surely, her father was like your father and gave her similar speeches about her actions, consequences, and protecting the family."

"I don't know if she got the same speeches as me and my brothers. My guess would be she didn't. As for her motivation for doing what she did to me, she wanted me to get her pregnant."

Dorian gasped and slammed her fist against the sofa cushion. "You've got to be kidding me! I hate her so much! What if whatever she slipped into your drink had killed you? What if you would've died?" she said. "She was reckless, selfish, and stupid! That... that, urgh! I don't even know what to call her!"

Dorian's anger-filled words pierced Lynix in the chest. He kissed the top of her head, hating that she was all riled up on his behalf, but he loved her for it. Besides maybe his mother, no other woman had ever come to his defense for any reason or cared enough to be angry on his behalf. Of course, that could be because he never let a woman get close to him before.

"Marisela assumed if she was pregnant with my child, then my father would force me to marry her," he continued. "Twisted thinking, I know. But that was her excuse."

"Please don't tell me she got away with what she did."

"I know you're not going to understand my reasoning, but I didn't want anyone to know about what happened—especially my parents or my other brothers. Maybe it's a guy thing, I don't know, but I was embarrassed and humiliated. Omari agreed to keep my secret, but I had to promise to go to therapy, which I did."

Lynix probably should've turned Marisela in, shared the video, and maybe even told his parents, but he hadn't. He and Omari did confront Marisela who'd apologized profusely. She'd been scared to death of what they'd do to her, especially after finding out there was a video. She cried and begged them not to turn her in. She also begged them not to tell her father. They had conceded, but she had to agree to stay away from Lynix forever and never speak of the incident.

They all had kept their word, and Lynix hadn't seen Marisela until that day at his parents' house recently. Technically, she had violated their agreement. She probably showed up for dinner that night thinking he wouldn't say anything about what had happened in college. And that's what he told Dorian.

"Did you see her on campus after the incident?" she asked, and snuggled deeper into him, probably getting sleepy.

"I finished out the semester, then transferred to the school Omari was attending. He and I were really close, and my parents didn't think anything of me wanting to go to the same university as him."

There was more that happened that night of the party and the next day, but Lynix felt Dorian had heard enough.

"Do you still have access to the video?" Dorian asked, surprising Lynix.

"Dee, there's no way in hell I'm showing you the video if that's what you're asking," Lynix ground out.

"So you do still have it," she said calmly, and he didn't confirm or deny. "I'm only asking because Marisela broke the agreement. That witch should pay. I'm just saying. She shouldn't be able to just waltz back into your life and stir up trouble the way she tried to do tonight."

Lynix had been thinking the same thing. He just hadn't decided how he was going to handle Marisela yet, but he would.

Dorian yawned loudly, then pulled out of his hold. It was after two in the morning, and no doubt she was tired because he was.

He pulled her onto his lap, liking the way she straddled him. "Stay the night with me?" he asked, hoping she would but prepared to take her home if she wanted.

She met his gaze and nodded. "I'd like that."

"To sleep," he added quickly, wanting her to know he wasn't trying to get her in his bed for sex. "Just sleep."

She smiled. "Fine. I think I can handle that."

Lynix stood with her in his arms, and she held on as he headed to his bedroom.

She placed a kiss near his ear. "I could get used to you carrying me everywhere."

He chuckled, feeling lighter than he'd felt in the last couple of hours. "It would be my pleasure to carry you anytime, anywhere."

Dorian rested her head on his shoulder and released a long sigh, and Lynix knew tonight was a momentous turning point in their life together. He wanted more than anything to tell her how he felt about her but not right now.

*Maybe tomorrow.*

# Chapter Twenty-Nine

Lynix eased his eyes open, and there before him was the most beautiful sight ever—Dorian. She was lying on her side, her face a few inches away and her legs entangled with his as she stared at him.

*Hmm*, this was what it was like waking up to the woman you loved.

In the past, he'd made it a point not to spend the night with a woman, and now he was glad he hadn't. That way this moment would go down in history as being another first for him and Dorian.

He reached out and pulled her closer to his body. "Good morning, beautiful," he said.

"Good morning, handsome. How do you feel? Last night's conversation was a lot. Are you doing okay?"

He heard the concern in her voice. It had taken him a while to fall asleep once they did get into bed because his mind kept replaying their conversation. He was glad he told her. No more secrets.

Now he needed to deal with Marisela once and for all. At least now, with Dorian by his side, he could handle anything.

"Lynix?"

"Oh, I'm sorry, sweetie. I'm fine and thanks for listening last night."

"I will always be here to listen, as long as you promise to talk to me."

He nodded. "I will, but you know that goes both ways, right? If there's something on your mind, or if you have a problem, or if you feel unsafe, anything, just know I will always be here for you. Okay?"

"Okay."

When she smiled at him, a warm, sensuous light passed between them. The heartrending tenderness in her eyes had his pulse jumping.

God, this woman...

If only she knew the effect her presence in his life had on him. He felt whole, like the emptiness that once resided inside of him was now filled with peace and love. And it was all because of her. His sweet Dorian.

She reached out and cupped his cheek. Her touch was so gentle and calming that his eyes drifted close on their own accord. He could stay like this forever.

"Are you going back to sleep?" she asked, and he reopened his eyes.

"Depends. What time is it?"

"Six o'clock."

He snorted. "Hell yeah, I'm going back to sleep. Don't you know there's a law that says, if you don't have to work, you're supposed to sleep in until ten?"

She laughed, and the sound warmed him.

"Why are you awake? It's too early, especially considering

we just got in bed a few hours ago." A yawn slipped through as if punctuating his words.

"I'm an early riser."

"Oh, then we're going to have a problem because I'm a night owl and rarely go to bed before one."

"You're right, that's a problem. I guess I'm going to have to give you a reason to get in bed a little earlier every night," she said, the sassy side of her personality peeking through.

And he grinned when he realized what she was saying—she was planning to spend more nights with him. Good.

"If you're in my bed, you better believe I'll be right beside you."

Her smile lingered but slowly turned serious.

"What?" he said. "What's on your mind?"

"I'm thinking..." she started but stopped, and then it was like she was transforming from his sweet, innocent, obsession to his bold, self-assured, hellcat. Oh yeah, this should be good.

"Tell me," he said. "What are you thinking?"

"I'm thinking I don't want to pretend anymore. I know we had an agreement, but I want to change the parameters of our deal."

His heartbeat picked up speed. "I'm listening."

"I want us to date for real. I want you to be my man, and I'm not saying that because of the beautiful gifts you've given me, or how you make me feel like a queen. I want to change the agreement because I love you." The last words were spoken barely above a whisper, but Lynix heard them loud and clear.

"*Finally*," he said and covered her mouth with his, kissing her with an urgency that left him breathless. She was his. All his, and he planned to treasure her like the queen she was.

He broke off the kiss. "I love you too," he said, cupping her face between his hands as he kissed her again. "I love you so damn much and yeah, no more fake dating because you're mine. My woman."

"I like the sound of that," she said, and the love he saw in her eyes had his heart thumping erratically.

"I think we should go away next weekend and consummate our relationship," he said and lay back against the pillows.

"Why wait until next week, and why do we have to leave? Can't we do that now and here?"

He shook his head. "I want your first time to be special, and I have ideas. We can fly to New York for a long weekend, have a picnic in Central Park, go on a carriage ride, do some shopping, then have a nice romantic dinner before we take in a show. After we leave the theater, we'll head back to the hotel where I'll have flowers and candles, and—"

"Stop," she said, her finger on his lips. "That sounds amazing, but Lynix, I don't need all that to make my first time with you special." She brought her mouth to his and nibbled on his bottom lip, then his top one. "What will make my first time special is being with you. Only you."

For a few seconds all he could do was stare at her. "Damn, Dee. That was the sweetest thing anyone has ever said to me, but are you sure you don't want to fly to New York?"

She burst out laughing and swatted his arm. "Oh yeah, one of these days we're going to New York, and no take backs on all that you said we'll do once we get there. But right now, I'd rather you make love to me."

"Whatever you want, sweetie."

Lynix took his time stripping her out of the pajamas and tossed them on the floor.

"You're so beautiful," he said, getting his fill as he took in her beautiful breasts and slim waist that flared into curvy hips. He couldn't wait to make love to her.

*My woman.*

He leaped off the bed and made quick work of taking off his T-shirt and tossing it next to her pajamas on the floor. But when he caught her watching him intently, a slow, cocky grin kicked up the corners of his mouth, and he slowed down. If she wanted to watch, he'd give her a little show.

He took his time sliding his basketball shorts and briefs down his legs. When he straightened, his dick was standing at attention and ready for action.

"You see how hard you make me?" he said, stroking himself.

"Yes, and I like what I see," she said boldly, checking him out while grinning. "You look incredible in clothes, but naked? Wow! And you're big... everywhere. Yeah, I like what I see."

Lynix laughed. "And it's all yours, baby, but let me grab something real quick."

He flexed his biceps and did a few bodybuilder poses that had her cracking up. When he finally made it to his closet, where he kept a box of condoms, and pulled out a few.

He stepped back into the bedroom to find Dorian still grinning, and he loved the spark of mischief in her eyes.

"You sure about this?" he asked, setting the condoms on the nightstand except for one which would go near his pillow.

She nodded, and her gaze stayed on his erection as he crawled on the bed toward her.

"Oh yeah, I'm positive. I want you, Lynix."

"And I want you."

He laid her back and covered her body with his, then kissed her slowly, wanting his love for her to be felt in every lap of his tongue.

She was his.

Dorian Priestly had finally said yes, and he was almost giddy with anticipation.

As their kiss intensified, their hands were all over each

other, touching, caressing, squeezing. And his skin tingled everywhere she touched him—on his arms, his back, his thighs, and he almost laughed when she squeezed his butt cheeks.

Definitely a hellcat, and he was here for it.

He eased away from her mouth and peppered kisses over her skin that smelled as fresh as it had the night before. As he enjoyed the feel of her skin, he whispered his love for each part of her body, and currents of desire coursed through his veins.

"Damn, baby..." he murmured as he worked his way to her breasts. He gently pinched her nipples, eliciting a hiss from her before he sucked one of her nipples into his mouth.

The erotic sounds she was making stoked his arousal, and he stroked himself while he continued to explore her body. He was going to enjoy making love to her. She was so responsive to his touch, his lips, and his tongue as he went back to feasting on her breasts again.

"I'm ready," Dorian said breathily as she squirmed against him. "I want to feel you inside of me."

"That's right, baby. Tell me what you want," he murmured against her heated skin, then lifted his head to meet her gaze. "And if I do something you don't like, tell me. Or if something doesn't feel comfortable..."

"Stop," she said, running her palm over the stubble on his cheek. "Stop looking so worried. I'm not going to break, and just because I haven't had sex doesn't mean I don't know how everything works. We got this, and I know you're going to take good care of me."

He almost laughed at her little pep talk. "You're right, I am going to take care of you. We'll take it slow, okay?"

"Not too slow because you already have me so turned on, I feel like I'm going to leap out of my skin."

Lynix chuckled and nuzzled her neck while sliding his hand down the center of her body. When he reached between her thighs, his pulse raced as he slid two fingers into her tightness, confirming just how wet she was for him. Though he wanted this first time to be nice and slow, considering how he couldn't wait to be buried deep inside of her, he might not be able to go slow at all.

Dorian dug her nails into his shoulder and lifted her hips as he fondled her. There was definitely nothing shy about his hellcat as she rode his hand. When he picked up speed, pumping his digits in and out of her, she matched him stroke for stroke.

"Lynix, I—I think..." Her words died on her lips as she bucked hard against his hand, forcing his fingers to drive deeper inside of her, and then she lost it. As her head brushed back and forth against the pillow, she clamped her thighs shut, holding him in place as she rode out her release.

Watching her twist, turn, scream, and dig her nails into his skin was hot as hell and had him hard as granite. Instead of giving her time to catch her breath, Lynix quickly sheathed himself and hovered above her, nudging her legs apart to make room for him.

She watched him through the slits of her eyes as her chest heaved.

He leaned forward and covered her mouth with his as his shaft bumped against her opening before he began easing inside of her. She was tight. Damn tight as he slowly slid between her slick folds.

She jerked her mouth from his. "Oh... my goodness," she whimpered, holding on to him as he slid in deeper. Inch by inch, he could feel her stretch around him, adjusting to his size. Being inside of her felt unbelievable, and it was taking all his control not to dive all the way in and give them both the release they wanted. But the last thing he wanted was to hurt her.

"Breathe, baby," he murmured, gritting his teeth as he

started thrusting. He needed her to relax because he could feel her tensing up. But damn, she felt incredible, especially with her moving with him, and he picked up speed. Driving a little harder and deeper into her.

"Oh yes, Lynix. Yes," she said.

Her eyes met his, and it was so sexy to watch her biting down on her lower lip as their hips pumped in sync.

"It feels so good." She moaned, and he could sense she was nearing another release as her moves grew jerkier and her hold on him tightened. Her eyes slammed closed. "Oh, my goodness. Oh my... I think... I think..."

"It's okay, baby. Let go," he crooned, knowing they'd be going another round after this one. No way once would be enough today. He'd waited too long for this. Too long to have her.

Seconds later, she screamed his name as she fell apart beneath him, but he couldn't stop. Her inner walls were snug around his shaft, feeling too damn good for him to hold on for much longer. He went deeper and harder with each thrust until a spine-tingling orgasm rushed through him and pushed him over the edge of his control.

Lynix collapsed on top of her, careful not to put all his weight on her as their chests heaved and their breaths mingled. Dorian held him tightly while his face was buried against her neck.

*Damn, that was amazing.*

He kissed her cheek but stilled when he felt wetness on her face.

"Dee?" He lifted onto his elbow and stared down at her. "You're crying. Shit, did I hurt you?"

"No." She shook her head vigorously. "You didn't hurt me at all."

"Then baby, why are you crying?" He wiped her tears and kissed her again. "Talk to me."

"For so long, I wondered if I'd ever love someone enough to give my body to them. I've wanted to, but it just never felt like it was time or the situation was right.

"I'm so glad I waited, and I'm glad I was able to share this experience with you. Thank you for making my first time special."

Lynix leaned down and touched his mouth to hers. Kissing her slowly and savoring this special moment in their relationship.

When the kiss ended, he looked at her. A few tears hung on her lashes, and her eyes glittered with so much love as she met his gaze.

"Thank you for trusting me with something so precious," he said as he caressed her cheek. "I love you, sweetheart. I love you so damn much, and every day going forward, I'm going to show you just how much."

"You already have, and I love you too."

"Are you sore?"

"A little," she said shyly. "But I want to do that again."

Lynix grinned. "Like I always say, whatever you want, sweetheart."

# Chapter Thirty

D orian made quick work of packing up some of the pastries she'd made that morning. It had been two weeks since the gala, and Bridget had insisted they come over for dinner. Of course, Lynix said no but eventually gave in to his mother, and Dorian had offered to bring dessert.

She just hoped his parents would like the lemon-blueberry mini cheesecakes, miniature key lime and chocolate pies, and peach fritters. She might've gotten carried away with baking, but she figured if fists started flying or an argument broke out between Lynix and his father, she'd just pig out on sweets and watch.

Glancing at the clock on the stove, she groaned realizing she only had fifteen minutes before Lynix arrived, and she didn't want to be the reason they were late.

She hurried to her bedroom for her shoes and handbag but took one last look in the mirror. The beige, sleeveless jumpsuit she'd chosen to wear was cute, classy, and with gold jewelry, it was perfect for dinner with the Mathews. Now all she had to do while at their home was remember she was there for Lynix.

Who cared what his father thought of her? Okay, she cared, but she wasn't going to think about how rude he'd been to her at the gala.

No, she'd just focus on how much fun she and Lynix have been having over the last couple of months. Especially the last two weeks since they officially started dating. It felt like they'd been together forever, falling into a routine effortlessly and seeing each other daily. It helped he was no longer on the police force. His schedule was flexible, and he was able to work around hers.

Dorian loved everything about the man, and their love-making was mind-blowing. Lynix was so adventurous in the bedroom... and the living room, bathroom, and even in the kitchen.

She giggled at the last thought and how long it had taken her to sanitize every flat surface in her kitchen after a particular wild night of sex. It had been worth it, though. The man knew how to get and keep her aroused while also making her feel cherished.

Definitely a keeper.

A knock on her apartment door jarred Dorian out of her thoughts, and when she rushed out of the bedroom, she remembered why she'd gone in there in the first place—to grab her shoes and purse.

She shook her head and laughed. With Lynix on her mind, it was easy to forget everything else. She had waited a long time to fall in love with an incredible man, and now that she had, she was going to enjoy him.

Just as she reached the door, her cell phone rang. "Oh, come on. I don't have time for phone calls," she murmured, then thought it might be Bridget needing them to bring something else.

Instead of greeting Lynix with a kiss like usual, she

unlocked the door and yelled, "Come in." Then she headed to the kitchen where she'd left her cell.

"Hey, babe," she called out and glanced over her shoulder, expecting to see him walk in, but it wasn't him.

She stopped in her tracks. "Shauna?" Dorian ignored her phone and backtracked to the woman who stood in her living room.

Her former boss didn't look as pulled together as usual. Her hair was windblown, sticking out in every direction, and the blouse and khakis she was wearing needed ironing. But it was her eyes and the smell of alcohol that made Dorian sorry she didn't look through the peephole before unlocking the door.

"What are you doing here?" she asked not so nicely.

"Rude much? I guess having a hotshot boyfriend has made you get a backbone," the woman said, glancing around before returning her attention to Dorian. "We need to talk."

"What could we *possibly* have to talk about?"

"We need to talk about you getting me and Rodney's job back," the woman snapped and moved closer.

Dorian frowned. "What are you talking about?"

"Don't act like you don't know your boyfriend got us fired. Playing stupid doesn't look good on you." She waved her hand up and down at Dorian. "Even in your fancy clothes."

"Wait. You guys were fired?" Dorian asked, ignoring the woman's insults. "I had nothing to do with that."

She was shocked Lynix had them fired and hadn't said anything. Still, she was glad he'd done it. Now the two people who had treated her like crap could get a taste of how she felt back then. And Rodney? He could go straight to hell.

"I know you were behind it!" Shauna's words slurred, and when she moved closer, Dorian stepped back. "You probably complained to Mathews, and he used whatever leverage he had to get the CEO to fire us, and it's your fault! And you're going to fix this mess!"

Fury clawed through Dorian. "Even if I could get your jobs back, I wouldn't. Neither of you deserve them. You especially. You're a horrible human being who's not qualified to have direct reports. Your ass should've been fired years ago!"

Shauna pointed her finger at Dorian, inches from her face. "I was a damn good boss," she seethed, anger sparking in her eyes. "I can't help it if you couldn't do your job. If you wouldn't have quit, I probably would've eventually fired you."

"Get out of my apartment," Dorian snapped and headed to the door, but Shauna grabbed her upper arm.

Pain pierced through her skin, and Dorian tried to shake free, but the woman's nails dug in deeper.

"Let me go!" Dorian yelled and swung at Shauna, catching her on the side of her face.

Shauna screamed. "Why you little..." She swung, missed, and Dorian shoved her as hard as she could, and watched her former boss stumble backwards just as the front door burst open.

With incredible reflex, Lynix snatched Shauna by the back of her shirt and righted her.

"What the hell are you doing here?" he roared, catching Dorian off guard with the rage in his tone.

"She was just leaving," Dorian said, rubbing her arm that was hurting and starting to bruise.

"Are you okay?" Lynix asked Dorian, still holding on to Shauna who was cursing and trying to kick and swing at him.

His attention went to Dorian's bare arm, and he must've seen the spot that was now red because his face turned into an angry mask.

"She put her hands on you?" he ground out, and without

waiting for a response, he pushed Shauna, not too gently, up against a nearby wall with her hands behind her back.

Dorian hurried to him. "Lynix, I'm fine, and she was leaving."

"You're damn right she's leaving, but she's leaving with an escort."

He didn't bother calling 911. Instead, he reached out to "a friend" who was on duty and arrived at the apartment within five minutes.

The next forty minutes was filled with answering the cop's questions, Lynix pacing the living room, and Dorian filing assault charges. In between time, she'd managed to contact Bridget to let them know she and Lynix would be late.

"If that was your attempt at trying to get out of going to dinner, it's not going to work," Dorian said once it was just her and Lynix left in the apartment. "We're still going."

He huffed and rubbed the back of his neck. "I figured as much, but seriously, are you sure you're all right?"

He had put ice on her arm while she answered the officer's questions, and it helped. Her skin wasn't as red and puffy, but her arm still ached.

"I'm fine, and thanks for coming to my rescue."

"Always, sweetheart." He tugged on her hand, pulling her to him, and gave her a quick kiss. "Now let's go and get this dinner over with."

# Chapter Thirty-One

Hours later, Lynix was sitting at his parents' dining room table with his father, waiting for Dorian and his mother to return with dessert and coffee. His mind drifted back to the scene at Dorian's apartment, and he couldn't help thinking about how bad it could've turned out.

To say he'd been shocked to see Shauna, and drunk at that, would be an understatement. Also seeing her reminded him that he hadn't told Dorian about the call he'd made. Though he didn't know the results of what happened after talking to the CEO about Shauna and Rodney, he still had planned to tell Dorian what he'd done. He was glad it had all worked out, and he'd make sure Dorian didn't have any more trouble out of her former boss or that ex-boyfriend.

Lynix stood and strolled over to the mini bar near the floor to ceiling windows for a bottle of water. "Do you want anything, Dad?" His father had been nursing a glass of whiskey through dinner.

"No, I'm good. Thanks, Son."

Surprisingly, dinner had gone well with conversation

flowing easily. Though Dorian and his mother carried much of the conversation, Lynix and his father chimed in periodically. They were getting along for a change. Granted, they hadn't said much to each other, but at least they weren't arguing.

"Dorian seems like a nice young lady, and your mother really likes her," his father said, surprising Lynix even more.

"Thank you. She's one of the nicest people I've ever met, and..."

He almost added he was going to marry her, but that might be a sure way of starting a fight, something he didn't want to do. His mother had warned them both that she wanted a nice, uneventful dinner while she got to know Dorian. So far, they'd done well in giving her what she asked for, and Lynix was happy because Dorian seemed to be enjoying herself.

"And her family is great," Lynix added. "I think you've met Zion before, right? He's the one who got married here on the property months ago."

His father nodded. "Of course, I remember him. He attended a few of our cookouts with you. Remember that time when he won the pie-eating contest?"

Lynix chuckled. "Yeah, that's right. Then he got sick and spent most of his time here in the bathroom."

His father laughed too. He had always been good at remembering faces. and names, which helped in the business world. Lynix shouldn't have been surprised he remembered Zion.

"I'm glad Wes was able to talk you into joining him at WBM," his father said, changing the subject.

This was the first time he'd brought up Lynix joining Wes's team.

"I like the idea of my boys working together carrying on the family business. I don't say it enough, but it means a lot to me.

And if you don't enjoy your new role, I'm sure your brothers can find another position for you in the company."

That had to be one of the nicest things his father ever said to him. This was also the longest they'd gone without arguing since Lynix could remember.

"Thanks, Dad. I'm sure it'll be fine."

"So the hours are good for you?" his father asked.

"Yeah, they're great. It gives me a chance to spend more time with Dorian."

His father sipped his brandy as he leaned on the back of one of the dining room chairs. "Does that mean the two of you are getting serious?"

"Very," Lynix said without hesitation. "She's it for me, Dad. Dorian is like no other person I've met, and I like who I am with her. She grounds me. Makes me happier than I've ever been in my life. We fit together perfectly."

"I don't know, Son. Now that you're working in the business world, who you have by your side could make or break a deal. I don't think you should rule out Marisela."

Anger stirred inside of Lynix, but he tried to keep his cool. "Dad, you need to get it through your head. There is no me and Marisela, and there never will be."

"I get that maybe things didn't work out back in college, but she's all grown up now. She's tough and bold, the type of woman who can hold her own and go to bat for you when needed. Dorian is sweet, but she's too meek for our world."

"You don't even know me!" Dorian's words cracked through the room like the wicked sound of a bull whip snapping through the air. She set a small tray of pastries on the table and looked like a beautiful, yet angry angel stalking toward his father.

Lynix wasn't sure whether to intervene or let her have her say. But considering how furious she was, he chose the latter. It was time his father got to experience the other side of Dorian Priestly.

"From the moment you met me, you judged me, but based on what? My looks? The way I talk? The lack of diamonds on my fingers and wrists? No, you based it on the fact that you don't know my people. That they don't run in the same pretentious circles as you.

"Well, you know what, Mr. Mathews, I don't care if you don't like me or if you think I'm too weak to be with your son. You're not the first person who's underestimated me, and I'm sure you won't be the last.

"But let me tell you something. No matter how you try to belittle me or make me feel less than, I'm not going anywhere."

When her attention turned to Lynix, and she walked toward him, his heart practically exploded out of his chest with the love he felt for her.

She stopped next to him but looked across the room at his father again. "I'm crazy in love with your son, and whether you like it or not, I'm here to stay. Not only because he's my heart, but also because he needs me. He needs someone like me who will *always* be in his corner. Who will always take care of him. Someone who will stand by him when jerks like you try to push the wrong type of woman on him. You would rather him be with someone who almost destroyed his life in a horrifying—"

"Dorian," Lynix said slowly, cautioning her not to say more about Marisela.

"Don't worry, baby. That's not my story to tell," she said, cupping his face between her hands and looking him in the eyes. "But he needs to know, and *you* need to tell him, today."

She kissed him hard on the mouth, turned for the door, but stopped when she saw his mother.

Lynix stood speechless. He didn't know how much his mom had heard, but he hoped she wouldn't insist on staying for the conversation he needed to have with his father. Because Dorian was right. His dad needed to know about Marisela, and hopefully after he did, he wouldn't bring her name up again.

His father set down his glass and walked toward Lynix. Instead of anger or frustration in his eyes, he saw concern. "What happened, son? Who was she referring to?"

Lynix glanced at the entrance to the dining room. He wasn't sure what Dorian had said to his mother, but they were gone. When he looked back at his father, he swallowed hard.

"She's talking about Marisela. There's something you need to know, Dad. Marisela drugged me."

# Chapter Thirty-Two

Still pissed at Mr. Mathews, Dorian's breaths came in short spurts while leaving the dining room with Bridget. She was so angry. Not just at Lynix's father, but also at herself. She hadn't planned to say so much. Heck, she hadn't planned to say anything, but the guy had picked the wrong day to insult her.

"What happened to my son?" Bridget asked when they reached the kitchen.

Dorian sighed and placed her hand on Bridget's arm. "I'm sorry for all I said in there. I apologize for disrespecting your husband."

"Honey, no apology necessary. He needed to hear everything you said and more. Not to sound condescending, but I'm proud of you. Don't ever let anyone, not even my arrogant, knuckleheaded husband, disrespect you or treat you less than you deserve.

"Now I want to know what woman you were talking about. Is it Marisela?"

When Dorian didn't respond, Bridget said, "I'll take that as a yes, and I respect you for keeping my son's secrets. I never liked that little hussy for him, but Weston and Karsten insisted the kids were perfect for each other. I knew Lynix would eventually come to his senses about her, but I was prepared to step in if he didn't."

Dorian wasn't sure what to say. So she kept her mouth shut.

"I know something happened in college," Bridget said, sounding more like she was talking to herself. "Lynix was quieter, more distant after that first semester, but trying to get any of my boys to talk about their problems or emotions was and still is impossible."

When the woman turned concerned eyes on Dorian, she groaned. "You're going to have to hear it from him or your husband. I can't betray his trust." She just hoped Lynix didn't hate her for insisting he tell his dad. If nothing else came out of the night, she hoped Lynix and his father could fix their relationship.

"Okay, since your lips are sealed, do you want to wash or dry? Because I gave the cook and housekeeper the night off."

Dorian laughed. There were two dishwashers in the kitchen, but some items probably needed to be washed by hand.

"I'll wash," she said, "but first, how about some dessert?" She pointed to the container on the counter, glad she'd left a few of the treats in the kitchen.

"Well, I've already tried the cupcake, and the lemon-blueberry mini cheesecake was life-changing. I can't wait to place an order with you. They both were delicious."

"Thank you," Dorian said, and they both startled when loud cursing and yelling filtered into the kitchen.

The words were angry, but Dorian could tell they weren't directed at Lynix. She was so proud of him. It was clear he had shared the story with Mr. Mathews. She just hoped it brought them closer.

"That's it. I'm finding out what's going on." Bridget rushed out of the kitchen, and Dorian was right behind her.

When they reached the dining room, they stopped at the door when they found the men in a tight embrace. Lynix was facing her, but he had his eyes closed, and she could hear Mr. Mathews saying he was sorry, he was so sorry.

"What happened?" Bridget walked over to her men. "You guys are scaring me, and one of you better start talking."

Mr. Mathews swiped at his face and blinked several times before shaking his head. "Come with me, honey," he said and started to leave the room.

"Dad," Lynix called out. "I need to be there when Marisela is confronted."

His father nodded, then turned to Dorian. "Young lady, I owe you an apology. I'm deeply sorry for my insensitive words and for making you feel like you don't belong in our family." He leaned in and kissed her cheek, and Dorian thought she would pass out in shock. "Welcome to my family." He gave her a slight smile and left the room with his wife.

Dorian went to Lynix who was watching her, and she couldn't read his expression. His eyes were a little watery, but it didn't look as if he'd been crying. She couldn't imagine how hard it had to be to tell his father the story.

"I'm sorry, baby," she said and slowly ran her hands up his chest. "I know I was out of order, but..."

Lynix pulled her into a tight hug, effectively cutting off her words.

"I don't know how I've gone this long without you in my life," he said, his voice thick with emotion. "Thank you for making me a better, stronger man, and for making me tell my father everything."

She leaned back to look at him. "I love you, and thank you for making me a better, stronger, self-confident woman. I've seen a change in myself, and I like it."

A slow smile appeared on his handsome face before he lowered his head and covered her mouth with his. The kiss was so tender and sweet, Dorian almost whimpered.

God, she loved him and would be forever grateful that he came up with the idea to fake date... even if she knew what he was up to.

* * *

Days later, Lynix and his father sat in Mr. Baldwin's home office waiting for Marisela to arrive. Lynix had thought telling Dorian about that night in college was hard, but it was even harder to share with his father. He had also shown him the video.

Lynix couldn't ever remember seeing his father break down, and something shifted between them. His dad had hugged him so tightly, he thought he'd crack a rib. But it was when he said, "I love you" that Lynix found himself getting emotional.

On some level, he had always known his father loved him, but the words were rarely, if ever, spoken. That went for both of them, and Lynix planned to make every effort to rebuild their relationship.

His dad had been livid. He had wanted to destroy Marisela. Wanted her to pay in every way possible, and he had been prepared to say to hell with his and Mr. Baldwin's friendship. But once he calmed down, they formed a plan to help Lynix put this behind him once and for all.

When they told Mr. Baldwin about what Marisela had done, he didn't believe Lynix. Not until he watched the video.

Then he'd been distraught. He knew his daughter wasn't an angel, but he had no idea she was capable of something so heinous.

After a lengthy discussion on how to handle the situation, Lynix had agreed he wouldn't do anything to publicly shame Marisela or her family. They were going to try to keep the information in-house but with some changes.

"Dad? Where are you?" Marisela called out.

"I'm in the study," her father said, and they all stood. Mr. Baldwin remained behind his desk, and Lynix and his father stood to the side.

"All right, Dad, I'm here. What's so imp..." Her words trailed off when she walked farther into the office dressed in a tennis outfit, and her eyes met Lynix's.

"I told you what would happen if you came near me again," he said, his words cold and unyielding.

Marisela looked frantically between all of them, but her eyes settled on her father. By his expression, Lynix was sure she could tell he knew everything.

"Daddy, I can explain."

Lynix held up a contract that he'd had drawn up to ensure Marisela never came near him or Dorian again. Not only that, but she was never to speak of him or the incident in college. She also had to agree to live in another country. That last part might not be a hardship since she often traveled the world, but she wouldn't see her father as often.

"Since a verbal agreement didn't work," Lynix said, "I took the liberty of having a contract drawn up. Your father has already approved it."

"Daddy, you have to let me explain."

"Sign the papers, Marisela," Mr. Baldwin said, and there was no room in his tone for an argument.

Once the document was signed and she received her copy,

Lynix and his father headed to the door. As he was leaving, he heard Mr. Baldwin say to Marisela, "Sit your ass down."

As he walked out of their home, Lynix felt like a weight had been lifted off his shoulders. He only wished he had done this years ago, but at least now he could move on with his life... with Dorian.

# Epilogue

**D**orian snuggled against Lynix as they rode in the horse-drawn carriage around Central Park. As promised, Lynix had whisked her away to New York City and had given her everything he had promised from the picnic in the park to shopping on 5<sup>th</sup> Avenue. Visiting The Big Apple had been on her bucket list of places to visit since she had binged watched Sex and The City years ago. She could honestly say the city had been everything she imagined and more.

It was their last day in New York, and the perfect evening. The setting of the sun, the city noises, and the *click-clacking* of the horse's hooves hitting the concrete had lulled her into a peaceful state. Dorian couldn't ask for a more perfect ending to a fabulous trip.

She squeezed Lynix's arm. "This has been the best weekend I've ever had, and I've had more firsts with you—which is the best part."

He smiled down at her and kissed her forehead. "I'm planning on us having a ton of firsts, and I'm glad you enjoyed the weekend. Since this is our last night here, is there anything else you want to do that we haven't done?"

They'd done several tours and hit all the major attractions, and they'd even walked across the Brooklyn Bridge. And something Dorian thought she'd never do—buy a hot dog from one of the street vendors. It had been so good, even though she did pray over it a few times between bites.

"Nothing I can think of," she finally said. "What about you? Anything else you want to do?"

"Nah, I think I'm good, except now that you mentioned it, there is one more thing. Jack," Lynix called out to the coachman.

"Yes, sir, Mr. Mathews?"

"Can you stop at that flower stand on the next corner?"

"Of course."

When they got close, Lynix waved over one of the older women who was selling the flowers. He requested three dozen red, yellow, and white roses, and he wanted them in a crystal vase.

When the woman hurried away to fill the order, Dorian said, "Why are you buying flowers? We won't be able to take them on the plane with us."

"I'm buying them because my woman loves flowers, and she hasn't received enough of them over the last thirty-plus years. So, I'm making up for lost time."

Dorian smiled and shook her head. He was always doing sweet gestures like that, and it warmed her heart.

"And once you're done enjoying them, before we fly out tomorrow, we'll leave them at the front desk of the hotel for other guests to enjoy."

"Dang, you are the most thoughtful man I've ever met."

"Yeah, and don't you forget it," he cracked, and they both laughed.

Once they were on their way with flowers in hand, Dorian reflected over the last few months. Her mother had finally embraced the idea of her dating Lynix and was now talking marriage and weddings. There was no pleasing the woman, but at least Dorian no longer had to endure her matchmaking schemes.

Lynix and his father had been spending a lot of time together, even golfing once a week. It was clear that Lynix was enjoying getting to know his father better. He had also started back going to therapy. After his run-ins with Marisela, and the way he reacted to her presence, he felt he still had issues to work through. Dorian was so proud of him. She knew admitting he needed help hadn't been easy, but he was determined to continue to work on himself.

It also helped knowing Maricela no longer lived in the US. Her father had put her on a plane hours after she'd signed Lynix's contract. From what Dorian heard, Mr. Baldwin planned on keeping her in check by threatening to stop funding her business ventures if she went back on the agreement.

Dorian didn't think about her much because her social life was on a whole new level. She was having a good time hanging out with Bridget and attending society events with her. Rubbing shoulders with some one-percenters wasn't as stuffy as Dorian thought it might be. And last weekend, they had attended a fancy, celebrity tea party that had been a blast.

She had to admit that going along with Lynix's hairbrained idea to fake date came with way more excitement and perks than she could have ever imagined. But most of all, she ended up with an amazing man who she absolutely adored.

"I was thinking," Lynix said, capturing Dorian's attention. "How about we experience one more first?"

Dorian grinned up at him. "Sure, what did you have in mind?"

He reached into his pants pocket and pulled out a small, velvet blue box, and Dorian's breath caught in her throat.

"I know we've only been dating a short while, but it didn't take long for me to know that you're the one for me. The joy I feel every day, knowing that I get to see your beautiful face and spend my days with you, is indescribable. You mean the world to me Dorian, and I love you more than I thought I could ever love another human being.

"So, to create another first, what do you think about us getting married?" he asked as he lifted the lid and revealed the most beautiful diamond ring Dorian had ever seen. "I love you, sweetheart. I want to wake up with you every day and fall asleep with you every night. I want to be the one you call when your raggedy car won't start." She laughed and punched him playfully. "I also want to have at least three kids, a dog, and a parakeet."

"A parakeet?" Dorian said, laughing again.

He shrugged, "Sure, why not? Basically, I want you to be my wife so we can have a lifetime of more firsts. I love you, sweetie. Will you marry me?"

"Yes! I will definitely marry you, and I can't wait to have those three kids, a dog, and even a parakeet."

He laughed and she grinned as he slid the stunning ring onto her finger, and then she kissed him.

"I love you, baby, and I'm looking forward to being your wife."

\*\*\*

***If you enjoyed this story, please consider leaving a review on review sites or social media outlets.***

# Next Book in the Series

T hank you for reading DARING TO LOVE YOU! I hope you enjoyed Lynix and Dorian as much as I enjoyed writing about them. The next book in the Priestly Family series is Cree and her mystery man's story.

Be sure to subscribe to my newsletter at https://sharon cooper.net/newsletter for sneak peeks of upcoming stories.

If you're new to my work, visit my website for a complete list of my books.

# Other Titles By Sharon

## Jenkins Family Series (Contemporary Romance)
Best Woman for the Job (Short Story Prequel)
Still the Best Woman for the Job (book 1)
All You'll Ever Need (book 2)
Tempting the Artist (book 3)
Negotiating for Love (book 4)
Seducing the Boss Lady (book 5)
Love at Last (Holiday Novella)
When Love Calls (Novella)
More Than Love (Novella)

## Reunited Series (Romantic Suspense)
Blue Roses (book 1)
Secret Rendezvous (Prequel to Rendezvous with Danger)
Rendezvous with Danger (book 2)
Truth or Consequences (book 3)
Operation Midnight (book 4)
Casino Heat (book 5)

## Finding Love Series
Legal Seduction (Contemporary Romance)
A Dose of Passion (Contemporary Romance)
Model Attraction (Contemporary Romance)

## Stand Alones
Something New ("Edgy" Sweet Romance)
Sin City Temptation (Contemporary Romance)
A Passionate Kiss (Contemporary Romance)
Soul's Desire (Unparalleled Love series)
Show Me (Irresistible Husband series)
His to Protect (Harlequin Romantic Suspense)

Sharon C. Cooper

His to Defend (Harlequin Romantic Suspense)
Business Not As Usual (Romantic Comedy)
In It to Win It (Romantic Comedy)
Kiss Me (Irresistible Husband – Contemporary Romance)
Mr. One and Only (Baes of Juneteenth)
Fiancé for Hire (Men for Hire)

**Priestly Family Series**
Believing in You (Contemporary Romance)
Finding You (Contemporary Romance)
Daring to Love You (Contemporary Romance)

# About the Author

USA Today bestselling author Sharon C. Cooper loves anything involving romance with a happily-ever-after, whether in books, movies, or real life. She writes contemporary romance, romantic suspense, as well as romantic comedy. She enjoys rainy days, carpet picnics, and family game night. Her stories have won numerous awards, including The Rochelle Alers Best Series award for her Atlanta's Finest Series (2022) and The Beverly Jenkins Author of the Year award (2021). When she isn't writing, Sharon loves hanging out with her amazing husband, doing volunteer work, or reading a good book (a romance of course). To read more about Sharon and her novels, or to sign up to be notified of her latest releases, visit www.sharoncooper.net